Undeath & Taxes

REUTS PUBLICATIONS

UNDEATH
&
TAXES

Drew Hayes

Cover design by Ashley Ruggirello
Cover art Copyright 2015 silinias/NokieSchafe/withmycamera/Giallo86 on DeviantArt.com

ISBN: 978-1-942111-17-7

REUTS Publications
www.REUTS.com

This one goes out to the people that buy the first round. You're doing the Lord's work, each and every one of you.

PREFACE

I ALMOST CERTAINLY DO NOT KNOW YOU; however, I shall assume you are a lovely person, and it is my loss for not having yet had the opportunity to meet you. Still, I must assume you and I are connected in some way, for the works you are about to read are selections from a journal of my memoirs. I compiled these not in the belief that the stories within are so compelling they must be told, but rather because I found my unexpected life transition to be so shockingly uneventful—at least initially. I place the blame for my aggrandized expectations squarely on contemporary media, filling my head with the belief that a ticket to the supernatural also put one on an express train toward coolness and suave charm.

This is simply not the case. Or, at least, it was not my case. I recorded my journeys in the hopes that, should another being find themselves utterly depressed at the humdrum personality still saddling their supernatural frame, they might find solace in knowing they are not the only one to have felt that way. Given the lengthy lifespan of many of the people with whom I associate, there is no guarantee they will have passed on by the time this is read. Therefore, names have been changed as I deemed necessary.

So, dear reader, whom I suspect is a wonderful person merely in need of a bit of reassurance, take comfort in my tales of uneventful blundering. One's nature is hard to change; sometimes even death is insufficient to accomplish such a task. But be assured that, while you might find yourself still more human than anticipated, you are far from the only one. You will eventually discover that under the movie stereotypes, imposed mystique, and over-all inflated expectations, each and every one of us is at least a touch more boring than our images would indicate.

And that is not a bad thing.

— Fredrick Frankford Fletcher

AN ACCOUNTANT IN THE WAREHOUSE

1.

AFTER MONTHS OF RELENTLESS TRAINING, hours of effort, and tests so great I didn't know if I would survive them, my work had finally paid off. Some months ago, when I'd first learned there were gaps in my knowledge, I'd had no real idea what I was signing up for. Now, with it finally done, I beamed with pride as I looked down at the starched piece of paper, a symbol of my accomplishment.

"Fredrick Frankford Fletcher," I read aloud, relishing the finely embossed print resting on the cream-colored background. "Certified Public Parahuman Accountant." (Parahuman being, of course, the term applied to all creatures of supernatural origin currently residing in the world.)

Learning about the parahuman world, through virtue of my own death, hadn't been nearly as disturbing to me as learning there were whole sections of laws, tax codes, and deduction options for my kind. This meant that I'd been doing my job without all the tools available to me, and, like working a calculator without a nine button, I found that utterly unacceptable. So, after four months of studying, certification tests, and a dreary weekend at a conference in a Seattle Holiday Inn, I'd closed that gap in my knowledge and gained the new accreditation to prove it.

Ah, but perhaps I should digress for a moment. My name, as stated on the certificate, is Fredrick Frankford Fletcher, though nearly all of my friends and acquaintances call me Fred. I am also an Undead American—a vampire, specifically—and an accountant. In fact, I ran my own company, which now had a whole new section of clients I could appeal to. The parahuman world is rich with magic, intrigue, and adventure, but it seems not a lot of folks like to do the job of crunching numbers come tax-time. I greatly prefer the latter to all three of the former, so I was happy to have found a niche where I could be both useful and make a tidy profit.

"I'm so proud of you," Krystal said, walking over and planting a kiss on my cheek. She nearly spilled some of the champagne in her cup (yes, I said cup) onto the certificate below. Of course, I'd already had it framed and protected by glass, but I still winced as the pale bubbly liquid surged up to the edge of the plastic container before plunging back down.

"Thank you," I replied, giving her a brief hug. Despite the fact that we'd now been together for over half a year, I was still shy about public displays of affection. Krystal, knowing this quite well, never missed the opportunity to embarrass me with such over-the-top actions.

"What does this mean?" Albert asked from the kitchen. He was my assistant (as well as a zombie), and a more loyal or well-intentioned person I could scarcely imagine. That said, Albert was not especially quick on the mental draw, possibly because of the . . . awkward circumstances surrounding his brain's condition at death. Which meant that, despite explaining it to him multiple times, he still didn't entirely understand the implications of my new title.

I walked out of my office—a small room in my apartment—and rejoined the rest of the party, which consisted of Albert, my aforementioned assistant, Neil, his best friend and an amateur necromancer, Bubba, a local therian (were-creature), Amy, Neil's magical mentor, and of course the aforementioned cup-using

Krystal. I'd invited them all over to celebrate my accomplishment, only to realize I'd forgotten the glasses for the champagne toast in my office. That had led to me getting mesmerized by the certificate yet again—a fact I am not proud of, but that I feel compelled to admit.

Crossing past the window—retrofitted with special glass that not only neutralized the sun's harmful effects on me, but that was also nearly indestructible—I glanced down and enjoyed the sight of sunlight dancing off the glasses in my hand. Having my home broken into the previous Christmas hadn't been a pleasant ordeal, but the opportunity to upgrade some of my abode's features had certainly paid off nicely.

"It means, Albert, that I am now far more attractive to parahuman clients," I explained as I joined the others gathered in the kitchen. "While I was allowed to do their taxes before, they'll now know that I'm aware of all applicable tax laws and viable deductions, meaning I can do a better job for them."

With great care, I set the glasses down and picked up the open bottle of champagne, filling the delicate containers one by one. Krystal merely stuck out her cup and motioned for a refill. I obliged, because nearly eight months of dating someone is long enough to understand what they will and will not bend on. At least she'd consented to toasting with champagne instead of beer, so this was her meeting me halfway. Once the glasses were filled, I hefted mine in a toast..

"Here's to progress," I said. "And to effort being rewarded."

"Fuckin' A," Krystal swore. "Here's to you, Fred. You busted your ass, and we're all proud of you." Her words, along with the smile she gave me, made me far less bothered by her choice to drink champagne from a plastic cup.

The others echoed their agreement, and we sipped the champagne. No, sorry, I sipped the champagne. Krystal knocked back her whole glass in a single chug, Bubba tried a swallow and then covertly set his glass down, Amy dropped two tablets in hers that made it glow blue before she gulped it down, and Albert and Neil had cider because they were under age. Technically drinking ages don't apply to the undead, but Albert had never shown any interest in alcohol. I think he was happy enough with his brain chemistry as it was.

"It truly is amazing," Amy said, her voice suddenly sounding a bit like a song-bird gargling wind chimes. "There's a lot of ground to cover; most people need at least a year to become a CPPA."

"Well, I've always had a head for numbers," I replied humbly. As a vampire, I wasn't anything special, but my accounting talents had never been a matter for debate.

"That reminds me," Bubba said, his thick drawl an oddly pleasant contrast to Amy's magically altered tones. Behind his back, Krystal stealthily took his mostly full glass and dumped its contents into her cup. He almost certainly heard her, but the situation worked out to his benefit so he stayed silent on the matter. "I've got your first client for you, if you want one."

"Sure," I readily agreed. "I've had to cut back on my own work in order to study, so I'm definitely looking to build a new pipeline of business."

"Suspected as much." Bubba reached into the pocket of his blue jeans and produced a worn business card. It had certainly been crisp when it entered his pocket, but Bubba was a large man, and everything he wore seemed to get battered faster than normal. "You already know the address, so just give him a call and set up a meetin'."

One glance at the card gave me reason to be both happy and full of dread. It was for Richard Alderson, head therian in my city and someone I'd had an outing with last winter. He was a good fellow, despite his terrifying presence, and it would be nice to see him again. However, Richard also had a houseguest—a dragon named Gideon who quite literally scared me catatonic, and I was in no great rush to see him again. Ever.

"Thought you might want to know, Gideon is out of town 'til the end of the week," Bubba added.

"Is he now?" My spirits perked up immediately. "I think I'll give Richard a call first thing tomorrow."

"Such a brave vampire," Neil chuckled into his glass of cider. The two of us had never really gotten along as well as the others, perhaps because he tried to kill me (along with several other people) the first time we met. Some first impressions are hard to shake, after all.

"Just one of those things," Krystal told him. "A dragon can suppress his aura around mortals, but vampires seem to get the full brunt of it even when it's dialed back. No one really knows why."

"I've conjectured that it's a trait evolved by their magic as a sort of natural defense. Since a vampire would be tempted by the dragon's blood, they developed a way to repel vampires, so as not to be caught unaware." Amy said all of this in a voice that now sounded like a cartoon chipmunk, and I noticed flowers in her hair, where previously there had been none. Amy's side-job was as a master alchemist, and she had a habit of trying out products on herself with alarming frequency. That said, she was easily smarter than the rest of us, possibly even if we were combined.

"Sounds odd. Even without the mind-crushing terror, I doubt I'd be much of a match for Gideon," I said. Gideon's official title was King of the West, and parahumans didn't bestow such monikers without good reason.

"Of course not, but you're on two opposite ends of the spectrum. There are dragons far weaker than Gideon, and vampires far more dangerous and ambitious than you," Amy reminded me.

That part was very true. I'd met the vampire who "made" me over Christmas of last year, and he'd been a piece of work. If not for Krystal, I'd have been dead. And this time, it would have stuck.

"I don't know about the ambition part," Krystal disagreed. "Didn't you see my man's new certificate? I think he's definitely got some aspirations."

"Yes, I do," I agreed, tucking the card into my own pocket. Tomorrow would be the first step toward those very aspirations. I intended to land a new client, and hopefully get some referrals.

It would be nice, familiar, and above all, safe.

2.

GETTING IN TO MEET WITH RICHARD PROVED
harder than I expected, but the majority of that fault
fell on me. I'd forgotten that, while he is a perfectly af-
fable and understanding man behind closed doors, he is
also the head of all therian society in our city, and that
meant there were certain procedures of respect I had to
follow. Therians (short for therianthropes, a term that
applies to all werewolf–like creatures regardless of which
animal form they actually take), are sticklers for ceremony and etiquette. Yes, I'd been surprised too, but Bubba

explained to me once that it was the best way to keep their animal instincts in line, making the human side of themselves constantly aware of their actions and the significance they held.

What this meant for my meeting with Richard was that I had to go to his place of residence—at an appointed visiting hour—and do a bit of bowing and thanking for the privilege of serving under him. This was done in his extravagant hallway at the top of the office building he called home, a myriad of other therians surrounding his marble throne and enjoying the show. It was a touch more extreme than therian supplicants had to go through, but that was mostly because vampires had never really gotten along with the were-community. If I were a particularly prideful person, I might have had an objection to going through it all just for a job. As it was, I treated it like I was in a tea ceremony. I might not understand the reasons for the actions required of me, but that didn't give me an excuse to ignore them.

Once an appropriate amount of groveling had been achieved, Richard (standing at least seven feet tall, his golden hair hanging shaggily down to his shoulders) rose from the cold marble seat he'd been resting on and gestured for me to accompany him to his private chambers. These were tucked away behind a thick wall that was only moveable by one with strength beyond a human's capacity. Only after that door had once again been sealed did he turn to me and allow his serious face to split into a wide grin.

"Thank you for coming, Fred," he said, his voice only a few octaves above a growl. I'd never seen Richard look totally human; it was possible he wasn't even able to. Richard was an alpha, a rare therian of such strength and power that he was considered unbeatable by anything short of another alpha. That status gave him his size, position of authority, and enormous strength, but I often wondered about the price that came with such blessings. In magic, I was slowly learning, there was almost always a price.

"Sorry about all the formality at the door," Richard continued, running a hand through his golden hair.

"Quite all right. I know your people have never seen eye to eye with mine. If it makes things easier, then I'm more than happy to accommodate."

"Any other week, I probably could have growled at my people and told them to piss off, but I need everything smooth right now," Richard explained. "I've got a lot of meetings this week with therians who were driven out of a nearby community. Supposedly, they're seeking sanctuary, though I'll be shocked if none of them tries to make a play for the throne."

"They'd have to be utterly suicidal," I commented, setting down my briefcase and surveying the room. It looked largely the same as the last time I'd been there—a generous space filled with cushy, reinforced furniture and a large television. I knew the door nearest to me led to a kitchen, next to that was Richard's room, and through the one after that would be the room belonging to his daughter, Sally. The other doors led to places I didn't know, but presumably one of them housed Richard's permanent guest: Gideon. "I mean, even aside from you and your gang of friends, who would attack the King of the West?"

Richard let out a low chuckle, the sort that would set your nerves on high alert if you heard it come from the dark shade of nearby woods. "Gideon does not intervene in my affairs. That too is part of therian society: if I cannot hold a position by my own strength, then I am not entitled to it. But no, I do not anticipate too much trouble with any who might think to become upstarts. They can challenge at the appropriate time and place, or I can put them down immediately if they think themselves above our laws."

"Right. As certain as I am that you can handle that, I'm here about your taxes," I reminded him. Talk of impending violence, even contained violence, always made me a little antsy.

"Of course, follow me." Richard strode forward with his sizable gait, easily crossing the room and flinging open one of the doors I hadn't yet been through to reveal a large office. Well, I say "large," but I suspect Richard would have been quite cramped moving about in it. There were boxes of paper all over the floor, three sets of filing cabinets, and a desk nearly overflowing with unsorted documents.

"Here it is," he announced proudly.

"What, exactly, am I looking at?"

"Forms, receipts, accounting ledgers, and other such paperwork I've accumulated in my time as this area's therian overseer," he explained. "I had it brought up from storage, assuming you'd need such things."

"You're not wrong about that," I agreed. "But I only need stuff from the last year."

"This is from the last year."

Being a vampire means never having to cough in shock; our impulses related to involuntary expulsion are wiped out in the conversion process. Habit, on the other hand, is making the noise anyway, because sometimes words fall short of your power to convey thoughts. Which is why I coughed loudly in unabashed shock.

"My territory is a large one, with many therians," Richard said. "And I am obligated to oversee this procedure for Gideon, as well. As you can see, the paperwork accumulates."

I took a deep breath (another habit I'd never seen a need to break) and steadied my nerves. "Richard, I have a point I want to raise with you before I try and tackle this mound of insanity. If I didn't, I'd feel like I was taking advantage of you."

"Do tell," he encouraged.

"You know I bill by the hour, right? And this is not going to be a quick job. I can do it, let's be clear, but if you have someone who is better acquainted with this material and charges less, then maybe you should go with them. I mean, who did your taxes last year?"

"No one," Richard admitted. "I just paid the bill the government sent me."

I nodded. In my training, I'd learned that, since parahumans often led somewhat more chaotic and no-madic lifestyles, they had the option to not submit taxes and just pay whatever the government told them they owed. Many parahumans exercised this option, which was a crying shame, in my humble opinion.

"If it's not prying, how much did they charge?"

Richard told me the number, and I made another chortled choking sound in the back of my throat.

"I can do it for cheaper than that," I assured him. "Definitely, far cheaper than that."

"Thank goodness," Richard said. "And thank you, Fred, for your concern over treating me fairly. I deal so much with politicians and backstabbers that it is a pleas-ant change to see someone show genuine kindness."

"Not a big deal. I just believe that good work and good service are the cornerstones to customer loyalty."

"I'll remember that," he said. "Now, if you'll excuse me, I need to head down for another meeting. You're free to start whenever you like. I'll also have one of my people wait in attendance and take you through a secret entrance when you want to exit or re-enter the building. No need to make you parade about every time."

"Wait, I'm supposed to work here?" I asked, though the answer was already quite obvious.

"Unless you'd like to haul all of this downstairs and across town," Richard said.

He had a very good point. I'd gotten so used to the digital age that the idea of trucking paper around hadn't even occurred to me. This was a useful lesson, though. Parahumans probably did most of their record keeping in the same manner as Richard. If I wanted to break into this segment of the market, I needed to adjust. And the sooner, the better.

"No, you're right; it's easier to do it here." I pulled my slim laptop from my briefcase and set it on the desk. "Fair warning, though, I do keep late hours."

"You are free to come and work anytime you like," Richard said. "I really only use this room for playing computer games and hiding from my assistants. Yell if you need anything."

With that, he was out the door, and I was left to start the nigh-impossible task of sorting through Mount Papermanjaro.

3.

I FIRST BECAME AWARE OF ANOTHER PRESENCE in the office after roughly three hours of work, but it was entirely possible that the person had been there for far longer than I realized—vampire senses might be exceptional, but I've always had a tendency to zone-out when working. Once I noticed, however, it was very difficult to ignore. Partially because, like someone drawing your attention to a rickety ceiling fan you were previously ignoring as white noise, it is very difficult to lose awareness once it is gained. And also partially because a toy unicorn was thrown at my head.

Credit to the pitching ability of my attacker; the plush figure struck me dead-center in the forehead, knocking my glasses somewhat askew. It is possible I let out a minor yelp of surprise, which I feel is perfectly forgivable given the unexpected interruption. I adjusted my glasses and glanced around, quickly scanning for any threats that required my special brand of dealing with (read: running away from). What I discovered was a small girl standing at the office door's entrance. Her blonde hair was pulled into a ponytail, and she wore pink overalls, along with a curious expression.

"Hello, Sally," I greeted, carefully tossing back her toy. "How are you today?"

"Bored," she replied, strangely enthusiastic given the negative news she was relaying. "Gideon is gone and Daddy is busy, so there's no one to play with."

I have never been particularly adept at picking up social cues, but this was a pitch slow enough for even me to get the speed of.

"Ah," I replied. "That does sound rather unfortunate. Your father has asked me to come in and help him with his work, so hopefully he'll finish soon and be able to play with you." It wasn't technically a lie, which was good, because I've found children strangely capable of sniffing out small deceptions despite their tendencies to wholeheartedly embrace big ones.

"But I'm bored *now*," she reiterated.

"Perhaps you could color in your books, or watch a movie."

"I tried. It's not fun without Gideon."

It had always struck me as a bit odd that the King of the West served as a daily playmate for Richard's daughter. I trusted that Gideon had his reasons; given his age and power, perhaps he simply took enjoyment in the innocent wonder only children could conjure. Still, it seemed strange. It also seemed like inadvertently angering his daily companion was not in my best interests.

"I suppose we could play a small game," I acquiesced. "But only if you promise to allow me to go back to my work when it's concluded."

"Promise!" Sally yelled excitedly, darting off to her room. From the rummaging sounds echoing forth, I presumed she already had a game in mind and was now excavating it from the rubble that was any child's toy chest. I glanced at the clock and wrote down the time. It would be unethical to bill for accounting work when I was merely playing with Sally, so I had to chart when I went on and off the clock.

I carefully shut the doors to the office and stepped out into the living room. A quick scan told me that the coffee table would likely be an adequate space for all but the most sizable of board games. Then again, I was somewhat out of touch with the entertainment options purveyed to children these days, so it was possible the dining room table would present a more appropriate option. I was heading toward the aforementioned dining room when I realized the level of noise from Sally's room had risen from merely "childish-roar" to "din of racket."

"Sally," I called. "Do you need help locating your game?"

The sound cut off immediately, which, in retrospect, should have been my first clue that something was amiss. Children do not cease noise-making so instantaneously, as I have now learned. At the time, I had no such wisdom, so I ignored the red flag. After all, I was in the headquarters of the most powerful therian in the entire metropolis of Winslow, Colorado. What safer place could there be?

"Sally?" I called again. This time, I received an answer, but it was not a verbal one. At least, not initially.

The two men who stepped into the living room had several hundred pounds and a couple of feet on me. They wore dark clothing and ski-masks, but tufts of fur stuck out from the eyes and mouth holes. Therians, transformed into their hybrid forms. Despite the fascination of their sudden appearance and evident heritage, the most eye-catching feature about these two was the limp girl in the taller one's arms. She had blonde hair styled in a ponytail and pink overalls, now stained with a small bit of blood.

As anyone who has read my previous memoirs will be keenly aware, I am neither an aggressive nor anger-inclined being. I leave such tendencies to Krystal, who possesses the training and power to back them up. That said, upon seeing Sally's body in their hands, I felt a curious prickle of cold in my stomach, and for the first time, I found myself wondering just how great a gap there was in the strength of a vampire and a therian.

"This him?" asked the smaller invader, light red hairs sticking out of his mask.

"Must be," said the taller one, his own fur a dingy gray. His eyes focused on me, and when he next spoke, there was a new level of harshness in his voice. "Don't move. The girl is just knocked out right now, but we can do a lot worse."

Whatever uncharacteristic fantasies I might have been entertaining vanished in a puff of reality. Sally's safety was first priority, and I had no reason to assume these men were bluffing. They'd broken into Richard's home and assaulted his daughter. These were actions of men either too bold or too stupid to care about the ramifications such an assault would bring.

I raised my hands slowly, demonstrating my surrender.

"What do we do with him?" This came from the smaller one, who I'd mentally dubbed Red on account of his fur color.

"Bind him," Gray instructed. "If we leave him be, he'll just come after us once we're gone."

I resisted the urge to cock my head in curiosity, but only because I feared for Sally's safety if I made any sudden movements.

"We could kill him," Red suggested. I decided that I greatly disliked the smaller of these two, not just because he'd tossed out the idea of ending my life, but because I have no great affection for anyone whose first recourse to solving a problem is murderous violence. Thankfully, Gray shut down that idea immediately.

"We want leverage, not a feud," Gray reminded him. "If we kill her bodyguard, Alderson is going to demand blood in return. Keep him alive, and we have another bargaining chip."

"Fine," Red agreed begrudgingly. He stepped toward me, pulling out a case from the fanny-pack resting on his hip. (Yes, you read that right. Evidently even criminals, unlike what films have led us to believe, sometimes have to put pragmatism over style and toughness.) As soon as he cracked it open, I recognized the scent: silver.

After becoming a vampire, I'd quickly learned that the myths about silver were one of the things the lore got right. It weakened me, to the point where I was scarcely able to move when bound in the stuff. What I hadn't known, until Krystal filled me in, was that silver did this to almost every kind of parahuman. It was a magic insulator, like rubber to electricity, and there were few supernatural creatures immune to its effects.

That was likely why Red used great care as he wrapped the silver chains around my arms, then wrapped those around my torso, never touching them with any part of his body aside from the exceptionally thick gloves. When he finished with me, he did the same thing to Sally. I was actually somewhat glad she was being hindered. Sally was a precocious child who'd grown up with a powerful father. Without some binding, she might take action that would get her injured, and I had every desire to see such an incident avoided.

"Done," Red announced at last, wrapping a thick blanket over Sally's chains, so that Gray could still carry her without encountering the silver himself. Even with their precautions, the proximity of the stuff had to be making them feel queasy. I was having trouble even standing, thanks to the amount of it encircling my body.

Gray nodded and scooped her back up. "You walk in front," he instructed me. "Say anything, try anything, vary from our orders in any way, and both of you are going to pay for it."

I demonstrated my understanding by moving forward, allowing myself to be nudged along at their discretion. I had no idea what was happening, but I knew Richard wouldn't take the kidnapping of his daughter lightly. I just needed to keep watch over her until he recovered us. I also sincerely hoped he wouldn't take too long.

4.

THE TRIP TO RED AND GRAY'S SECRET lair was largely uneventful; they put a rough canvas bag around my head and stuffed Sally and me into a black van. Even in the world of cinema, these tactics were cliché. I should know. I watched an absolute plethora of films about people with more interesting lives than me.

During the ride, I did my best to stay calm. This endeavor was somewhat handicapped by my tendency to arrange things in mental lists when faced with a seemingly insurmountable situation. For organization and paperwork, it's a godsend of a habit. When kidnapped and being held hostage by criminal therians, it was somewhat less effective. Nonetheless, the thoughts came unbidden, and I had soon numbered all the issues currently facing me:

1. Sally and I were in the hands of people who either meant us harm or would inflict injury if conditions were not met.

2. Since they had entered and led us out through a secret entrance, it stood to reason that Richard's security had been compromised. That likely meant they had someone on the inside, which could hinder our rescue.

3. Gideon was out of town, but even if he weren't, he wouldn't be able to intervene.

4. My own friends would likely lend aid, but only if they were contacted in time. And given Richard's stance on "defending his position," that scenario seemed unlikely.

5. I had less than five hours until sunrise.

That last one was actually a bigger concern than its list position would indicate. I'd gone to Richard's establishment in the relatively early evening; however, I'd burned several hours on the entrance and making a dent in the paperwork. Assuming this didn't turn into a protracted situation, that left me with at least some time before the sun's rays pierced the horizon,. Once that happened, my only hope would be if my captors kept us in a place without any exposure to sunlight. Given that we were hostages, that seemed like a reasonable possibility, hence its low position on the list.

I heard brakes engage as the van came to a halt after nearly thirty minutes of driving. Rough hands directed me out the door. I managed to make it to a standing position without taking a tumble, although barely. Vampire reflexes and dexterity are lovely, but a blindfolded klutz is still a blindfolded klutz. Besides, being wrapped in silver meant I was in far from peak condition. More shoving had me walking at a brisk pace. Inwardly, I wondered why they didn't take the bag off. Was there some incredible secret I'd be privy to if they allowed me the gift of vision? I doubted it. More likely, it simply didn't occur to them.

Our group passed through a doorway, after which I was hustled over to what turned out to be a small corner of the building. I learned this because the bag was at last removed, and I could finally take in my location: a dilapidated warehouse that could have easily served as the set for a low-budget action film. I began to wonder if I wasn't the only one present who had spent too many nights alone on the couch with a pile of movies.

"That the bodyguard?" This was a new voice, different from Red or Gray, and it drew my attention to the other creatures present in the building. There were roughly five of them, possibly more; with my senses smothered by silver, I was limited to noting only those directly in my line of sight. Each appeared either human or therian, which didn't surprise me given the context clues Red and Gray had dropped. The one who had spoken was a stocky man, shorter than the others and in full human form. In spite of his comparatively diminished stature, he held an air of authority that kept every eye in the room on him, my own included.

"Has to be," Red informed him. "Vampire would be strong enough, 'specially if he's fed off an alpha, and he surrendered as soon as we threatened the girl."

It said a lot to me that Red had jumped to the conclusion that I must be an employee because I cared that a little girl was being threatened. At his words, I realized I hadn't seen Sally for a bit, and my eyes darted about furiously. I quickly found her; she was roughly twenty feet away, still bound in silver. She was awake, but remained silent. I prayed she would continue to have the good sense not to speak. This was not a situation where antagonization would benefit us.

While I'd been looking at Sally, the shorter man had turned his direct attention on me. He strode over with careful, measured steps. Even though I was bound in silver, he was cautious. This was probably an intelligent attitude to take with most captured parahumans, however, in my case, it was a bit wasted. Silver or no, I was not a challenge to him, let alone him plus another four therians.

"What's your name?" His eyes were a light yellow, like the color of fresh bile.

"Fredrick," I responded. I didn't want to lie if I could avoid it; he seemed like the type to take such things personally.

He raised a slight eyebrow. "Fredrick?"

"Most of my colleagues and friends call me Fred," I admitted after a moment.

"Fred the Vampire, huh? Fine, you can call me Orson."

I nodded my head, but said nothing. Every word I spoke risked getting us into worse trouble. Best to use them sparingly.

"So, Fred, are my people right? Are you Richard's guy?" Orson's tone was casual, while his face was as serious as a man giving a eulogy.

"Yes, I work for her father," I replied. It was true, though likely not in the way he was interpreting it. It seemed prudent not to allow him time for follow-up questions that would undo the assumptive deception, though. "And he is not at all going to be pleased with your actions. Return us now, while there is still time, and perhaps some bit of mercy can be shown to you."

Orson snorted; it was a loud, powerful sound that rebounded off the warehouse's walls. "I know Richard is going to be pissed. I knew that when we planned this whole thing. But what was our other option? Live like second-class parahumans? Scrape and bow and beg for a place at his table? To hell with that. I ruled my last town, and I'll rule this one too."

"It was my understanding that Richard's position can only be taken by one stronger than him. Taking Sally won't make you more powerful."

"There are many kinds of strength, Fred," Orson said, eyes narrowing just a touch. "Richard has the physical kind, but I've got the mental kind. When I issue my challenge, he's going to let me win, because I've got something he loves more than his position."

"Daddy hates his job," Sally said. Her soft, high-pitched tones reached every ear in the room. She stared at the floor as she spoke, as though there were no one else around her. "He hates it. He does it 'cause it has to get done, liking cleaning up a room."

"There you go, then," Orson said, allowing a toothy smile to slice across his face. "Richard will be free of a job he doesn't like, and I will take my rightful place as ruler."

"I hate when people die," Sally said. This time, everyone grew slightly still at the sound of her words. "I'm sorry."

Orson gave the small girl his full attention then, the wicked grin now erased from his face. "What are you sorry for?"

"I don't think anyone should die. Dying is really bad. It means you leave people lonely. I still miss my Mommy. It would be better if no one ever had to die."

"You don't have to worry," Orson told her, using what I think he believed to be a comforting tone. It sounded more like a gentler form of threatening, which, perhaps, was the best he could manage. "As long as your dad does what we tell him, everything will be fine. No one is going to die."

Sally lifted her head, finally looking at the people surrounding her instead of the ground. I'd expected any number of expressions to be on her face: terror, pain, panic, any of these would have made sense, given the situation. What I saw instead was grief; a terrible sadness etched into her tiny face, suddenly seeming so much older than it had any right to appear. With great care, she looked at each man present, as if she were memorizing their features. When she finally spoke again, her words had a gravity that could have pulled satellites from orbit.

"You are. You're all gonna die. I'm so sorry." With that, Sally began to cry, a soft, shivering sob that was almost noiseless as the tears ran down her face.

Orson was momentarily taken aback by her earnest concern, but quickly recovered. Clearly, he was too much of a professional to take the implied threats of a child seriously.

"Oh, to have the fantasies of youth again," Orson said loudly, his voice breaking the somber spell cast by Sally's warning. "I'm sure she thinks her father will come bounding in the door to rescue her. We know better, don't we, boys? By now, he's probably worried himself into a panic. When we deliver the ransom note, he'll kiss our feet in gratitude at the chance to get his daughter back."

I'd seen Richard fight before, and not when things were especially serious. If I'd stolen his daughter, I wouldn't let that set of werelion jaws anywhere near my body, even if he feigned surrender. Right about then, I began suspecting these five had bitten off more than they could chew, but not more than could chew them.

"All right, I'm done talking to the hostages. Shove them somewhere out of the way and stick a guard on them," Orson ordered. "I've got a challenge to get ready for."

5.

SALLY REMAINED SILENT AS WE WERE
DRAGGED off to another corner of the warehouse. We
were close enough to hear the others in a general sense,
but picking out more than a few haphazard words at a
time was beyond my capabilities. Red ended up being
stuck with guard duty, taking a seat on an aged wooden
crate and setting his gaze so it fell on us. He appeared
bored, and I didn't much blame him for that. A silver-
bound vampire and a therian child, also chained in silver,
don't make for very exciting guard-duty. If he'd hoped

for unexpected action, we were not the crew to deliver it. Eventually, his attention waned, and he began checking his phone more often, evidently becoming engrossed in some internet reading.

"Sally," I called. My words were soft, but not a whisper. I didn't want Red to think I was plotting anything, yet, at the same time, I didn't want him overhearing unless he put a mind to it. He gave the sound of my voice no apparent consideration, so I continued. "Sally, are you all right?"

She gave me a small bob of her head. The tears had stopped flowing; however, her nose was still runny and the area around her eyes had turned a puffy red.

"It's going to be okay. We'll get out of this just fine." Admittedly, after her strange prediction, I wasn't entirely sure which of us I was trying to reassure, but being the adult in the situation made me feel that it was my duty to at least attempt some consoling.

"He's going to be mad," Sally said, her own voice in hushed tones as well.

"No one will be mad at you," I told her.

"Not at me. At them. He's always mad when I get taken."

My next trite phase died on my tongue as I soaked in her words. "Sally, does this happen often?"

"Used to," she replied glumly. "People want to hurt Daddy, but Daddy is too big. They try to hurt me because I'm small."

I wasn't certain which part revolted me more: how resigned Sally was to the fate of being constantly kidnapped, or the knowledge that therian society was so cutthroat that such things were acceptable. Then I recalled her assessment of their impending death. Perhaps acceptable was not the correct phrase for the methods these people were employing. In a way, it made a psychopathic kind of sense. Winslow was a pretty sizable city, and there had to be lots of therians in it. Trying to take Richard's position by force was laughable—even Krystal considered him one of the strongest were-creatures she knew. So the only method remaining was to attack his weakest point, the daughter he loved so dearly. If this had happened before, then Richard clearly had some sort of Sally retrieval system in place. Otherwise, he'd have been killed or deposed long ago.

"I'm sorry they took you," I told her. "And I'm sorry I wasn't able to stop them. No one is going to hurt you, though. I promise."

Tears welled up in the sides of her eyes once more. She turned away, looking at the raftered ceiling looming over us. I wondered if she was trying to picture the sky outside, or if she was just gazing at the reality that surrounded us.

"Edmund, come give us a hand. We're loading the truck." This voice came from the main part of the warehouse, and at a guess, I would have said the speaker was

Gray. To my momentary surprise, Red let out a sigh, put away his phone, and rose from his seat. In my time with them, I'd forgotten that Red was a nickname I'd assigned him, not his genuine moniker.

"Coming!" Red/Edmund yelled. He shot a single glance our way, the meaning of which was abundantly clear, and then headed off to join the others. They exited amidst a myriad of sound indicating heavy lifting. Obviously, they weren't that concerned with us making a break for it, which was sound judgment since our silver chains were locked to the chairs we currently sat in.

Still, I expected to feel a soft flutter of relief at not being under someone's watchful eye, but that relief didn't come. What arrived in its place was an unexpected sense of dread, a deep-down, to the soul of my being, terror. I'd have cried out for help if I could have found the courage to move my tongue. Anyone, any*thing*, was better. I would have gleefully welcomed back our kidnappers just to rid myself of such panic. Somewhere, though, in the few coherent portions of my mind, a piece of me recognized the sensation. The last time I'd felt it, there had been some subtlety and nuance; it hadn't been nearly as overwhelming.

Then again, the last time I'd felt it, Gideon hadn't been pissed off.

"I thought they'd never leave," said the voice of a child who was centuries too old to be one. Gideon stepped out from behind some boxes, clad in a small tuxedo that must have been custom made for his tiny body. He looked much the same as he had the first time I saw him—a tan-skinned child somewhere between six and eight years old, dirty blonde hair mussed in every direction. The key difference this time was his eyes. Their violet color had always sparkled, but tonight, they positively burned. I didn't need many guesses to know the cause for that change.

"I'm sorry," Sally blurted out as soon as he arrived. "Daddy said you were on a trip, and I didn't want to ruin it, but I got scared and I—"

"Hush, Little Wyrm," Gideon told her in gentle tones. "I'll always come for you. You never need to say sorry when I appear." He managed a far better "soothing" voice than I had, not that it did me any good; I literally cowered in place. Had I not been chained down, I'd have been running into the night. It was strange, part of me was still coherent and rational enough to understand what was happening, but every animal instinct in my body was overpowering that part, demanding we escape.

"But your trip . . ."

"Is a silly trip that I can go back to when I please," Gideon reassured her. "You are what is most important. After all, friends look out for each other, don't they?"

Sally nodded. This line of reasoning jived well with her understanding of acceptable practices. "Don't be too mean to them, please. They didn't hurt us."

At the mention of there being more than one person captured, Gideon gave me the smallest flicker of attention. I shook so hard that I knocked my chair over. I expected the loud noise to echo through the empty warehouse, but no such racket arose. He turned back to her, and I was ratcheted back down to my previous level of soul-quaking dread.

"I will be as gentle as possible," Gideon told her. "If they are willing to properly apologize, there is no need for me to be harsh. For now, why don't you take a short rest? I'm sure you're tired after so much excitement." His irises brightened for a fraction of a moment, and seconds later, Sally's own eyes began to droop.

"No . . . I'll . . ." Sally opened her mouth, letting out a loud yawn that again failed to echo. "I'll stay . . ." And with that, her small head fell to her shoulder, the sandman's sudden charms too much to resist. Gideon stayed crouched by her side for a moment longer, just enough time to tear away her chains as if they were made a Play-Doh. (I'm still not certain if dragons are immune to silver's power, or if they're simply so strong, it doesn't make a difference. In the end, the concern is largely academic, because the results are the same.) He pulled her carefully into his arms, then set her down on the floor. Only when she was comfortably resting did he turn his attention to me once more.

"Blood-eater," he greeted, all softness gone from his voice. "I will keep this brief; the spells I cast to slow the fools outside will wear thin soon. I require your assistance tonight. What is going to transpire in this warehouse is not something I wish to expose Sally to, not even as she slumbers. You will be entrusted with her safety. You are to leave this place and use those dead legs to carry her back to Richard with every ounce of speed available to you. Should anything more happen to her, there will be consequences."

At the word "consequences," I spasmed so hard that I nearly snapped a chair-leg, which was no small feat considering my strength was reduced by the silver.

"Right, the terror," he muttered. The small boy put his hands on his tuxedo-clad hips, clearly contemplating a rogue idea. He could have been like that for minutes or hours—time had grown wonky in my perceptions—but finally, he reached a conclusion.

"What I am going to do, I do purely out of regard for Sally," he informed me. "Technically speaking, I will violate several unspoken laws of dragon pride, as well as a few ardently spoken ones." A small, dangerous smile danced on his lips. "But what is the point of being a king, if one cannot ignore the rules when it pleases him? So rejoice, blood-eater, because I am going to remove your fear. Just remember, what you are about to experience is merely a single drop of my power. If you want to see how deep the well goes, then fail in safely delivering

Sally home. I will show you every bit of my strength then, and you will pray for Hell to accept you just so you can be free of me."

With that not at all utterly terrifying warning, Gideon stepped closer to me. As he did, he raised his right hand. The nail on his thumb began to warp and extend until it was no longer a nail, but a small copper-colored claw. He pressed the tip of it into his index finger until the flesh parted. A single droplet of blood welled up before the wound sealed itself closed.

Gideon leaned down to the shivering lump that was my body and carefully pulled open my mouth. I could no more have resisted him than I could have beaten Bubba in a beer chugging contest. My lips parted, and Gideon wiped the small bit of blood on my tongue. I swallowed involuntarily, because my vampire instincts demanded that blood be consumed, and then it hit me.

If Gideon's presence had filled me with incomparable dread, his blood had me overflowing with a blast of power. My silver-dulled senses all came rushing back, even stronger than they'd been before. The world exploded in color and sound, and I felt like I was hearing the entire city thrumming in my ears. My muscles spasmed like they would explode. I jerked in surprise and heard a dull crunch as the chair became splinters. But even through the head-swimming amazement of it all, I noticed one change above the others: my terror at Gideon's aura had completely vanished. Aside from the blood-high, I was back in my normal frame of mind, which was a whole other level of incredible relief.

After a moment to compose myself, I slowly rose from the ground. My chains lay in broken chunks around my feet, but that was likely Gideon's work. Even on dragon-blood, silver is silver, and I am a vampire. I looked over and found him staring toward the central part of the warehouse, where the sound of softly scuffling feet was beginning to echo.

"Control yourself, blood-eater," Gideon instructed me, making no attempt to soften his voice. With my perked up hearing, I realized the sound was dying out a few feet away from us. Evidently, he'd cast more than just a spell to slow down our kidnappers. "Most of the effects will fade soon, though you will find my presence far more tolerable from now on. For now, you should have all the power you need to get my . . . Sally home safely. Take her. *Now*."

I did as I was told, not just out of fear of Gideon, though that certainly played a healthy part in my actions, but because I could hear the murder in his voice. He was right, what was about to happen was nothing that Sally needed to be around for. I scooped her up from the ground, set her over my shoulder in a fireman's carry, and then scouted my options. There was a window roughly forty feet in the air with the glass broken out.

Even for a vampire, that was a hell of a jump. With my momentary boost, however, it felt laughably easy.

Gideon stepped forward, coming into view of the rest of the room.

"Good evening, gentlemen. My name is Gideon, and I have come to speak with you about the young girl you stole this evening."

Taking the cue, I leapt up and through the window while their attention was focused on him. They might have sent pursuers, but if so, they never came near me. With the dragon blood in my system, I was an undead blur, racing through the streets as fast as my power would carry me.

Unfortunately, thanks to amped up hearing, it wasn't fast enough to outrun the first of our kidnapper's tortured screams.

6.

RICHARD RAN HIS HANDS OVER HIS
daughter's head for the umpteenth time. She was still
passed out, though whether it was from fatigue or Gideon's spell, I had no idea. Getting her back had been easy;
I could have smelled my way across town, even if I hadn't
been familiar with Winslow's layout. Richard had met me
at the entrance to the building, probably saving my life,
since a vampire showing up with a kidnapped therian is
not exactly a trust-inducing scenario. If I'd been thinking, I would have realized that before the cacophony of

growls began, but that damned dragon blood still had me somewhat loopy. I was finally calming down a bit when Richard at last satisfied himself that she was really back safe and stepped into his living room to talk with me.

"Wine?" He asked, his voice a deep rumble that spoke to how draining his own evening must have been.

"Please," I responded.

Richard stepped into his kitchen and returned with a bottle of pinot noir. He pulled out the cork with practiced ease, then poured us each a large glass. Motioning to one of the unoccupied chairs, he indicated for me to sit. I complied, accepting the wineglass as I did, and soon, he took his own perch in a larger piece of furniture. We sat in silence for several moments, both delicately sipping on the wine. It was an exceptional vintage, and I made a mental note to get the year and label from him later.

"You must have questions," Richard said at last. I'd seen Richard partially dissolved by magical-monster acid before, but I couldn't ever recall seeing him appear so weary.

"I do have some things I'm curious about," I admitted. "However, I know privacy and secrecy is a large part of your job. After tonight, I understand why a little better. I'd be content if you could just tell me what happened, keeping the strokes as broad as you need to."

"I owe you far more than that; however, it is a fine place to start," Richard agreed. "My security was compromised by a bloodline I wasn't aware of. The therians from a neighboring community were driven out by forces it is best you remain ignorant of. I was prepared to take them in, as I told you, but it seemed they weren't content with merely joining my town's citizens. Their former leader wanted to take my job. One of his cousins works for me. Not high up enough to officially know about things like Gideon or the secret entrance, but connected enough that he was able to piece some bits of it together."

"He turned on you?" Perhaps it was naive; however I'd always seen therians as intensely loyal. It had seemed to be a staple of their culture.

"I'm a figurehead," Richard explained. "Orson is blood. Blood means a lot to my kind. Family, the pack, those we share blood with, these things are so sacred that many of us consider them holy. He owed loyalty in two directions, and he chose to honor the one that he saw as his true pack. I don't begrudge him that."

"So, what happened to him; the guard who leaked your secrets?"

"I didn't begrudge his choice, but he still betrayed a loyalty. Do you really want to know more than that?"

"Point taken," I said quickly.

"Anyway, Orson decided to use Sally against me. He knew about the entrance, and he knew she was guarded, so he sent up thugs with silver to snatch her while keeping me busy with diplomatic bullshit. Once he had her, Orson planned to ransom her back to me at the cost of my position."

"You know as much as I do, and I was there to hear them talk about it," I commented.

"The traitor was . . . interviewed before judgment was passed." Richard took a longer sip of his wine. I wondered if Sally had been right, if Richard truly did hate his job. He certainly didn't appear to be taking any enjoyment in the more savage aspects of the position.

"I see. I suppose we were lucky they didn't know enough to be aware that the King of the West was your daughter's bodyguard." I kept my tone neutral. This was a subject I dearly wanted to broach, but had well-founded suspicions would be taboo in Richard's book.

"He is not her bodyguard," Richard corrected me. "It's well known that I play host to the King of the West; however, Gideon rarely leaves this room. If he does, he appears as you know him, as Sally's friend and playmate. Who would imagine that a dragon of such tremendous power would take the form of a mere child?"

"Who indeed," I concurred. "One thing does strike me, though. Earlier this evening, you told me Gideon couldn't meddle in your affairs and that he was out of town. Him crossing untold distances to save Sally . . . that seems well within his scope of power; however, it also seems as though retrieving your kidnapped daughter would fall well within the realm of meddling."

Richard turned his glass carefully in his hand, examining the last bits of wine clinging to its surface. "I don't know much about taxes, but there are loopholes, right?"

"I prefer to refer to them as alternate means of revenue classification. That said, yes, there are definitely loopholes in the tax code."

"This is a loophole in the parahuman code," Richard replied. "Or maybe I should say just the therian code. We have a stricter one than any other type of creature, probably because we're all so stubborn and willful that we need to be. I told you the truth when I said that Gideon can't get involved with my affairs, not unless I want to truly be a powerless figurehead. A leader who can't handle his own problems is not respected or obeyed by the pack. However, what Gideon did tonight wasn't technically involving himself in my affairs. Kidnapping Sally was a personal insult to him, and as her father, I allowed him first right of retribution. It was a move that earns my pack favor from a powerful ally, so no one can say my actions weren't for the good of my people."

"Seems tenuous," I pointed out.

"No question about it. But I stuck to the letter of the code, and that's what matters," Richard said, allowing himself a slight, relieved smile.

"I suppose it's a good thing she and Gideon are such good friends," I commented.

Richard's smile slid away, replaced by a heavy look in his eyes. After the night he'd already endured, it struck me that perhaps I should let the conversation die out. In fact, I was about to tell him that I was going to head back to my paperwork when he spoke once more.

"They're betrothed, actually."

"Beg pardon?" My mouth might have been hanging a touch bit open in shock.

"In a roundabout sort of way, they're betrothed," Richard sighed. Now that the dam holding back his secret had burst, the truth came pouring easily out of him. "There are conditions that must be met, the most important of which is that Sally must agree to wed him of her own free will when she comes of age, but should all things be satisfied, then Gideon has my blessing to wed my daughter. In our world, that makes them betrothed."

"I . . . um . . . wow . . . ." (Forgive the lack of eloquence, I was still half-muddled on dragon blood and had just been hit with a doozy of culture shock.)

"It was the only way I could keep her safe," Richard continued. "An alpha of my size is either a leader or a target. Any community I tried to settle down in had a leader that saw me as a potential threat, even though I had no aspiration to take over. It didn't matter. They'd come after me through my family. For a while, I kept moving around, trying to find somewhere safe. That strategy ultimately cost me Sally's mother. After I buried my wife, I decided to take on different tactics. I came to Gideon for help, and he made me the proposal that he would take the form of a child Sally's age. He would grow up with her, be her best friend, her ever-present protector. And if he could win her heart, he would wed her."

"I'm going to ask something, and no matter how I turn it about in my head, it seems terribly untactful," I told him.

"You want to know why Sally, right?"

"I do. She's an adorable girl with a shockingly big heart, but it seems like a lot of trouble for a wife. I'd imagine there are all sorts of parahumans who would be eager to be with someone of Gideon's power."

"You're not wrong," Richard said. "The reason why Gideon asked to marry her is something we both keep secret. I've already told you more than some of my top people know, because I felt you deserved some answers after what happened tonight. And because I like you, Fred. I've met many vampires in my time, but you're the first one I think I've ever enjoyed being around."

"Thank you," I said sincerely. I raised my glass and gulped down the last bits of wine. From the way Richard kept glancing down the hall to where Sally slumbered, it was clear where he wanted to be. And I did still have a job waiting for me. "I enjoy your company as well.

Unfortunately, I must forgo indulging in much more of it, as I have work to do."

Richard's eyebrows rose inches in surprise. "Fred, after everything you've been through, I think you're entitled to take the rest of the night off."

"Are you joking?" I asked. "I'm still running strong on the power of Gideon's blood. With this much energy, I feel like I can work for days. Now is the time to tackle that massive mound of monetary evaluation. Unless you think my work will keep you both up?"

"No, we'll be fine," Richard replied, letting out a soft chuckle—the first laugh I'd heard from him since my return.

I stepped back into the office, shut the doors to keep my noise from permeating through the rest of the home, and took my seat at the desk. Glancing at my watch, I quickly jotted down the time under my first note, left all those hours ago. I was officially back on the clock.

7.

WITH SEVERAL KEYSTROKES, I SAVED MY FINAL version of the documents, closed the program, and powered down my computer. That accomplished, I allowed myself to indulge in a long, uncoordinated stretch. Vampires don't actually get stiff or sore—at least, not doing the sort of activities I'd undertaken since my change— but stretching still generated a positive feeling. I didn't particularly know why, I was just thankful it did. After three solid days sitting in Richard's office, it would have felt vastly unsettling not to top things with off with the gentle tingle of a good limb extension.

"I got the last load of boxes done," Albert informed me, stepping into the office. He'd been brought over on day two, once I'd gotten things sorted enough to begin the digitization of the massive pile of documents. Albert wasn't always the swiftest study; however, once he learned a task, he could be trusted implicitly to carry it out. In our time together, I'd grown to rely on my assistant more and more. If he ever got a better job offer, I might have to talk with Neil about whipping up another zombie or two.

"Good work," I said, slipping my laptop into my computer bag. My eyes slid around the room once, double-checking to be certain every receipt, document, and piece of uncategorized clutter had been dealt with. Once I was satisfied we'd gotten all of it, I slung my bag over my shoulder and walked out of the office to join Albert.

My zombie assistant was hefting a large machine—our portable scanner, which he'd brought from the my office. I'd decided it was better to handle all the documents on site, especially in light of the recent events. Watching Albert heft the machine was somewhat entertaining, given that it weighed far too much for someone of his size to comfortably carry and the feat was only possible due to his undead strength. The sight of such a slender fellow holding such a cumbersome object still tickled the part of me that appreciated simple, vaudevillian comedy.

"Go ahead and take the scanner down," I instructed him. "I'll see if Richard needs anything else, and then meet you at the car."

"Can do," Albert replied.

He began tottering forward, and I quickly realized that he'd need help getting through the massive stone door. I pushed it open with one arm, surprised at how light it momentarily seemed. While the initial rush from Gideon's blood had faded after a day, some of the effects were longer lasting. Once Albert was safely through, I allowed the giant marble barrier to slide back into place with a hefty thud. It was so loud, in fact, that it drew the attention of the man I'd intended to go seek out.

"Fred," Richard called, greeting me from down the hall. He was in Sally's room, where he'd been almost exclusively since the kidnapping. The giant of a man was squatting down beside a plastic table, fake teacup clutched daintily in his hand and a gleaming plastic tiara perched atop his golden mane of hair. "Are you finished already?"

"That I am," I told him, patting my bag for emphasis.

"Hold on a minute," he instructed, beginning to rise to his feet.

"Daddy, that's bad manners," Sally chastised. She took a sip from her own teacup, which appeared far more appropriately sized grasped in her small hand.

"Oh, sorry," Richard replied. "May I please be momentarily excused from the tea party?"

"Of course," Sally said.

Even if I'd been dumb enough to laugh at someone like Richard, I'd still have kept my mouth shut out of respect for the situation. Despite seeming unaffected by her ordeal, Richard was clearly concerned about any emotional scars his daughter might have gained. While I'd been working on his taxes, Richard had scarcely left the apartment. Business was done by headset, and with great rarity. Only once had one of his aides convinced him to attend a meeting in person. I didn't know what had transpired there; all I knew was that after he returned, no one even hinted at the idea of his leaving Sally again.

Gideon had also shown up to check in on her, never bothering to even so much as greet me, which I was perfectly fine with. I'd done all I could to shove his strange engagement out of my mind. Pulling at that thread seemed as though it would unwind nothing but trouble, and I'd already had more than my fill for the quarter.

Richard walked over, teacup set down but still wearing the tiara. "So it's all done, right? I just have to cut a check?"

"At this point, I'll put together a report breaking down your fiscal obligations and how much each deduction will allow you to retain—"

"Yeah, um, if you were going to just ballpark it, how much would you say I owe? Not that I won't read your report, of course . . ." Richard glanced awkwardly away, certain I would see the truth in his eyes if he met my own. Even with the avoidance, I knew he would likely give my comprehensive report a brief skimming at best. Oh well, I would still make it. What the client did with the information wasn't my concern; I merely took satisfaction in knowing that I had done the job to the best of my abilities.

"If I were going to do a ballpark estimate, I'd say you'll be looking at about half of what you paid last year," I said.

"Really? Half?" Richard's face lit up in surprise.

"Roughly speaking, yes. As head therian, you are actually able to write off a tremendous amount of your expenses as business-related, since so many facets of your business interact with your daily life. Add in a few other deductions for all the parahuman staff you employ, not the mention the break for Gideon—"

"Break for Gideon?"

"Dragon's don't actually pay taxes," I informed him. "When the country was founded and the treaties were signed, they were incredibly adamant on that point. Which, given their penchant for gold, is hardly surprising. Anyway, Gideon pays nothing, but since you're lodging and feeding the King of the West, who is the equivalent of a high-ranking diplomat, you are entitled to an enormous break on your own financial duties to the government."

"Damn," Richard said, shaking his head and sending his golden locks tumbling about. "I guess I've been overpaying all this time. Even with your fees, paying only half of what I did last year will be a big windfall."

"It would be," I agreed. "If that's what you were going to pay. I think, however, that you misunderstood what I meant. You aren't going to pay half of what you did last year."

"Then what do I owe?" Richard asked, worry seeping into his large eyes.

"Nothing. When I said you were looking at roughly half of what you paid last year, I meant that's what the government would be sending you. Your deductions were so enormous that you were actually entitled to a refund."

Richard made a noise in his throat that was somewhere between a choke and a snort.

"That is . . . a *lot* of money."

"I'm aware," I said, doing my best to repress the prideful glow I felt burning in my chest. There is no feeling in the world quite like seeing the beaming face of a satisfied client. This was the part of being a CPPA I'd looked forward to most. So few parahumans took good care of their finances that I was confident I'd be able to improve the fiscal situation of anyone who hired me. Starting off with a well-known client would certainly help that process along.

"FYI, if you have one of your people get a reasonably priced scanner and make your document-keeping digital, I can probably manage to do this in the same amount of time next year, even without a boost from Gideon. Cost of equipment and labor should run less than what you'll save on my fees."

Richard stared at me for another few moments, then let out a sonorous laugh that nearly shook the paintings from the walls. Before I could react, he scooped me up in a two-armed hug and gave a mighty squeeze. If not for the residual dragon-blood in my system, I might have been concerned for the state of my spine, but my already impressive tolerance to damage was still heightened so much that the pressure barely registered.

"You are a very strange vampire," Richard said, setting me down at last. "But a good man. And clearly an excellent accountant. If you ever need anything, please feel free to call on me."

"Actually, there is something you could do for me," I replied, reaching into the pocket on my bag and pulling out a small stack of business cards. "If you know anyone else looking for a good CPPA, send them my way. Advertising in the parahuman community is largely word of mouth, so recommendations are key to my business."

"Have no worry, I will absolutely be sending anyone in need of accounting to you," Richard assured me. "I'd have done that anyway. There aren't many parahumans who do what you do."

"You know what they say, find a niche and fill it," I replied.

"That, you have certainly done," Richard said. "I wish you good luck in all your upcoming ventures. And remember what I said, you can call me freely if needed."

"I appreciate it," I told him. "But Albert is really all the help I need. Feel free to give me a ring though, if you have any questions about the report, or just need to chat. It seems like this place can get a little lonely sometimes."

"Your offer is heard and remembered," Richard said, a strangely serious expression suddenly cresting his face.

"Daddy, the tea is getting cold!" Sally yelled from her room.

"You must excuse me," Richard said, reaching up carefully and making sure his tiara was still attached. "If the tea gets cold, I have to wait while she brews a whole other imaginary pot." He headed back toward his daughter, an earnest smile apparent beneath his beleaguered facade.

For my part, I merely headed down through the building, out the front door, and into the night. Even a block away, I could see Albert waiting in my car, cheerfully entertained by the passing motorists. I felt great at that moment, suffused with the sort of contentment only attainable after a job well done.

After a few moments of basking in the sensation, I let it slip away, relegating it to nothing more than a memory as I resumed my journey toward the car, eager to get back home and check my messages. Who knew, maybe I'd already gotten a bite on another job. There were a lot of parahumans in Winslow, Colorado, and I was now officially the man they could turn to with their accounting needs. It had the promise of being a very interesting new page in my career, and I was genuinely excited to start.

I just hoped the next few jobs would be at least somewhat more tame than this one turned out to be.

AN AGENT AT THE CONVENTION

1.

"OKAY, ONE MORE LOAD SHOULD DO IT!" Krystal announced happily, her face sweaty but beaming. Bubba and I looked around her apartment with considerable doubt. There were still at least ten boxes remaining, and even with two us sporting enhanced strength, the unwieldiness of such burdens made lugging them down the stairs of Krystal's apartment a highly suspect proposition.

"If you say so," Bubba muttered at last, pausing to take a drink of his beer. "What all you got in these boxes, anyway?" Bubba spoke with the sort of twang one would expect from someone sporting such a moniker. His frame (massive, with ample muscle), wardrobe (Baseball caps, jeans, and flannel), and occupation (truck driver) also fit well within the bounds of appropriate stereotypes. These small conformities only highlighted the unexpected bits: his wisdom, gentleness, and unashamed homosexuality being a few examples.

"Mostly stuff for the booth," Krystal said. Somehow, she still managed to look sexy, even in a pair of gray sweatpants and an old T-shirt from the high school we'd both attended. Krystal had been significantly wider of frame back then, so it hung loosely on her in a way that I found appealing, but couldn't quite understand. Slung over her shoulder was a large duffel bag, nearly bursting it was so full. She hadn't let it out of her possession since Bubba and I arrived and had begun loading a significant number of boxes into the back of her pickup.

"Don't agents have teams to set this stuff up?" I asked, hefting a large box that would have thrown my meager back out when I was still alive. Thankfully, one of the boons of a being my type of parahuman was a hardier frame. Krystal was also parahuman, but one of incredible rarity and power. That was part of why she worked as an Agent (an emissary from the secret branch of the government charged with keeping peace and upholding treaties in the parahuman world), since, in a world of big bad monsters, Krystal was near the top of the heap. Sometimes, her job involved putting down supernatural beasts that had decided to chuck our covert existence and go hog wild. Other times, like this upcoming weekend, it involved a more diplomatic set of tasks.

"Fred, agents are highly specialized resources," Krystal reminded me. "They aren't going to take time out of their day to come help me set up a booth for CalcuCon."

"Your entire organization cannot be made up of just agents," I pointed out, setting my box back down. "There must be people who make coffee, clean restrooms, and mop up the messes after you leave a wake of destruction. There is always grunt work, and I know you well enough to presume you are not the one doing it."

"*Fiiiine*," she said, stretching out the word like a cat basking in a sunbeam. "I could have put in a request for a moving and set-up team, but it's a shitload of paperwork to deal with and I found employing the boyfriend-labor to be far easier. And Bubba will do anything for a case of beer and a well-prepared steak."

Bubba nodded his agreement, setting two boxes on top of each other as he began constructing a teetering tower he would then lug down the stairs. The truth of the matter was that Bubba would do anything for Krystal. She'd been his friend for a long time, and just last Thanksgiving had saved him from a company of dracolings that had had enough debt on him to make him a slave for life. Pointing this out at the time would have been impolite, however, so I shifted topics.

"I still find it mildly insulting that you named a convention solely based around the idea of parahumans congregating "CalcuCon," as if no other parties might want to come to that," I grumbled.

"First off, I didn't name it. CalcuCon has been around for like twenty some years," Krystal informed me. "Second, no, you're not the only nerd drawn by that name. We've had plenty of applicants try to sign up for it over the years."

"How do you dissuade them?" Parahumans weren't exactly a secret on par with nuclear launch codes, but great pains were taken to keep the veil of disbelief drawn across society's collective eyes. Letting them come to a place where we gather en masse, without hiding our natures, would be the height of unacceptability.

"Red tape, usually," Krystal said. "Lost applications, extra fees piled on top of extra fees, constantly changing dates, and overall horrendous customer service. We make the experience so terrible no one wants to come, let alone try again the next year."

"I think my cable company has been stealing plays from your book," Bubba remarked, as he set a fourth box on the pile.

"Other way around. Every couple of years, we have someone set up a Castcom account, just to see if they've come up with any new tactics. They never fail to disappoint," Krystal replied.

"How big is CalcuCon, anyway?" I interrupted. All I'd been told was to pack a bag and come help lift things, so now I had to gather information on the fly. I was largely unbothered by it all though; this was pretty much par for the course with Krystal. "If there's a large enough presence, perhaps I'll get a booth to advertise my accounting services next year."

"It's pretty damn big," Krystal said. "Several thousand parahumans make the trek for it. That's why I've got to set up an Agency recruiting booth. This is a chance to reach lots of people we'd never otherwise get a chance to court."

"Seems like people would be coming to you, not the other way around."

"Agents ain't exactly universally beloved in the parahuman world," Bubba informed me, setting the last of his boxes on top of the pile. "Lots of folks grew up with their parents treating them like the bogeyman, the sort of thing that gets whispered about, but is hopefully never seen. You know how you get an uneasy feeling in your gut when a cop starts driving behind you, even if you ain't speeding?"

I nodded. My general anxiety meant that even the possibility of a confrontation with authority was enough to spur a bout of nausea—at least, back when I could have such things.

"Amp that up by a few dozen degrees, and that's how lots of parahumans feel when they hear about or see an agent. Even if we ain't doin' anything wrong, we understand that that person can completely wreck our shit. It doesn't exactly lead to warm and fuzzy sentiments."

"Which is precisely why we do things like set up booths at CalcuCon," Krystal jumped in. "We want to take every opportunity to let people know we're not the evil gestapo, and we'll play nice as long as they do."

"I suppose that might help soften your image," I agreed.

"Oh no, we don't try to do that," Krystal said, giving her head a shake that sent tumbles of her blonde hair bouncing about. "We like the terrifying image. That's something we work hard to preserve. The Agency is fine with being perceived as a horrifying monster, so long as it is a just, well-intentioned horrifying monster."

"That is slightly disturbing," I said, and then sighed, piling my set of boxes in a manner that imitated Bubba's technique.

"Think of it as preemptive shock-and-awe," Krystal urged.

"I would prefer not the think of it at all," I replied. With a mighty heft, I lifted my pile into the air and was nearly knocked off balance by the unexpected lightness of my load. This was not due to the boxes being packed with nothing but Styrofoam or other such silliness, but because I still hadn't really grasped my current strength. Ever since I'd had that drop of dragon blood several weeks back, my physical power and senses had been exponentially heightened. For a more classic, action-oriented vampire, this would have been a blessing of incomparable worth. For me, it meant I'd broken three keyboards and pulled the handle off my refrigerator. I couldn't wait for the effects to fade and my more manageable level of augmented power to return.

"That's the best strategy," Bubba concurred, lifting his own set of boxes as well. A cursory glance around the room told me that, even with Krystal pitching in, there was still going to be another trip up here before we were finished. Evidently, my girlfriend reached the same conclusion.

"Well, damn," she muttered. "Looks like I was off. I thought you two could do heavier lifting."

"If we try and carry any more than this, we're likely to drop the whole lot during our descent down the stairs," I pointed out.

"Excuses excuses."

"You could always set down the duffel and lift a little more," Bubba tossed out.

"No can do," Krystal replied. "The contents of the duffel bag have to stay with me at all times until we reach the convention. No exceptions."

"Oh. There must be something really valuable in there," I noted.

Krystal let out an unladylike snort, the sort of characteristic that endeared her to me. "I wouldn't really say 'valuable,' just needy."

"Needy?" I asked.

"Like a colicky baby," Krystal affirmed. She bent down to pick up a box, and as she did, something in bag shifted, striking her in the back of the head. "Ow! Look, assholes, I might have to bring you along, but pull that shit again and I won't bother with any polishing or lighting."

These words were clearly directed at the duffel bag, a fact which Bubba and I noticed and pointedly chose not to comment on. In the parahuman world, you learn that asking questions often leads to answers you either didn't want or don't understand. Sometimes, it was better to just accept things as they were and focus on the task at hand.

"We're ready when you are," I told her.

"Yeah, I'm ready," Krystal said, grabbing the final box she would carry. "Let's get this done. We've got a long drive ahead of us. On the plus side, after this run we should only have one load left."

Bubba and I exchanged glances, then began the awkward trek down the stairs and into the street, where Krystal's oversized truck was waiting for the next round of boxes.

2.

HORBON, NEVADA WAS A TOWN ROUGHLY AN
hour's drive north of Las Vegas. Its claim to fame was
not any particular aspect the town itself possessed, but
rather its quasi-adjacent location to other, more tourist-
friendly towns. Horbon capitalized on that convenience
in a rather ingenious method—they billed themselves
as an economic way-station between popular locales.
With an airport that hosted cheaper flights than either
LA or Vegas, along with budget-friendly hotels and accommodations, Horbon was the place people went if

they wanted to pop by one of the well-known cities, but didn't feel like spending enough money to stay there. This, quite understandably, made Horbon a favorite of many companies looking to do off-site meetings and conventions without having to reallocate budgets.

It was this desirability as a host city that had led Horbon to build the massive convention center that Bubba, Krystal, and I were hauling a small cart through. Piled atop the cart, secured by a few thin strands of rope (and a whole lot of hope) were the boxes we'd hauled over from Winslow. The drive had been largely un-eventful, save for Krystal's always adrenaline-inducing driving. Her handling of an automobile was beyond ex-ceptional; however, her aggressive personality often led to tight turns and accelerations that left me wondering how my undead body would fair in a head-on collision. Thankfully, we'd arrived in one piece, and, after Krystal grabbed us badges and a cart, we began the process of locating her booth.

I was struck with surprise at how busy the floor seemed, given the late hour. We'd gotten an early start, so our arrival put us in at roughly three in the morn-ing, and the area was positively bustling with people. Most were setting up their own booths and displays, but there were plenty who were merely standing by, watch-ing the process of creation unfold around them. Given that the convention officially opened at ten—still seven hours away—I'd expected more attendees to do their work in the morning. This was my error in thinking, as I'd forgotten that parahumans tend to prefer the night whenever given a choice. For me, that choice was mandatory, thanks in no small part to my severe sunlight allergy. For others, it was simply a matter of tradition or preference. This observation resulted in my being struck by a thought, which I then realized I should have had before ever leaving my apartment. My vampire survival instincts were usually exemplary; however, I did have a tendency to get caught up in things when my girlfriend began leading us off on unexpected errands.

"Krystal," I said, pushing the cart along carefully while she and Bubba manned the sides, watching for any falling boxes. "Do we have safe accommodations? I know sunrise is still some hours away, but I just realized that I don't know where I'll hole up. I suppose I can sleep in the truck, since the windows are enchanted to keep out sunlight."

"Really? Freddy, you iron your socks. I don't see you being comfortable passing out in the back seat and getting your khakis all wrinkled," Krystal teased. "We get rooms as part of the deal. Not that you have to leave the floor, if you don't want to. The Agency helped build this whole place with a shell company, so it's about as parahuman friendly as you can get. The windows protect vampires from sunlight, several breaker systems help minimize the electrical short-outs one sees with mages, hell, we've even got a special warding system to keep the worst effects of a full moon at bay."

"What happens during a full moon?"

"Lots of stuff," Bubba informed me. "Full moons are powerful things; even humans can sense it. It puts therians on a transformation hair-trigger. The younger among us can't retain human form at all. Then you've got how it impacts mages and their spells, pretty much any kind of water creature, and don't even get me started on the fey."

"Couldn't have said it better," Krystal surmised. She turned away from the boxes to pull out a large piece of folded paper, which she then unfurled and studied. "Okay, according to this, we're in section C, row one-thirty-two. Where the hell is that?"

"Over there," I replied, pointing to an area some distance away.

"How do you know?"

"The section lettering is in place," I replied, motioning to the colored boxes with letters painted on them that were hung from the ceiling. They dangled down from a massive metal catwalk that criss-crossed over the entire ceiling. "Also, some of the booths have their numbers displayed. Not a lot, but it only takes a few to figure out the basic set-up. Assuming no deviation, C-132 should be in the area I pointed at."

"Last time I worked one of these, it took me over half an hour to find my spot," Krystal mumbled, putting the paper away. "Plenty of slacking off time. But noooo, I had to bring my boyfriend: the numbers expert."

"I would say it's less numbers expertise than basic pattern recognition," I corrected.

We hauled the boxes over to the area I'd indicated, and sure enough, there was a booth waiting for us. My first thought upon seeing it, however, was that I must have been mistaken, because this booth was already manned. Or, wo-manned is perhaps a better phrasing. The person in question was currently setting up lights that would presumably illuminate a name or logo when the booth was complete. She was so absorbed in her task that she didn't register our arrival until Krystal spoke.

"June?" There was something about her voice when she said June's name, some indefinable quality not normally present, that was my first clue that this might not be the happiest of surprises. Krystal didn't sound mad, or annoyed—tones I well accustomed to dealing with—no, she sounded . . . perhaps uncertain is the closest description, and that was not a sentiment I was accustomed to seeing from my girlfriend.

The woman, June presumably, turned away from her project to look at us. She was strikingly beautiful, but in a way I found somewhat off-putting. Her high cheekbones, blue-white hair, and gleaming eyes presented a sort of otherworldly aesthetic. June was beautiful in the way of a painting, or a sculpture, something that was pleasant to admire, yet brought forth no desire to touch. Of course, had she been an actual painting, I feel relatively certain the artist would have dressed her in fine silken dresses, rather than the paint-stained overalls and gray T-shirt that currently adorned her lithe form.

"Krys!" June yelped, nearly dropping a light bulb in the mad dash to run over and embrace Krystal. She hugged the blonde agent with gusto, dispelling much of the inhuman aura I'd associated with her. "Oh my goodness, I haven't seen you in over a year! No one told me you'd be working the booth with me."

June released her hold and flashed all three of us a dazzling smile. It created a curious sense of disharmony in me, as the logical, human part of my brain was warmed by the genuine outpouring of emotion. In contrast, the vampire part of my brain, hardwired like the predator it was, flashed a warning of danger. I'd been trying to ignore that part as often as possible recently, this being no exception. If she was a friend of Krystal's, then I didn't need to fear her, regardless of whether or not her kind was dangerous to mine.

"This is a hell of a surprise," Krystal said at last. "I thought you were doing long-term work in New Mexico."

"I was, but the situation took care of itself," June replied. "Gremlin infestation was so deeply rooted that I spent months trying to find their queen, and then guess what she went and did."

"What?"

"Tinkered with a damn meth lab and got herself blown to kingdom come," June replied, letting out a laugh that reminded me of sleigh bells during Christmas.

"Gremlins like to mess with technology," Bubba whispered to me, correctly assuming my ignorance. "Make it go haywire, glitch out, that sort of thing."

I nodded, easily able to imagine how that tendency around a methamphetamine laboratory could lead to disastrous results.

"Anyway," June continued, "how have you been? I want to hear all about your life. After the engagement fell through, I feel like we lost touch, which is a damn shame."

"Engagement?" I really didn't mean to interrupt; the word slipped out of my mouth completely unbidden. Given the chance, I'd have stuffed it back under my tongue without hesitation. Unfortunately, one of my vampire abilities is not the reversal of time, so the exclamation remained and the consequences of it began.

"I'm sorry," June said, giving Bubba and I her full attention. "I was so caught up in seeing Krystal that I let my manners slip. My name is June Windbrook, and, like Krystal, I'm an agent. We've known each other since her recruitment."

"Bubba Emerson," Bubba said, sticking out his impressively sized hand. June accepted it, the handshake almost completely obscuring her own dainty digits from view. "Old friend of Krystal's."

"Fredrick Frankford Fletcher," I said, mimicking Bubba's offer to shake as I felt a familiar sense of social awkwardness wash over me. Should I introduce myself as her boyfriend? We were in a committed relationship, after all. But I didn't know the rules surrounding agents and dating. Perhaps playing it aloof was a better strategy. Besides, June's mention of an engagement still had me curious as to the full expanse of her connection to Krystal. "Krystal and I went to high school together, and we're currently . . . um . . . well—"

"Freddy is my boyfriend," Krystal said, ending my suffering with a mercifully swift assertion. Relief washed over me, but as the hand I was shaking grew cold and stiff, I realized I wasn't the only one who'd had a reaction to her words.

"Boyfriend?" June asked. Her eyes looked me up and down once more, this time with an appraising gleam. I couldn't fault her for her skepticism. With my khakis, glasses, clean button-down, and fresh sweater vest, I hardly looked the type to be romancing a beautiful woman like Krystal, let alone an agent.

"Yup, boyfriend," Krystal confirmed.

"How lovely," June said, finishing our shake and giving me a polite smile. There was no warmth in this expression; it was done clearly for the sake of formality.

"Listen, Krys, I still want to catch up, but I could really use a break. Do you mind taking over the booth while I run and get a coffee?"

"Not at all," Krystal replied. "We brought the rest of the stuff, so we'll keep the set-up moving along."

"Thank you." June grabbed a small handbag from behind the booth and walked away at such high-speeds that it seemed like she was sprinting. Within moments, she was out of sight, and I began unfastening the ropes that had done a surprisingly good job of holding the boxes in place.

"Hey, Bubba, why don't you go get us checked into our rooms. I'll want a shower when this is done, and waiting though the line at reception won't be fun," Krystal said.

Bubba said nothing, merely took the hint and headed down the convention's long hallway. Once he was gone, Krystal turned her attention on me.

"Freddy, you never need to do that."

"Do what?" I asked.

"Be afraid that I'm ashamed of you, of what we are." Krystal took my hand away from the rope I was having an unexpectedly hard time unknotting and held it in her own. "I know how you are, and I know you get worried and all, but I'm proud to be with such a sweet, caring man. Introduce yourself as my boyfriend, because I'm sure as hell going to introduce myself as your girlfriend when the tables are turned. Okay?"

"I . . . okay," I said, abandoning all hope of pretending that wasn't exactly what had just happened. "Sorry, it's just intimidating meeting another agent. I felt she would expect you to be with someone more like you, a tough, powerful parahuman."

"June's expectations have no impact on my dating life. Trust me on that one."

"Good thing, because she seemed pretty disappointed in your selection of men," I pointed out.

"Don't take that personally. June was just a little upset seeing me in a relationship at all. She had to know it was coming eventually, but I think she's been pretending otherwise."

"Why would it bother her for you to have a boyfriend?"

"Because," Krystal said, her voice growing several degrees more timid. "That engagement she mentioned? It was mine. I was supposed to marry her brother."

3.

AFTER LAST CHRISTMAS, WHEN I WAS NEARLY killed by Quinn, my crazed vampire sire, Krystal and I had taken the time to have a long talk about our relationship: both what we wanted from it and where we hoped it would go. Part of this was discussing previous relationships, and while I had little to add on that point, Krystal did inform me that she had been engaged when she was younger. So, I was not taken by surprise at the declaration of her previous status, merely by being confronted with the sudden reality of it. Krystal didn't like to talk about her former fiancé, and I had never pressed the subject. He'd always been a nebulous existence, something I was aware of in an intellectual way, but that had lacked any sense of substance.

That sentiment faded rapidly after having met his sister. I was, admittedly, not the most perceptive of people when it came to socially oriented things; however, I did have the skills of a solid accountant, and that meant I could do basic math. Krystal was an agent, and June was an agent who had known Krystal since she was recruited. If June's brother was Krystal's former betrothed, that meant he was probably an agent as well. These people were like action heroes mixed with Greek legends—they commanded fear and respect amongst entities that were accustomed to being the ones everyone else was afraid of.

As we unpacked the booth and set things up, I found myself wondering more and more how she had gone from being with an agent to spending her time with a . . . me. The one upside to my distraction was that I lost track of the work, and before I knew it, Krystal had dropped her duffel bag on one of the booth's flat surfaces with a jingling thud.

"Finally." As she moved her hand away, the jingling in the bag seemed to grow louder, despite the fact that she was no longer touching it. "Hold your damn horses. Let a girl pop the crick from her spine first." She leaned backward until a crackling noise came from her vertebrae and she sighed with relief. That done, she reached into the bag and began to unpack its contents.

"Are we expecting a fight?" I asked.

"Technically, an agent is always ready for shit to go down, but no, I'm not worried about anything in particular today."

"Then why did you bring an entire duffel bag of weaponry?" I was watching in a mixture of curiosity and fear as Krystal pulled out ancient instruments of battle, one after the other. The majority of them were swords, but there was also an occasional axe or mace tossed into the mix.

"These aren't for fighting. Well, I mean they are for fighting, but not against anyone here. Shit, I hope not anyone here, I'd be in for a nightmare of reports if that level of violence went down. Anyway, these are for people to take."

"Wait, instead of bookmarks or pens like most convention booths, you give out weapons?"

"No no, the only people who can take these are the ones who own them." Krystal paused, then held up the blade in her hand. "Sword of the Vengeful Moon. Can only be wielded by a therian who is destined to find revenge on someone who has wounded them." She set it down and pulled out a small hand-axe. "Axe of the Bloody Poltergeist: meant for a warrior who will topple the wicked and dead." Down it went, and she began taking more out of the bag. "Dagger of the Angry Ogre.

Mace of the Wild Stag. Sword of the Demon God. Blade of the Unlikely Champion." The last one rattled in its scabbard as she said its name, and Krystal smacked the pommel with the back of her hand.

"These are magical weapons, ones that have some aspect of destiny to them. The Agency keeps them safe, but they're meant to be out in the world and getting used. Damn things will get antsy if they stay put away too long: falling off shelves, lying in that perfect way so you trip over them, that sort of thing. Every now and then, we pull some out—usually the ones that are making the most racket—and see if they can find new owners. When people come by, I'll let them try to draw or wield any weapon that calls to them. If they can, then it's theirs."

"Aren't you worried about what people will do with them?" I asked. "Some of those sounded pretty dangerous."

"They are, but if we don't let the weapons out regularly, then our warehouse will blow up, or thieves will break in, or something. Destiny isn't the sort of thing you can fight long-term. This way, at least we know who to keep an eye on. Plus, if they pull one of the more powerful ones, I get to shove a recruitment form under their nose."

My eyebrows went up without bothering to ask my brain if that was okay. "Those things can make someone agent-level powerful?"

"I'd say it gives them the base requirements. There's still a lot of training to be done after that, but the gist is, yeah, they can." She set the Blade of the Unlikely Champion on the table, and I felt my eyes drawn to it. It was in its scabbard, a simple black-and-gold piece with a matching hilt. The harsh florescent convention lights seemed to soften when reflected off its shiny surface.

"How does that one work?" I asked.

"Old-school style, just pull it out," Krystal said. She glanced at me, and I suppose something in my face must have given away what I was wondering, because she kept going. "Of course, drawing or wielding one of these isn't all power and picnics. When you take a Weapon of Destiny, you become a part of its fate. A lot of these end in untimely death, and almost none of them allow for a peaceful life."

I looked away from the sword and back to my girlfriend, who wore an uncharacteristic expression of concern on her face. Perhaps we might have talked things out right then and there, but Bubba came jogging over with two small envelopes in his hand.

"Krystal was right about the check-in. I thought I would never make it through that line," Bubba said. "I'm a little down the hall from you two, but we're on the same floor." Bubba handed Krystal one of the envelopes, which she immediately passed to me.

"Freddy, why don't you go rest a little," she said. "Since I'm on the Agency's dime, you can rent some fancy flicks on the pay-per-view system."

"Don't you need more help getting everything set up?"

"The booth is done; all that's left now is to shine and position the weaponry so it doesn't throw a hissy-fit." The distinct sound of clinking metal answered Krystal's words, but it stopped immediately when she glared at the pile of blades. "Plus, I feel like I should talk to June, and that will be a little easier without you here. Just at first."

"I haven't actually seen her since we arrived," I said.

"She's been around, but keeping her distance. I'm not trying to brush you off, promise, but she is a friend. Just a complicated one."

"I understand." I accepted the envelope from her, noting the floor and room number written on the outside. "How long do you want me to stay gone?"

"Give me two movies, or until sunrise, whichever comes first." Krystal leaned in and gave me a light, but unexpectedly tender kiss. "I know how you like those foreign snoozefests that run for half a day, and I don't want to be down here by my lonesome for the entire morning."

"You might like one of those snoozefests if you paid attention, or bothered to stay awake through them."

"Maybe, but with those requirements, I don't think we'll ever find out." She pulled back slightly and glanced over at Bubba. "As for you, seeing as you actually need things like sleep and food, take some downtime as well. Both my helpers are officially off duty for the rest of the night."

"Call if you need us," Bubba said. This was more for form than anything else; the sorts of things Krystal couldn't handle were the sorts of things we weren't likely to be able to do more than die in front of.

"Go. Sleep. Watch movies. Drink blood. Shoo." Krystal gave us the brushing motion with her hand, which Bubba and I took as our cue to head upstairs.

As we walked down the tile hallway, Bubba's heavy-booted, thudding steps filled the hall with sound, and a thought struck me.

"Bubba, you've known Krystal a long time, right?"

"Years now," Bubba confirmed.

"Did you ever meet her former fiancé?"

"Just once."

"What was he like?" We boarded our elevator, and Bubba pressed the number "13" on the panel. Somehow, I wasn't surprised that a building the Agency had helped construct wouldn't be bothered about having a thirteenth floor.

"He was handsome, but most of his kind are. Strong, too. The sort of man who looks you in the eyes and you just inherently know he can take you down in two moves flat. Well-spoken, good dresser, more or less what you'd expect an agent to be."

The elevator came to a stop, and the doors opened.

"I couldn't stand the fucking guy," Bubba continued as we exited.

I twisted my head in surprise. Bubba usually managed to find the good in everyone he dealt with or spoke of.

"Why not? He sounds amazing."

"It had nothing to do with him. At least, back before the break-up. I just hated the effect he had on Krystal. And that's all I'm telling you, since you're obviously digging for dirt."

"Nice to know I'm still awful at subterfuge." I passed a familiar assortment of numbers and realized I was at my door. "My stop, it seems."

"I'm further down," Bubba replied. "I'd offer to talk things over with you, but Krystal was right, I do have to sleep at least a little."

"Please, by all means. I'll be fine."

"No, more likely you'll keep being worried and a bit obsessive." Despite his accusing words, Bubba's tone was surprisingly gentle, and a soft smile spread across his wide face. "But nothing I can say will stop that anyway, so I won't bother. Just remember: you're the one she wants to be with. Try and hang on to that when the worry gets too strong."

"I'll do my best," I promised. It was the only response I could truthfully give him.

4.

TWO MOVIES AND A PACKET OF BLOOD LATER,
I was heading back toward the main convention floor. As
I passed through the lobby, I saw a line of attendants
snaking out from the registration booth—these would
be the actual attendees, rather than the people working
behind the scenes. I had been to a convention before,
something comic-book based that I'd attended in the
fruitless hope of meeting people on par with my level of
social skill. At that registration, people had been dressed
in all manner of strange and elaborate garb, some so

encumbered by their outfits that even basic movements required concentrated effort.

Such was not the case at the Calcucon registration line. If anything, people looked exceedingly normal; almost aggressively so. It was such a bland arrangement of beings that I would have fit in perfectly, and that was saying a lot. It struck me as strange, but only until I passed through the wide white doors that separated the convention area from the rest of the building.

Stepping through, I was immediately struck with wonder at the number of inhuman beings casually walking around. Though the convention didn't officially open until ten, many attendees were already wandering around and checking things out. There were several therians shifted into their hybrid forms, a couple of mages with telltale glowing enchantments around their bodies, other undead that I could only recognize by smell and paleness, as well as a few centaurs and winged creatures I only knew from my CPPA courses. Even the more mundane beings had horns, or strangely colored eyes, or extra arms. Only then did it strike me why the registration line had seemed so unimpressive.

The people out there *were* in costume. They'd come from the outer world, where they had to blend in with regular people. Only in here, in the safety of a space specifically set aside for them, could they cast aside their false faces and live as they truly were. In that moment,

I genuinely appreciated how fortunate I was to be a parahuman that could blend so naturally into society, without the need for elaborate costumes or costly illusion enchantments.

I meandered my way through the convention floor, noting how many more booths had sprung up in the relatively short time I was away. Many of the business-based ones caught my eye, advertising things as ubiquitous as parahuman-friendly home retrofits to services as niche as at-home hoof-cleaning. It seemed I would indeed have to grab an information packet or two before we left; getting in front of a crowd this size could do wonders for my budding business.

At last, I came to the Agency's familiar booth. I hadn't realized it at the time, but the booth Krystal and I set up was much larger than the surrounding ones, occupying a space big enough for three normal-sized stalls. Either they were trying to create a subconscious image of size and power, or they were expecting to draw a big crowd. Regardless, things looked more or less the same as when I'd left, with only minor exceptions: the signs were a bit straighter, and the weapons more symmetrically laid out.

The one large exception was that June had rejoined Krystal at the booth. Both women were sitting on stools behind one of the display tables, clutching cups of coffee next to empty pastry bags, and June was smiling at my girlfriend with the same warmth she'd shown in her greeting. As they realized I'd arrived, June's demeanor cooled slightly, though not as intensely as I'd been expecting.

"'Bout time," Krystal said, hopping off the small stool she'd been perched on and giving me a quick peck. "Bubba got down here half an hour ago. We already sent him on a coffee-run."

"What do you call that?" I pointed at the still steaming cup in her hands.

"I call it free convention pisswater, because I wouldn't sully the good name of coffee by comparing it to this."

"Yet you're drinking it anyway."

"Still caffeinated," Krystal said, giving a half-hearted shrug as she took a sip. "And, unfortunately, June and I have to be extra alert. Seems there's been a bit of thieving going on already."

"Already? Were you expecting it?" I asked.

"There's always something," June broke in. "People misplace items they're sure they brought or a mage accidently teleports some boxes to a different place and sooner or later someone starts crying thief. Parahumans of so many cultures don't often gather together in one spot like this, and some have literally ancient grudges against others. Paranoia gets a head start before common sense can even get its shoes on."

"Of course, sometimes there really is bullshit afoot," Krystal added. "Those grudges aren't just for posturing, and every now and then, things get real bloody, real fast. More often than not, though, it's just some misunderstanding. But in case it's the first one, we'll be on alert."

"Doesn't the convention center have security?"

"We've got a few head-crackers for minor incidents, but as agents, we're the top of the food chain if things need handling." Krystal said this with the sort of strange pride I'd never understood before last Christmas. After learning about her abilities, as well as seeing them in action, such tones made perfect sense to me. In a world of terrifying things, Krystal was one of the scariest. And she relished that fact.

We were interrupted as Bubba came jogging up to us, two tall, white containers held easily in each of his massive hands. His eyes were darting about, and a visible expression of relief came over his face when he saw Krystal. Bubba plowed through the remaining bystanders between us, which might have caused an incident if he hadn't been doing it to reach the agents' booth.

"Think we got a situation down the hall," Bubba said quickly. "I passed a group of mages who were prepping some sort of ceremony to lock down the hall and prevent any more stealin' in here. I don't know a lot about magic, but that seems . . ."

"Like it'll fry the whole electrical system, breaker system be damned," Krystal finished. She grabbed the gun at her waist and pulled it clear of the holster. "Those fucking idiots. Bubba, lead me to them. Fred, you stay here with June. We can't leave the weapons unattended, and this is dangerous."

Without another word, Krystal sprinted off in the direction Bubba had come from, the sizable man doing all he could to keep up. Unlike Bubba, Krystal didn't plow through the crowd. Instead, she screamed enough threats and obscenities to get them clearing out ahead of her. Agent Krystal Jenkins was a lot of things, but subtle was not one of them.

"Of course she grabbed the action and left me on guard-duty," June grumbled from behind me. I glanced back to find her picking through the remains of a blueberry muffin, pressing the crumbs to her thumb and licking them off. It was oddly disharmonious, seeing such an elegant being indulged in such unglamorous actions.

"You know Krystal, always the first to rush in."

"Yes, I do know Krystal. Very well, in fact." June's tone stayed neutral, though I felt like it did grow noticeably frostier. She finally looked up from the muffin wrapper, having gotten every piece worth consuming. "What I don't know is you, Fred. Since we're here anyway, why not come sit and chat with me a bit?"

Vampires are attuned enough to the predator/prey dynamic of the parahuman world that I could sense the danger in her words, but I walked over and plopped onto a stool anyway. That side of me was instinct and guttural reaction; it ran on preconceived notions of what was dangerous based solely on what people were. Some of the best friends I'd made since turning were in that category, and so far, the most dangerous enemy I'd faced was one of my own kind. Instinct was well and good in the right situations, but I refused to let it dictate how I treated or reacted to the people around me. What they were was not the same as who they were, and I knew that better than anyone.

All of that said, I still had to suppress a chill of fear as June's eyes bored into my own.

"As I'm sure Krystal told you, I'm a vampire, turned over a year ago. More interestingly, I run my own accounting firm, and just got my Certified Public Parahuman Accountant License, so I've been looking at expanding the parahuman side of my business. I love good wine and movies, plus I can put together a cheese-plate like nobody's business. How about you?"

June blinked, a brief but unmistakable expression of surprise flitting across her face. Perhaps she'd been expecting bluster, lies, or mere embellishments, but she clearly hadn't been prepared for my honest self-summary. She recovered within moments, regaining her distant and authoritative air.

"I'm half fey," June said. "Been an agent for over thirty years, on both sides of the realm, and have the skills to take down any kind of parahuman in a matter of seconds." Her expression softened just a bit as she let the implied threat wash over me before she continued. "Also, I like shopping, and I'm a bit of a foodie."

"Oh? There's a gastropub in Winslow you should try if you're ever visiting Krystal. Their deconstructed salmon cakes are downright incredible."

"Went there back when you were alive, huh?"

"No, they just opened two months ago," I replied.

"Most of your kind prefers to stick with the red stuff." Her eyes narrowed the slightest bit, as if she were trying to see through a lie I wasn't actually spinning.

"I wouldn't know. I've only met two other vampires, and neither made me eager to go replicate the experience."

"Yeah, I heard about—"

The air was filled with a tremendous crackling as lightning seemed to shoot between the florescent bulbs suspended from the catwalk, filling the entire area with blinding light. Fast as I was, June was far quicker. She planted a hand firmly on my chest and pushed, sending both me and my stool sprawling backward. By the time I landed, she was standing over me, dagger in one hand and gun in the other. In that moment, I was sure she was seizing the opportunity to kill me, removing me from Krystal's life permanently.

Only later did I realize she was trying to protect me.

The lightning died out, along with all of the florescent lights. Normally, this would have caused no issue for me, or any of the dozens of other parahumans with exceptional night vision; however, even vampire eyes require time to readjust after a blinding flash.

It only took half a minute for me to get my bearings, and as I looked down the aisle, I noticed a small figure laden down with objects, dashing about in a way that meant they were unimpeded by the darkness.

Moments after my vision returned, the area brightened as the emergency lights on the walls and ceiling kicked on. I pulled myself up, unaided by June. At first, I took this as intentional, but when I made it to my feet, I realized she wasn't even paying attention to me. Her gaze was fixed firmly on the portion of the booth where the weapons were sitting. Only now, instead of being neatly and symmetrically organized, there were three distinct holes in the pattern.

Three spots where magical weapons of importance and destiny had been resting only a minute prior.

5.

"SON OF A BITCH. I DO NOT WANT TO DO the paperwork on this," June said, staring at the empty spots with a furrowed brow and slight sneer.

"You seem to be taking the theft of such important items surprisingly well," I noted.

"That's because they can't be stolen. I mean, yeah, people can take them away from us, but those things have destiny wound around them. Wherever they end up, that's where they're meant to be. It's why we take them out every now and then: keeps them in circulation so there isn't a need for a jailbreak."

"So Krystal told me. Does that mean we don't need to retrieve them?"

"Are you brain-dead on top of being normal-dead? Of course we have to retrieve them. Until they're official-ly claimed, those things are Agency property. If I admit to losing three of them to some sticky-fingered jerk, then I'm going to get a massive earful. And so will Krys, for that matter."

On cue, Krystal came treading back over, Bubba in tow. "I had to crack one of those dipshits in the back of the head, but I got the spell stopped before it did too much damage. Maintenance says they can have the lights fixed in about an hour, so overall, not my worst headache at one of these things." She stopped talking and noted both of our somber expressions. "Why do you two look like someone pissed in your cereal?"

"There may have been a very slight misplacement of three of our specialty items during the blackout," June admitted.

Krystal's eyes wandered over to the display, where she found the same triple gap we'd previously observed. "Really? Fucking really? We were gone for five minutes, tops, and someone got away with three of those damned things?" She looked over at the two of us, and we both shrank back under her fierce gaze. "Do we at least have any leads? Sight, smell, something?"

"Too many parahumans moving around with unique scents," Bubba said. "Even if you had something to smell that you were sure was the thief's, you'd need a master tracker to find them in here."

"I caught sight of someone scampering away in the dark," I said, keeping my voice respectfully low. "There's no way to be certain it was the thief, but they were moving through the darkness like they'd expected it."

"Not a bad plan, actually," Bubba said. "Rile up some mages, get them to create a distraction, and then sneak by and grab stuff from right under an agent's nose."

June bristled visibly at his observation, but she had no real comeback for it. The items were gone, and she'd been the one on guard. Like or lump it: Bubba was right.

"Right, first things first. We have to put the rest of these things away now," Krystal said. "Having our weapons stolen is bad enough, but if people figure it out, we're in for way more shit from the home office."

"Why does that matter more?" I asked.

"Image, reputation, call it what you want. Part of the Agency's power comes from the fear we instill. We are the nightmare of parahumans, and it needs to stay that way. Agents need to be seen as flawless, unstoppable beings, because that sort of reputation allows us to end a lot of conflicts before they start. If we can find the items before word gets out that they were stolen, then we can keep things civil. However, if it becomes known that someone stole from the Agency, we'll have no choice but to make an example of them. A very brutal one, at that," June said.

"I really just meant that I didn't want to get bitched out, but June isn't totally off base," Krystal admitted. "For the thief's sake as much as ours, we need to get those weapons back." She paused to look at the display once more. "By my count, we're missing The Axe of Withering Trees, The Sword of the Furious Sun, and The Blade of the Unlikely Champion. None of those will be easy to conceal, so our thief's best option to stash them. That leaves us a two-pronged approach: one team hunts the thief, while the other searches for the weapons."

"Let me track our culprit," June volunteered immediately. "This fool slighted my honor as an agent; I wish for the chance to redeem myself. Besides, I'm more gifted in terms of hunting prey."

"Can't argue with you there; you're the right fit for thief duty." Krystal looked at Bubba and me, a slightly worried expression drawing across her face. "Freddy, you're the only one who has actually caught a glimpse of this person. That means you should probably be on the hunting team too."

The way she structured her statement, she was clearly giving me the chance to object or raise some reason why I would be a bad fit. Krystal realized that pairing me with June made the most sense; however, she respected my feelings enough to give me an out. I greatly appreciated the gesture, but I couldn't very well take an easier path just because June made me uncomfortable. It wouldn't be right, and after seeing June move, I felt confident she could handle any threat we might encounter.

"I agree, June and I will try and find the thief."

"Good call. Bubba and I will pack up the rest of the weapons and get them somewhere safe, then start scouring the hall for any signs of the hidden merchandise." Krystal reached behind the counter of the booth and produced a small sign that read "Back in 5 minutes." She plunked it onto the center of the table. "The convention opens officially at ten, which is when we need to be on duty. That gives us a little under two hours to hunt this douchewad down before our manpower gets halved. At that point, we'll also have to report the theft to the home office."

"So soon?" June said, her eyes widening considerably. "We could at least wait until the end of the day."

"No, that axe is way too powerful to lose. Even if we catch hell for it, we'll need to call in a full team to sweep the place. It will probably ruin the con for everyone, but there's no other choice. So, let's make these next two hours count." Krystal grabbed a handful of the remaining weapons and began piling them into their former duffel bag, which she'd yanked out from under the display.

June grabbed my shoulder and jerked me forward. "You heard her, we're on a clock. Which way did you see our thief going?"

"Toward the north entrance." I pointed in the direction I'd last seen the strangely waddling figure dart off. It was thick with bodies already, making even seeing to the end of the aisle a difficult task.

"Figures they'd go toward the most crowded part," June snapped. "All right, Fred, stay close and don't fall behind. When I start hunting something, I lose track of everything else. Lose me, and there's no way of knowing when I'll realize you're gone."

With that, June hurtled forward, darting gracefully down the aisle, nimbly weaving between the various parahumans like a ballet dancer gliding between raindrops.

I might have been more inclined to appreciate the aesthetic appeal, if I hadn't been tasked with following such a display. Instead, I awkwardly bustled my way through the crowd with hurried apologies.

6.

IT TOOK LESS THAN FIVE MINUTES FOR US to scout the general area our thief had headed into and confirm they were no longer around. Despite the various parahumans meandering about, June was surprisingly methodical in keeping them mentally organized as she dragged me to each section and asked if anyone matched what I saw. Truthfully, I shouldn't have been surprised by her skill, but I was accustomed to Krystal's style of problem management, which was . . . less organized, to put it nicely.

"If the thief came this way and isn't here anymore, that leaves us with limited options," June declared, once the final area was pronounced to be thief-free. "They could have doubled back and gone to another part of the floor, but Krystal was right about those weapons being bulky as all hell, not to mention noticeable. There probably wasn't time to stash them before the lights came back on, so if I were in their shoes, I'd have left the convention floor and found a place to squirrel the goods away before coming back."

"It makes sense, but it's equally possible they ran this way momentarily and then shifted course, or found cover in one of the booths."

June nodded her head toward a white-painted door that nearly blended in perfectly with the ivory-colored walls. "There are only two exits out of this whole area besides the main doors, and our thief happened to run right at one of them. True, it isn't concrete, but sometimes this job is about playing the odds. Besides, I have a feeling in my gut that says the weapons went this way."

"Forgive me for asking this, but I'm relatively unfamiliar with the capabilities of fey. At least, beyond the old stories and literature. Is this gut feeling an actual magic, or are we merely talking about intuition?"

"Fred, when you've been doing this job as long as some of us have, there is nothing 'mere' about intuition," June said. "I actually can sense magic within a certain range, but no, this isn't that. It's just decades of experience telling me to follow this route."

"A well-made point," I conceded. Though I had peeked behind the curtain a bit in terms of seeing agents without the bluster, that didn't change the fact that they were highly capable at their jobs. If June said the thief went out the door, then it behooved me to trust her judgment. Besides, it wasn't like I had any better idea to put forth.

We exited the main floor and came into a stone hallway, clearly meant only for emergencies and staff, since it lacked the more upscale décor of the rest of the convention center. Before us were a set of rising concrete steps and a short hallway that led to a door with a bright red "Exit" sign hanging above it. Even just seeing it left me a touch uneasy, as I knew beyond that door was bright, beautiful, deadly sunshine. If June wanted to follow the trail that way, she would have to do it without me.

"We go up," June said. That command made me feel both worried and at ease, since, as much as I'd dreaded the idea of telling June I had to quit, the chance to exit the hunt had been extremely appealing.

"What do you think is up there?" I asked. "The hotel is attached, but it's a separate building, so it can't lead to the rooms."

"Smart money says this is how they access those catwalks near the ceiling. With the main lights down from the spell, it's pitch black up there, and no one is looking up at them anyway. Perfect place to hide stolen magical weapons."

"If you're right, our thief seems to have done an awful lot of planning for a spur of the moment pilfering. Being at the booth just as the lights went out, having this place already in mind, it all screams to significantly more pre-meditation than I'd suspected."

June gave me a long, cool stare, then artfully raised one of her eyebrows by the barest of inches.

"I, um . . . I watch a lot of mystery movies and shows," I admitted, caving under her authoritative gaze.

"Then you realize our only advantage over this jerk is that, while the thief you described is short and hobbly, we are both capable of incredible speed. So we should quit yapping and start climbing."

"Of course." I barely had time to get the words out before June was off, barreling up the stairs with the same grace she'd demonstrated in maneuvering through the convention hall.

Now, as a vampire, I'm pretty spry myself, and since having a drop of Gideon's blood, I'd been even more so, yet I still had to push myself to keep up with her as we climbed flight after flight. Had it been a straightforward race on flat ground, I likely could have overtaken her, but when adding the nimbleness needed to corner and climb, she easily became the faster of us. If she was only half fey, I shuddered to think what a full-blooded one could do. Suffice it to say that the fey had joined the ever-growing list in my head of parahumans to avoid slighting or angering. Thus far, it included every type of parahuman I'd met, as well as a few I'd only heard about.

Even with our exceptional speed, it took us nearly a full minute to ascend the high reaches of the industrial stairs. At last we came to a small platform with a door marked "Employees Only."

"That just seems cruel," I said, pointing at the sign. June shot me a curious glance, so I continued. "It makes more sense to have the sign at the bottom. Imagine if someone was all the way down there, curious about what was at the top, and they climbed that whole set of stairs just to be disappointed. Sure, it's not a big deal for us; however, that might have been truly taxing for a human."

"Fred, stop talking."

"My apologies. I was just struck by how it—"

"No, Fred, stop talking because I need to concentrate," June said, her voice surprisingly patient. "I can feel a slight trace of magic up here."

"Ah. Right. Shutting up now."

June closed her eyes and inched carefully toward the door. She pressed her slender fingers against its cold metal surface, face so close that if the door were flung open it would easily break her nose, or it would if that exceptional speed of hers didn't extend to her reflexes as well as it did to her legs. It was hard to say how long she stood like that; time spent trying to be quiet and still tends to stretch out in odd directions. Thankfully, June finally broke the silence, and with good news at that.

"They're here," she said softly. "I can't be sure where, or if the thief is still around them, but I can tell they're nearby." She reached around to the small of her back and removed her gun from its holster. It was smaller than Krystal's sidearm—my girlfriend preferred the sort of weapon that could cleave limbs off bodies with a single shot. June's was smaller and built for precision. It matched her personality well.

"From here on, things get dangerous," June warned. "Normally, I'd tell you to wait out here, but we're going into a situation with an unknown parahuman whose capabilities are a mystery. The one thing we do know, however, is that they're adept at staying hidden. Add in that it will be dark as hell up here, and that means I need as many eyes as I can get, especially vampire ones, just in case our villain tries to get the jump on me. All you need to do is play lookout, no trying to be a hero and getting involved. Just because our thief has been peaceful and working in the shadows doesn't mean they have to. It's entirely possible that this person has plenty of power to throw around and just prefers the convenience of staying hidden. That option won't exist when they're cornered, so you'd better brace for anything."

I gave a small nod to signal my understanding. Much as I loathed getting tangled up in these situations, June was right about plunging into the unknown. It was always dangerous, and my extra vision might very well make the difference between a successful surprise attack and a thwarted failure. June clearly wasn't my biggest fan, and she'd done little to ingratiate herself to me thus far, but it didn't matter. She was important to Krystal, and that made her important to me. Such is the burden of love and friendship.

"I'm going to pull open the door in a minute. When I do, I'll jump forward, in case anything is nearby, and as soon as that happens, I want you to do a quick scan for our thief. If they try to bolt, give me directions. If they rush us, give me a warning. Under no circumstances, *none*, are you to pursue or engage. Clear?"

"Understood," I said.

June gave a half-hearted roll of her eyes, then grabbed the door handle firmly in her clutches.

"One, two, three, go!"

7.

JUNE'S VOICE HAD BARELY STOPPED reverberating in my ear by the time the sound of the door opening reached me. She was through it almost faster than I could track, gun held at the ready as she stepped onto a metal grating. Not wanting to fall behind, I quickly peered over her shoulder and scouted the area.

We were at the top level of the convention center, with black metal catwalks stretching across the ceiling like a steel spider's web. The railing only came up to roughly hip-level—which I felt had to be some sort of safety-code violation—and they had black sheeting covering everything up to the rails. While this undoubtedly made it easier to walk around and not accidently slip a leg through a gap, it also created an excellent area for someone of small stature to duck down and hide.

"See anything?" June asked.

"No movement, but with the sheeting in place, it's impossible for me to say for certain we're alone," I admitted.

"What about a scent?"

That, truthfully, hadn't occurred to me. Smell was one of the senses I'd used the least since my death, at least in a capacity beyond detecting floral notes in a decanting merlot. It was undeniably useful, as Richard had demonstrated late last year when I first met him, but it didn't generally provide much utility in my day-to-day life. Practiced or not, it was one of my skills though, so I decided to give it a try.

I inhaled deeply, mentally pushing aside the selective attention I generally kept in place. The world around me seemed to come alive in a symphony of scents. Metal was what hit me first, sharp and clear, followed by the more mellow odors of grease and oil. Next came the soft crackle of ozone I assumed was from the now shut-off light bulbs. I caught a strong whiff of June as well, which was a curious experience altogether. It's hard to put down exactly what June smelled like—the closest I can come is to say it was like the scent of roses blooming in the snow. These were the most prevalent scents that hit me, but there were so many smells overall that I nearly lost count. Unfortunately, none of them were things that sang out as "weapons" or "thief" to me.

"Sadly, that appears to be a bust as well," I said. "How about your tingle?"

"Just so many ways you could have phrased that better." June sighed. "It got stronger when I opened the door, but it isn't exactly a compass. I know there's magic up here, but the where is pretty much a crap shoot."

"Now would be an excellent time for some more intuition."

"No, now would be a great time for methodical searching," June countered. "I'll walk in front, you watch from behind. We go row by row until we've either cleared the area or found the weapons. If our thief is up here and makes a break for it, let me handle it."

"You won't get any argument from me," I assured her.

June nodded and started forward, moving to the nearest catwalk. They were set up like parallel lines, running across the ceiling to allow access to lights at any given point. At both edges and in the direct center were catwalks that ran perpendicular, so that one could access the other walks. We'd started out on one of the edges and went through a run of grating directly in the middle.

While we could see most of it just by looking directly down it, there were a few areas at the corners of the intersecting walks that were hard to view without getting close. As we neared the first such area, I held my breath (not that it mattered if I breathed), but June and I walked past without finding either the thief or the stolen goods.

We cleared the next row just the same, and the next, and the next. By the time we hit row five out of what I estimated to be twenty, my nerves were beginning to calm down just a touch. In fact, I was so relaxed that I barely jumped at all when June broke the silence by speaking to me.

"Tell me something, Fred: what are you hoping to get out of a relationship with an agent?"

"Um . . . do you mean . . . marriage? Because, while I don't particularly object to the idea, Krystal and I haven't even been dating for a full year, so we've yet to discuss that sort of long-term possibility."

"No, not marriage. I mean, why are you dating her? Krys's attraction I sort of get; after what happened with my brother, she would obviously have been more into guys who were stable and trustworthy. But you? You're clearly a coward, and I don't mean that maliciously. You should be scared. You're a soft man in a very dangerous world; fear is the logical reaction. It just makes me wonder why such a logical, non-confrontational, insecure guy like you would really want to be with an agent.

We invite chaos and carnage wherever we go, and being around us means never knowing peace or safety. What makes a guy like you want to date someone like that? My guess is that it's convenience. Krys was the only girl willing to give you a shot, so you decided to be with her whether it really made you happy or not."

For a moment, there was no sound, save the soft rattle of the grate shaking with our steps and the gentle murmur from the convention floor below. With a question that loaded, I assumed June was prepared to tear apart whatever justification I offered up. She wanted to rip into the relationship Krystal and I had, and no amount of clever responses was going to change that feeling. So, with no options for glibness or avoidance possible, I fell back on the one thing I knew I could defend.

I told the truth.

"You know, in the beginning, I think that's probably exactly what it was."

June didn't stop walking, but her pace did slow down noticeably.

"Back at the reunion, through the LARP where we met Neil, perhaps even into Vegas, we were probably together simply out of convenience. She was interested in me, which fit my requirements, and I was safe, which fit hers."

"Then I—"

"However, that is only where things began, the reason *why* we started our relationship." I made no apology for cutting her off as we approached the intersection of our current row, steps moving carefully. "As we grew to know one another, we realized how well we complemented each other, and genuine affection began to grow; the kind born of true adoration, instead of just convenience. So, to answer your question fully, what I get from Krystal is simply that I get to be with Krystal. Not a woman, not an agent: Krystal. I am . . . very fond of her, and she's the one I want to spend my time around."

"Cute speech," June said. "Couldn't quite get the L-word out though, huh?"

"I am not very good at showing emotions," I admitted. "But even if I were, I was raised to believe the first time a man admits to loving someone, it should be to that person's face, not said in secret conversation behind their back."

"That's surprising," June said.

"Not at all, it's a perfectly reasonable sentiment."

"Not that, ding-dong, *that*." She pointed to the corner, where our current catwalk intersected with the length-wise one. There, sitting unguarded, were the three weapons we were currently looking for. The one I had been unable to look away from only hours earlier, The Blade of the Unlikely Champion, sat poised atop the other two.

"Oh. Yes, that is rather surprising."

June holstered her gun and bent down toward the pile. "Surprising or not, this takes a lot of pressure off of us. Let's get these back downstairs. Then we can hunt this stealing prick down."

As she hunched over, a small, shockingly quick blur bolted forth from the shadows and struck, hitting her on the ass and sending her sprawling over the railing without so much as a moment to react. It happened so quickly that she still had a weapon clutched in her hand as she was sent airborne. June tumbled over once, allowing me a perfect view of the terrified look on her face as the world suddenly disappeared beneath her, and then began to plummet toward the all-too-distant convention floor below.

Just like that, I was suddenly stuck on a cat-walk, alone, with the thief whose glowing yellow eyes were already turning in my direction.

8.

HAD I FACED THIS SITUATION EVEN A MONTH sooner, there would have been a very different outcome. Then, even with all the physical blessings that vampirism had provided, I simply would not have been fast enough to react. But that was before I'd been given a single drop of Gideon's blood. Vampires can take on abilities from other parahumans by drinking from them; it's what makes us both powerful and feared, even among other supernatural creatures. True, Gideon had only given me one drop of his blood, but Gideon was one of the oldest known dragons in the world. That made his blood *extra* potent, and gave me the edge I needed to keep the day from turning into a tragedy.

As June tumbled over the railing and the thief turned their attention toward me, I bounded over the edge as well, jamming my foot into the small gap between the metal sheeting and the grated walkway. The distinct and (unfortunately) increasingly familiar sound of bending metal reached my ears as I stretched forward, hoping against hope that my makeshift anchor point was enough to hold the both of us. Of course, that would only matter if I could reach June in the first place.

The shove had sent her over, but thankfully hadn't flung her far, which meant I was merely racing gravity instead of distance as well. Even with that, it was still close as I lunged forward and tried to grab the back of June's foot. She saw me out of the corner of her eye and kicked on reflex, bringing it a few precious inches closer to my face. It was a very close call.

It just wasn't close enough.

My long fingers closed on air as she fell away, and for a moment, my own undead heart defied gravity by sinking into my stomach despite my upside-down position. June hung there, slowly falling away, and I was powerless to reach her. All I could do was hope that half-fey were resilient enough to survive a fall from twenty staircases up.

At least, that's all I thought I could do in that brief yet never-ending instant. Then I realized June was forcing herself into a somersault so that her upper body would face me. It didn't make sense why she would bother—her arms were shorter than her legs, and those were already out of reach—until I saw the flash of gold and black clutched in her left hand. Her plan finally sank in, and I readied myself for one more shot at saving her. June finished her flip and faced me, thrusting her arm and the object clutched within it toward me. My fingers stretched to meet them, and this time they managed to close firmly.

Firmly around the hilt of The Blade of the Unlikely Champion.

I must confess now, that, upon hearing that name, I'd wondered if perhaps the destiny that had driven it from its protective housing was a path that was meant to bring it to me. Forgive the egotism, but do we not all, on occasion, like to believe we have it in us to be better versions of ourselves? That if the moment were to call on us, we could respond with previously unseen strength and courage? It is that persistent delusion on which I blame the brief moment of fear that rippled through me when I grabbed The Blade. What if I were its chosen one and accidentally unsheathed it? On top of the implications and responsibilities, June would be taking the long-drop for sure.

Luckily, it turned out The Blade of the Unlikely Champion had at least some standards in choosing its wielder, as it remained so firmly rooted in its sheath that I would have sworn the two were welded together. We hung there only for a moment, then I pulled myself up with my leg and took hold of the grating with my free hand. It was far from anything I would ever call "safe," but it was also a far sight better than we'd been even two seconds prior.

"I can't believe it," June said, face surprisingly stoic for a woman dangling over a massive fall.

"Me neither. Where were these reflexes when Krystal dropped my favorite decanter last week?"

"Actually, I can't believe that was the choice you made," June said. This time, however, her voice didn't come from the end of a sword. It came from directly above me, where she was standing with her hand outstretched. "Come on, I'll pull you up."

My eyes narrowed, a gesture which certainly would have been more intimidating if my glasses hadn't been knocked askew in the hurried rescue. "You can teleport?"

"It would be more accurate to say I shifted my position in the world, but your version isn't entirely wrong." June wiggled her fingers, still waiting for me to take her hand. Part of me dearly wanted to slap it away, but I wasn't quite so certain that I wanted to get back on her bad side while she was standing there and I was merely dangling.

With a small and defeated sigh, I reached up, sword still in hand, and she took hold of my forearm. Whether it was magic or strength, I have no idea, but June hefted me back onto the catwalk as easily as if she were moving a sack of foam.

As soon as I was safe, I noticed the hooded figure that had struck her sitting nearby, face still obscured by shadows, save for its glowing yellow eyes. It made no attempt to attack either of us, nor did it go after the weaponry. It didn't take me long to put things together after that.

"This was you, wasn't it? This was you all along. That thing is a friend of yours, and you had it steal the weapons when you pushed me down."

"That 'thing' is a brownie, a spirit that serves the fey, and his name is Grelthidolk. And he's a very good boy, too, yes he is." June reached down and scratched the back of the creature's hooded head, which resulted in the brownie kicking one leg against the metal grating.

"What about the things that were stolen before our weapons?"

"What did you think I was doing while you and Krys were putting the booth together?" June shot back.

"Okay, enough of the what and how, just tell me one thing: *why*? You're an agent, you're supposed to be the good guy. Why on earth would you steal these things?"

"First off, you can't steal what belongs to you," June pointed out. "And as an Agency rep, these are technically my property as much as Krys's. Secondly, I never took anything from the others, just moved stuff about so it would be misplaced. We told you paranoia runs rampant at these things; it only took a nudge. As for why, that should be the most obvious part: I wanted to test you."

"How in the high heavens was this a test for me?"

"You can tell a lot about a person by the way they react when they don't have time to think," June said, bending down and grabbing the other two weapons. "It gives you the sort of look at their soul that can't be faked. If you'd gone after the weapons, keeping them and, by extension, Krys safe, then I'd have known you were a dedicated man. The sort of fellow who would always put the mission first, regardless of what it was. If you'd gone after Grelthidolk, then I'd have known you were a vengeful man, the kind who would never tolerate harm coming to the people you loved."

"And if I dive unnecessarily over the edge to try and save you, what does that say about me?"

"That you're kind, and a little dumb. I am an agent, after all. You don't think something as simple as a fall could kill me, do you?"

"I didn't really register that at the time."

"No, you didn't, which is exactly the point. When you had no chance to think, only to react, your default setting was saving the woman who has made it very clear that she doesn't like you." June sighed as she hauled the weapons under her arms. "Much as I hate to admit it, you may not be as bad of a match for Krys as I thought. Damn, she's never going to let me live it down, either."

"You're going to tell her about your crazy plan?" Don't get me wrong, I'd already intended to her in about her friend being a total nutjob, I just didn't expect said nutjob to have the same idea.

"Of course, I have to tell her the results. She figured out what I was doing as soon as the swords were gone. That's why she set the time limit for 'calling the home office.' It was her way of saying I had to wrap it up before our jobs started."

My mouth opened and closed several times as I reached for words, but found only a general sensation of being aghast. It wasn't that I found the idea of Krystal allowing her friend to put me through the paces so unbelievable, it was the opposite. That sounded so much like something Krystal would agree to that I was having trouble finding any sort of argument. At last, I gave up, and accepted the plain truth that had been laid out before me.

"Does she do this to your boyfriends too?"

"Only the ones I get serious with," June said. We began heading down the catwalk and toward the exit, Grelthidolk trailing us several steps behind. "She's not always as nice as I am, though. There was one boyfriend that she terrified so much, he still won't set foot in a carnival. He goes on trips when they come to his town."

"I would like it on the record right now that I do not want to hear that story," I said.

"That's probably a good call, but you're the one who has to stop Krys from telling it. After all, you're her boyfriend." June gave me a surprisingly warm smile, one that in no way began to make up for what she'd put me through, but was still pleasant nonetheless.

"I am indeed, which means I know enough to ply her with martinis and leave her to torment you all afternoon."

"You know, Fred, you might be more dangerous than I give you credit for."

9.

TWO DAYS LATER, WHICH I AM HAPPY TO report passed without incident, Krystal and I wearily entered my apartment and dropped the few remaining boxes on the floor. I'd agreed to let her use the extra space in my storeroom for her more mundane items, until she had time to haul them back to their central office—a gesture I made mostly out of concern for my own free time. My apartment was on the third floor, while Krystal's was on the seventh in a downtown loft. Since I knew I'd be roped into lugging them about either way, moving them from my place was the less annoying endeavor. Bubba had agreed with my logic thoroughly, and was downstairs unloading the truck to make for faster trips up.

Her only non-mundane object was the duffel bag, still stuffed with mythical weapons of destiny, though less than there had been when she set out. Two of them had found their owners at the convention—poor, unsuspecting souls that were suddenly thrust onto the Agency's radar as June and Krystal got every scrap of information they could about them. The duffel bag and its contents would certainly not be staying at my home; Krystal just refused to leave them in the car while we unloaded. After what June had pulled, I hardly blamed her.

"Hey, Fred, I'm in the back!" Albert's voice rang through the room as soon as I entered. My live-in assistant had been left behind to catch up on a plethora of filing.

"Come out when you reach a good stopping point," I yelled back. "We've got some boxes to move."

"Son of a bitch," Krystal swore. I turned to find her rubbing the back of her head. A familiar black-and-gold hilt was sticking out of the duffel bag, the zipper seemingly having gone down of its own free will. From the glare on her face, it didn't take much effort to figure out what had happened.

"Quit being a dick." Krystal dropped the duffel bag roughly on the counter and poked the sword fiercely, clearly unashamed of talking to an inanimate object. "You got to go be held by people. You even had a bit of an adventure. If you were that desperate to find a wielder, then you should have picked one of the dozens of people who tried to unsheath you."

The sword, quite obviously, said nothing.

"I'm just glad it didn't choose me," I said honestly. From the leather messenger bag at my side (a purchase I'd found too well-crafted and fairly priced to pass up), I produced a small, cellophane bag and set it on the counter.

"Freddy, you know you're my heroic number cruncher, but you aren't exactly fit to be a champion, unlikely or otherwise," Krystal said. "Hell, for one thing, you're too smart. Champions are usually the type who charge into battle, odds be damned, believing they can triumph because right is on their side. You have to be a little bit of a moron to pull that sort of shit."

"Says the woman who battles monsters every day," I pointed out.

"Says the woman with access to the powers of a devil—one of the most dangerous supernatural beings we know of—who battles monsters every day. My fights are rigged; I'm the one with the staggering odds to win."

"Unless your opponent is a fellow agent who steals weapons." I set the cellophane sack next to Krystal's duffel bag. Inside was a plastic clamshell package containing a pair of custom headphones with headstones on the side and a medium-sized T-shirt adorned in magical symbols. The shopping at various booths had been incredible, and I'd felt Albert at least deserved a few souvenirs, since he hadn't gotten to come.

Krystal rolled her eyes, a motion so theatrically exaggerated I half expected her to call stage left for her line. "How many times can I say I'm sorry? June's just a little . . . protective. Even though the engagement fell through, I think she still sees me as sort of a younger sister. Doesn't help that she was one of my mentors when I first started the Agency."

"I don't fault you for June's actions. However, you were complicit in them by letting her drag me off. In fact, you encouraged us to group up."

"My options were to let her pull that stunt, which I knew was in a controlled environment and probably safe, or stop her, in which case, she would have just tried again. Only, in that second version, it might not have been as safe or controlled, and I might not be there to shadow you in case things go bad."

The discovery of Krystal waiting in the stairwell, scowl fixed firmly in June's direction, had done much to mollify my concern. It was reassuring to know that, even if she was willing to throw me into the clutches of her insane half-fey friends, she at least wasn't willing to do it without making sure I was okay. Despite being almost as bad at talking about her feelings as I was, Krystal still managed to show me she cared, and that meant a great deal to me.

"What do you need me to do?" Albert asked, walking out of my office with his usual grin spread across his face. Though I wasn't always keen about having a roommate at my age, it was hard not enjoy being around the ball of positivity that Albert usually embodied.

"First up, I brought you souvenirs," I said, pointing to the cellophane sack next to the duffel bag. "My way of apologizing for leaving you behind. Once you've opened those, start moving the boxes into the storage closet in the back of the office. We're going to get another load from the truck."

"Can do, boss! And thanks a lot for bringing me souvenirs."

"Thank you for working so diligently," I said.

Krystal and I headed back downstairs as Albert pulled open the sack and began to remove his presents. I'd meant to remind him that I'd moved the scissors to the far drawer from the stove—those clamshell packages could be a pain to open without a sharp implement—but it slipped my mind as I tried to calculate how many more of these trips would be required to finish unloading. As we stepped outside, lit only by the soft glow of streetlights, and I saw the pile that Bubba had pulled from the truck's depths, I readjusted my estimate.

It took a few minutes to get loaded down with just the right number of parcels to maximize my productivity without risking me losing my grip and dropping the lot, but eventually, Krystal and I made our second journey up the stairs and into my apartment. As soon I entered, I noticed Albert coming back from loading the previous boxes in the closet. Resting around his neck were the headphones I'd brought him.

"Oh good, you found the scissors," I noted.

"Huh? Oh, no, I couldn't remember where you moved them to when you reorganized the kitchen," Albert said. He grabbed a large amount of the boxes from Krystal's arms, and they both set their loads down.

"Did you use a kitchen knife, then?"

"No, I remembered your lecture about food and plastic utensils needing to stay separate," Albert replied. "I just borrowed one of the display swords you guys brought in." He walked over to the kitchen counter, where, I realized for the first time since entering, one of the weapons had been taken entirely out of the duffel bag. "I was worried they'd be dull since they're pretend, but this thing actually cuts super well."

"Oh, no fucking way . . ." Krystal muttered under her breath.

With a single motion, Albert picked up and easily unsheathed The Blade of the Unlikely Champion. The steel shone in the light, an unnatural glow cascading across its smooth surface. Krystal's eyes widened visibly, and I dropped my boxes unceremoniously to the ground. For his part, Albert finally realized something was amiss as he stared at our shocked and uncertain faces.

"What? Did I do something wrong?"

A SWORD IN THE CATACOMBS

1.

"AGENT JENKINS, WE'RE CURRENTLY AN HOUR outside our destination. Obscuring protocol must be enacted before the wheels touch down." The voice—male and authoritative, with just a hint of fear underlying the strong tones—crackled over the intercom. This plane belonged to the pilot, it was his domain, but that didn't change the fact that he was hauling a menagerie of beings who could kill him with the barest effort, and the most dangerous of us all was the one he was ordering around.

"Calm your ass down," Krystal said, leaning across me and punching a white button just below the speaker.

"It takes less than five minutes to put the damn bags on their heads. I'm not making my friends ride like that until I have to."

"Just be sure they're covered in time."

Krystal rolled her brown eyes so hard, I was amazed they didn't detach and continue going across the floor. She pulled herself back into a seated position. I was momentarily surprised; she usually never missed an opportunity to be publicly draped across my lap in an effort to make me embarrassed or panicked. Even for Krystal, though, there were situations serious enough to dampen her ever-present levity.

The plane we were on was large and beige on the inside, with enough seats to accommodate roughly twenty people, by my estimate. I had no idea what the outside looked like, since I'd had my head in an enchanted bag when we boarded and there were no windows anywhere in the cabin. Krystal had always made light of the amount of secrecy enacted by her employer, but this was my first time actually seeing the extent of it.

Krystal and I were seated across the aisle from Neil and Albert. Two seats up were Bubba and Amy, who appeared to be playing a game of Go Fish. Neil and Albert weren't doing much, just talking quietly about a new movie in a franchise they were looking forward to. It might have seemed like a semi-normal experience, if not for the gold-and-black sword clutched tightly in Albert's hand. He'd been holding it ever since drawing the thing three hours prior. To be honest, I wasn't sure if he was even able to let it go. Those weapons had more agency than I'd expected.

I had been both surprised and impressed by Krystal's efficiency in handling the situation. After Albert drew The Blade of the Unlikely Champion, she'd vanished into the hall, pulling out her cell phone as she went, and returned five minutes later. In that time, she'd called the Agency to arrange transportation and had told Amy to bring Neil to my apartment. After that, we were all put in a van—a van I'm certain hadn't been there the last time I went down to unload boxes from Krystal's truck—and fitted with hoods that dulled even my enhanced senses. She'd refused to tell us where we were going or what was happening, revealing only that "protocol had to be followed." It was out of character for her; Krystal usually treated us as equals despite her somewhat authoritative position. That had me far more on edge than the fact that Albert had been chosen by a Weapon of Destiny.

"I don't suppose, now that we've reached the point of no return, you could give us a hint of what's going on?" Neil had let his conversation with Albert lapse while I'd been lost in thought, and was now staring across the aisle at Krystal.

"What makes you think this is the point of no return?"

"We're up in the air, and when we land, I'm certain you'll have dozens of armed agents waiting to make sure we all toe the line like good children. Even if you tell us that we're all off to be killed, there would be nothing we could do."

"Oh? Hey, Amy, do you have any potions that would let you survive a fall from several miles up?" Krystal asked.

"I've got one for floating that I have all the ingredients for, plus I know a couple of minor levitation spells I could cast on the fly," Amy replied. "Got any twos?"

"I swear you've got some way to cheat at this game," Bubba grumbled as he took a card out of his hand and gave it to her.

"It's really all in the math," Amy said with a shrug.

"With a potion and a spell, that means Amy could save herself as well as her apprentice," Krystal continued. "Meanwhile, a drop like that isn't enough to kill a therian or a vampire. Not unless they land in a way that decapitates them."

"Or it's sunny out," I reminded her.

"Right, yes, or there's sunshine. Now, we all know I'm not dying on impact, and any damage Albert might suffer can be patched with a quick spell from you, his aspiring necromancer friend."

"I take your point—we could still destroy the plane or leap out of it, so we're not truly at a point of no return," Neil said.

"My point was that there really is no point-of-no-return. You guys could still leap out of here and escape. Or you could ask that we turn the plane around. Hell, you could have just refused to come along with me. It's not like I pulled a gun on you."

"But you told us to come with you," Neil said.

"Yeah, because that's what I was told was the right move for everyone." Krystal looked around, realizing that the rest of us were staring at her as well. "Wait, did you all think I was holding out on you?"

"You have been pretty tight-lipped since Albert pulled out that sword," Bubba said.

"For the love of . . . guys, I haven't told you what's going on because I don't have a damned clue either. I called up the chain to report the sword being drawn and was informed that they would send transport immediately. What Albert did is . . . unprecedented, and I think they want to make sure that there isn't some hidden danger to him or us."

"Has that sword never been drawn?" Amy asked.

Krystal shook her head. "No, it's had a very lively past. The issue here is that a Weapon of Destiny has never chosen a zombie before. Not once, in all the history we're aware of."

"Never?" Albert spoke softly, addressing someone besides Neil for the first time since Krystal had explained to him how big a deal unsheathing that blade was.

"Never," Krystal said. "Them choosing undead is pretty rare to begin with, but occasionally, a vampire or Ghoul Lord will manage to wield one. Zombies are a different matter."

"I wonder why?" Albert stared down at the sheath in his hand, clearly overwhelmed by the events of the last few hours and the consequences he was now facing. My heart went out to him; I knew that feeling all too well.

"Not many zombies are like you, Albert." Amy leaned her seat back, nearly smacking my knees, so she could peek through the cushions and address the rest of us. "Most are resurrected to do chores and menial labor, so very little consciousness is warranted. To produce a zombie like yourself requires a powerful mage, a determined soul, and a strong bond between the spell caster and the zombie."

Neil and Albert exchanged a slightly embarrassed glance, both being a bit too young to be comfortable on being called out on the depth of their friendship. Growing up together as outcasts, there was no doubt they loved one another like brothers, but that was not an easy thing to talk about, especially in front of a group of strangers.

Krystal let them off the hook by steering the subject back on course. "Anyway, it might not be a bad thing. Hell, it might not even be a *thing*. But the Agency tries to be careful when anything new pops up. Magic is unpredictable, and mixing two that haven't been combined before is just as dangerous as slapping a few unknown chemicals together. Could be that nothing will happen, could be you just made mustard gas in the sink. For my money, that's why they're transporting us somewhere: to check you out in a place that minimizes the odds of you hurting anyone, yourself included."

"I trust you, Krystal," Albert said. "If you think this is where I should be, then I'll come along."

"If they were going to do anything I wouldn't approve of, I doubt they would have let me bring everyone else with us," Krystal said. I blinked in surprise. It hadn't even occurred to me that she'd dragged us along purely as some sort of litmus test. Sometimes I let myself forget that, despite her generally flippant attitude, Krystal was immensely skilled and experienced. And, obviously, dangerous.

"Don't worry, I won't let anything happen to you," Neil reassured him.

"We're all here for you," I added, feeling some sense of responsibility. I tried to keep my promise a bit vaguer than Neil's though. The simple truth of it was that, if the Agency decided to do something to Albert, I highly doubted we would be able to stop them in any way. All we could do was trust Krystal, hope for the best, and try to keep Albert calm.

"Let's hear them out before we start planning a counterattack," Krystal said. She leaned back over me and punched the white button, activating the intercom to the pilot. "Hey! Who am I meeting on the ground, anyway? By now, they should have told you the receiving agent."

"Ma'am, that information really shouldn't be shared with others able to overhear—"

"Just give me the damn name, Skippy. I'm the agent, and I'll decide what is and isn't classified." She lifted her finger for just a moment and glanced up at me. "These fucking guys. They all want to act like we're in a damned spy movie all the time. Honestly, if they ever actually made it to field work, they'd spend seventy percent of their time weeping from boredom."

I pointedly avoided asking what they would spend the other thirty percent doing. Seeing only a small bit of Krystal's work-life had told me the answer far too clearly.

"I'm told that the agent goes by the name Arch." The pilot was clearly miffed about being ordered around, but luckily, he was smart enough not to try and push back against Krystal. I was sure the door armoring him off from the rest of the plane was well-built and nigh impregnable. I was equally sure that Krystal would find a way to tear it to shreds, and then give the pilot a similar treatment.

"Arch? You're sure about that?"

"Yes, ma'am. Very sure."

Krystal let go of the intercom and slid back into her seat before addressing the rest of us. "That's perfect. Arch is an old friend and one hell of an agent. If he's meeting us, we're in good hands."

As the rest of cabin fell back into card games and conversation, Krystal's hand wormed its way down from armrest and found my own. Our fingers interlocked, and she gave my hand a firm squeeze. Despite her efforts to keep everyone calm, I suspected that whoever Arch was, it might not be such a great sign that he was waiting for us.

I squeezed her hand back, then chanced a quick glance to Albert. For his sake, I hoped I was reading Krystal's body language incorrectly.

2.

ARCH SMOKED LIKE MOST MEN (EXCLUDING those such as myself) paid their taxes: it was a begrudging action done without evident pleasure and observed purely from necessity. By the time we'd been taken out of the van—emerging in a vast corridor that seemed to be carved entirely from stone and lit by haphazardly strung lights— and walked over to greet him, Arch had already burned through one cigarette and stuck another in the mouth of his perpetually scowling face. An expression that was all the more striking given his youthful appearance; he'd have been lucky to pass for over twenty-one. It might have been confusing, were I not already all too familiar with how deceptive parahuman appearances could be. The sole exception to his apparent youth were his eyes; one glance told me they'd seen far more than I could imagine.

We walked together as a tightly packed group, save for Krystal, who was several steps ahead of us. If she was at all worried about the location we'd arrived at or the man greeting us, she kept it well hidden. She strolled eagerly ahead, grabbing her fellow agent's hand and pulling him close in a bastardized mixture of a hug and a handshake.

"Arch, you sack of shit, I haven't seen you since Quebec. How've you been?"

"Busy. Too damn busy," Arch replied, as he returned her embrace. For a moment, I was afraid that his cigarette would catch her hair on fire, but when they parted, there were no wisps of smoke curling from Krystal's blonde locks. It made me wonder if she could even be burned. Given her supernatural heritage, there was bound to be some inherent resistance to fire.

"You brought the kid with you, I assume?" Arch's voice matched his eyes well. Despite its youthful nature, the tones were harsh and weathered. His gaze ran across us, clearly searching for Albert. It wasn't a very difficult task, since my assistant was the only one holding a large, ornate sword in his hands.

"My friend, Albert, was more than happy to come along," Krystal replied. She didn't quite make it a correction, but she put it forward with enough force to get the meaning across.

"Yeah? How nice for you." Arch walked over to us, and I realized that I couldn't hear his footsteps. Generally, I tried to block out the excess information from my vampire senses; however, this situation had me so on edge that I could have practically heard a cockroach let out a weary sigh. I increased my focus on him and was able to pick up the sound of his steps, but only barely. Whatever Arch was, I couldn't place it. From his looks and scent, he seemed completely human. Then again, the same could be said for Krystal . . . most of the time.

"Your name is Albert, right?" Arch said, eyes on the only zombie in our midst. "Before we go any further with this, would you mind knocking out the prerequisite demonstration?"

"Wh . . . what?" Albert tilted his head like a cat watching dust fall through a sunbeam.

"He wants you to draw the sword," Neil explained. "Whatever we're here for is based on you being the one it chose, so he wants you to prove that first." His own voice was calm and, for once, generally polite. Usually, that was a tone Neil reserved solely for Amy, who was his teacher (and who he had a not-so-secret crush on).

"Oh. Sure thing." Albert gave a small grin and, with no visible effort, pulled out The Blade of the Unlikely Champion. It slid free of the sheath and all but glowed in the pale yellow light of the cheap bulbs dotting the ceiling. "Ta-Da!"

"Damnation," Arch said, eyes widening a bit as he stared at the previously concealed blade. "I can't believe that thing finally picked someone else." He looked away from the sword then, and seemed to really take Albert in for the first time. My assistant appeared sixteen, and always would. He was wearing the same thing he'd had on when working: a black T-shirt, blue jeans, and old sneakers. Arch said nothing, but his sour expression made his feelings a little too clear for my tastes.

"All right then," Arch said at last. "We've got a zombie wielding a Weapon of Destiny. I'm assuming one of you is the contract holder, but for the life of me, I'm not sure why Agent Jenkins brought the rest."

"I brought them because they're Albert's friends too, and I thought he could use some support during whatever lies ahead," Krystal shot back. "But yes, I brought the contract holder. It's my boyfriend, Freddy." She jabbed an index finger in my direction.

"Wait, I'm a what now?"

"A contract holder." Neil sighed, all traces of his good-boy voice vanished. "Zombies need to work to keep their focus and not cause trouble. The contract holder is the person they're serving. You get the labor, and in return, you have to provide the zombie with lodging and care."

"That . . . that sounds a lot more like slavery than employment," I said, suddenly very uncomfortable with the implied arrangement I had with my friend.

"It was, originally," Krystal said. "But in modern times, it's not much different than any other job. You're allowed to fire Albert, and he's allowed to leave you for a better gig. Neither of you owns the other. That's why you're called the contract holder, instead of the zombie holder. All you're holding is the agreed upon work arrangement, for now."

"How exactly is he the contract holder, if he doesn't know any of this?" Arch asked, eyeing Krystal suspiciously.

"Freddy didn't create Albert. He just stepped in when Neil was deemed unfit to hold Albert's contract anymore. I took care of the paperwork for them to ease the transition."

"Uh huh." Arch glared at her for a few seconds longer, and then let it go. Clearly, he knew Krystal well enough to realize that critiquing her adherence to protocol was as productive as demanding stones dance the cha-cha. "Well then, Freddy, was it?"

"Fredrick Frankford Fletcher," I corrected. "Though most people do refer to me as Fred."

"Fred, then," Arch said, clearly a touch relieved not to have to use Krystal's ridiculous nickname for me. "Fred, as current contract holder, I must inform you that your asset is going to be put at risk by order of the Agency. Should any harm come to him, you will be within your rights to demand compensation or suitable replacement. You may not, however, stall or stop the coming events on grounds of your contract. I can cite precedent, if you require it."

For many people, that quickly spoken mangle of terms and releases would have been incomprehensible; however, those people had never sat through the mind-numbing processes required to become a Certified Public Parahuman Accountant. I took Arch's meaning quite well, and I didn't like it one bit.

"My 'asset,' as you called him, is an independent and fully-cognizant Undead American, obliged to the duties and taxes required, and protected under all parahuman laws. I may only know things from the fiscal side, but I'd be willing to bet heavily that there are laws stopping you from compelling Albert to put himself in harm's way."

Arch tilted his head back in surprise; evidently, he hadn't been expecting that response. "Of course I can't make him get hurt. Didn't Krystal explain this on the plane ride? We're going to put Albert through the paces to make sure nothing bad or dangerous happens when you mix a zombie with one of these crazy weapons. But since I don't know what will happen—which is the whole fucking point, after all—I'm legally required to tell you that he might get hurt. For all we know, just swinging the thing could make him explode."

Albert's eyes grew wide, and he quickly stuffed the sword back in its sheath, while I took a moment to be thankful for the fact that vampires were ill-suited to blushing. Arch was right, that was more or less exactly what Krystal had already explained to us.

"Right. Right, she did mention something along those lines. I apologize. I just heard what you were saying . . . it was a mistake on my part."

"It's fine. Honestly, I prefer you being pissy about it to being apathetic. Some contract holders seem to forget that the guy who washes their dishes is powered by a human soul." Arch turned from me and looked at Neil. "Since you're the only person here wearing a trainee collar, I take it you must be Neil, the one who raised Albert."

It was my turn to be surprised. Just from Krystal's off-handed statement, Arch had deduced that the mage who brought Albert back would be among us, and that he'd been put into apprenticeship. The obsidian black collar around Neil's neck matched the bracelet on Amy's left wrist. Unless he was within a certain proximity to her, all of his magic was completely sealed. Given that Neil had tried to kill around a dozen people, myself included, I'd felt the punishment to be a bit light, but the parahuman world has its own rules and repercussions.

"Neil is my apprentice," Amy said, speaking for the first time since we left the van. Her eyes were clear and her expression was purposely neutral, which terrified me. Amy was a prodigious alchemist and tended to use her products liberally, meaning she was almost always in some state of altered mind. When she wasn't, however, the full weight of her tremendous intellect shone through. I was good with numbers and generally smart, but Amy was a no-holds-barred genius. And she'd come to this meeting with a completely clear head.

"But he wasn't when he raised the zombie," Arch countered. "So I'm just talking to him. Neil, as the creator, I am obligated to tell you that your creation will be put at risk by order of the Agency. Since you do not hold his contract, you are not entitled to any compensation, however, you do retain the right to mend or reacquire his remains should the worst happen."

Neil nodded solemnly, his eyes flickering between Albert and Arch.

"Finally, Albert, as a bearer of the sword," —Arch took a breath as he glanced at the re-sheathed sword in Albert's hand— "you have been chosen by a Weapon of Destiny, The Blade of the Unknown Champion. You are to be tested at dawn, to determine if you can safely fulfill the role of Weapon Bearer without putting others at risk. If you are able to surrender the sword by that time, you may be excused from this trial."

"What do you mean, 'if I can surrender it'?"

"When weapons of destiny choose their wielders, it's not a thing they let go of easily," Arch explained. "If they did, I'd be asking if you even wanted to do any of this. No, once they've got you, it's almost impossible to break free. Still, it has happened on occasion, so it's only fair that we give you the chance."

"Why do they get to test him at all?" Neil snapped, his composure finally beginning to crack. "Just because he's a zombie, what gives you the right to put him in harm's way?"

"I'd have expected a mage to understand." Arch's words were directed at Neil, but his eyes were looking at Amy. "Untested magical combinations can be incredibly dangerous, and those swords don't choose owners haphazardly. If it's in Albert's hands, then it's a question of when he'll use it, not if. Now, the Agency doesn't have the right to tell him how to wield that blade, so long as he doesn't use it to break laws, but we're damned sure going to make sure that there aren't any unexpected side effects that put innocent people at risk."

"It's okay," Albert said, putting his free hand on Nick's shoulder. "I don't want to hurt anyone, so I'm fine with checking things out here first."

"You could give up the sword," Neil suggested. "Between Amy and I, we're sure to find a spell that lets you abandon it."

"If you're going that route, you've got three hours to do it in," Arch informed them. He finished his cigarette, tossed the butt into a pocket in his jacket, and then pulled out a fresh one. "Come with me. We've got some rooms set up so you can relax until it's go time. Do whatever you want until then, but be ready by sunrise. The whole place is underground, so those of you with light-aversion will be fine."

Arch began walking down the dry, stone corridor, and, with no other options before us, we followed.

3.

WE WERE SPLIT INTO PAIRS FOR OUR ROOMS:
Neil and Albert, Amy and Bubba, and Krystal with me.
The rooms themselves were like the rest of the facility—fashioned from stone and lit with hanging bulbs
that seemed precariously close to flickering out at any
time. At least they came with beds. Well . . . perhaps
"cots" is a more apt descriptor for the flimsy, twin-sized
mattresses and faded sheets. The whole affair struck me
as surprisingly low-end. I'd always imagined Krystal's
organization to have near unlimited funds and all sorts

of posh, high-tech accommodations. It was only when I paused for a moment and considered the situation that I realized why everything here was so cheap; it was all meant to be disposable. After all, it wouldn't make sense to have a facility for testing unstable magic filled with all sorts of pricey accoutrements.

All the same, I was thankful that the moon was still overhead, as I had no compunction to sleep on such an unsanitary affair. Vampires are able to sleep during the day, but we're not especially compelled to; although, going too many days without rest can lead to a bit of loopy lightheadedness that's somewhat inconvenient. Still, I credited that more to a psychological need than a physiological one. Undead or alive, everyone needs the cobwebs swept out on occasion.

"I'm going to grab a quick nap," Krystal announced, once we were through the roughly attached wooden barrier that served as a door.

"Is this really the time for it?"

"Hell no, but I'm running on almost two days with no sleep thanks to all the convention work, and sooner or later, my body will start showing symptoms of fatigue." She pulled off the thin red jacket she'd been wearing, revealing a black tank-top and gun holster. The holster came off next, then her boots. Usually, when we were out, she pared down the ass-kicking gunslinger look, but the convention had been all about repping her agency, so she was in full gear. For a moment, I thought she would throw modesty to the wind and lose her blue jeans as well; however, she merely pulled back the white sheet and laid down. Whatever trepidation I'd felt about such sleeping accommodations, Krystal clearly didn't share them.

"You going to just stand there, or you going to come lay with me?"

In another context, I'd have feared she meant that in the biblical way, but as soon as she'd hit the bed, exhaustion had already crept into her voice. She was so strong, so indomitable, that I often genuinely forgot that even Agent Krystal Jenkins had limits.

I laid down next to her, staying on top of the sheets and trying not to think about how thoroughly my clothes would need to be dry-cleaned when I got home. My arm found its way around her body, and I pulled her close.

"You're worried, aren't you?"

"Albert is wielding a Weapon of Destiny, something no zombie has ever done before, and we're here to make sure that doing it won't turn him and those around him into pudding or something. If I wasn't worried, I'd either be an idiot or a sociopath." She put her hand on mine—the one currently resting against her stomach.

"It isn't just that. You've been more on edge since you found out Arch was overseeing things. Is he dangerous?"

"Holy shit yes," Krystal said. "Arch is one of the most deadly people in the Agency. If I ever go off the deep-end and start murdering innocent people, he's the one they'll probably send to kill me."

"Pity that wouldn't work on you."

Krystal was silent for a moment, idly tracing her fingers across the back of my hand. "Freddy . . . you know I can die, right?"

"Of course, but only until your devil passenger comes to your aid."

"No, Freddy, I can die for real. If someone were able to kill me in devil-form, was able to put that thing down, I'd die right along with it."

"Oh." Somehow, that hadn't occurred to me. I'd only see her draw on that power one time, and it had been beyond terrifying. She'd torn a previously unstoppable opponent into nothing more than charred remains. The idea that there were things out there stronger than that . . . well, it reminded me just how fragile we all truly were. "And Arch, your friend, you think he'd be able to do that?"

"It's not like he'd get a kick out it or anything, but yes, if given the orders, Arch would kill me without hesitation." Krystal patted my arm reassuringly. "That doesn't change what I said earlier though: he's a good man and a friend. Arch is only someone you should be afraid of if you've done some serious shit wrong. He's not going to attack any of us, or anything crazy like that. I'm not scared at all of what Arch is going to do. I'm scared at what his being here signifies."

"Are you going to make me ask?" She was clearly shifting the topic away from things as serious as her own mortality, and I felt no inclination to stop her.

Krystal elbowed me in the ribs, one of her favorite close-proximity attacks. "You watch enough action movies to know the basics of how law enforcement works. There's beat cops, detectives, SWAT, administrators, all these different divisions of labor to put the right people in the right situations. The Agency works similarly, in that every agent is rated for certain situations. I'm called in for either covert work—things that require a little flirting and diplomacy—or when it's time for some scorched earth."

That made sense, seeing as Krystal the Human was pretty, tenacious, and could be charming when she wanted; whereas the other version of Krystal was barely contained violence fashioned from claws and fire.

"Arch is different," Krystal continued. "He's rated to do damn near everything, and do it well, but even we don't always have fires to put out. That leaves him with down time, and, since he hates administrative work, Arch's favorite pastime is training and recruitment."

A ghostly shiver ran up my spine (no mean feat for a body already at room temperature).

"You think he's not just here to test Albert, but to try and convince him to join your organization?"

"It's possible. When it comes to evaluating talent and potential, we've got damned few agents who are as good at it as Arch. If he thinks Albert's got some real power with that sword, then it would almost be irresponsible of him not to try and talk him into signing on."

I pulled her a few inches closer. "But Albert would still have to agree to it. He can't be drafted or anything like that, right?"

"No, he'd still have to make the choice himself. The Agency has some ability to compel service, but that's only during special circumstances, like war. If Albert says no, then that's the end of it." Krystal stifled a yawn at the end of her sentence, barely getting the words out before the voluminous expulsion of air forced its way out.

"Then I don't think we have anything to worry about. I mean, aside from the potential of pudding. Albert isn't the danger-seeking sort. I seriously doubt he'd be tempted by any offers Arch could present."

"Don't be so certain about that. Albert is a lot like you."

"Exactly. Not the sort to be pulled into life-threatening shenanigans if he can help it."

Krystal let a small smile tug at her face, just barely visible from my horizontal position behind her. "You're cute. A little thick at times, but cute." She patted my hand, and then turned over in the small bed to face me. "But what you aren't doing is helping me sleep. Give me an hour or two, and I'll be bright-eyed and bushy-tailed for sunrise."

"You know, I used to really like that colloquialism. Now, it just makes me wonder if you'll actually have a tail when I see you again."

"Well, if I do, we know it will be bushy." Krystal moved her face across the small gap between us and kissed me. It was sweet and delicate, the kind she only gave just before bed or first upon waking. "Now, go take a walk or something. I don't know that I believe in beauty sleep, but if you don't leave me be, you're going to see some ugly-awake."

"Message received," I said, sliding off the cot and back onto the stone floor. I didn't even make it to the door before the first of Krystal's snores tumbled into my ears. Before I opened it, I paused to glance back at her. She was sprawled out, one leg hanging so far off the edge of the bed that it was amazing she hadn't fallen entirely out of it.

I'd have liked to believe her ability to sleep so easily signified that she wasn't all that afraid for Albert, but we'd been together too long for me to kid myself with such delusions. Krystal was a warrior; she took her rest when she could. If we'd been besieged by dragons and had a thirty minute window for sleep, she'd have nodded off just as easily.

No, Krystal was worried about Albert, and after hearing what may be in store for him (even if things went well), so was I. It was hard to imagine him being tempted by the sort of life the Agency could offer, but in my time since becoming undead, I'd learned one very important rule about the parahuman world:

You never knew what was or wasn't possible when dealing with our kind.

4.

I'd spent a lot of my life lying to Albert. The others might have thought his cheerful, sometimes admittedly dopey nature came from the unique circumstances of his death, but the truth was that those had only exacerbated a previously existing condition. Albert was always quick with a smile and an open heart. He was so trusting, even when we were kids, that I suspected the world couldn't help but take advantage of him.

I never lied to hurt Albert; I lied to protect him. I would tell him we weren't hanging out with a group of people because I disliked them for one reason or another, never admitting that the truth was because I knew they'd tease him. I assured him that girls would come to us later in life, when our natural talents and charm were not hampered by the limitations of high school, doing my best to keep him from realizing how low on the social totem pole we sat.

I told him that I hadn't gone to his funeral; that I'd been too busy working on the spell to bring him back. I'd actually sat in the front row, next to his mother and father. I'd tried to say my goodbyes when he was lying in the casket, but I couldn't make the words come out. I tried again when we went to the cemetery, but still got nothing. When they were lowering him into the ground, I tried one last time to let go of my best friend. I ended up crying so hard that I fell out of the chair. I couldn't do it. I couldn't let him pass on.

That was the day I resolved to do anything, follow any avenue, to bring Albert back into my life.

As we sat on our respective cots, Albert staring at his sword and me at my ancient tome of necromantic magic, I wondered what sort of lies I might have to tell him before this ordeal was over. All I could think about as my eyes skimmed through the scrawled spells was what was coming at sunrise. I didn't really need to study the words; I'd long ago committed the ones I could work on the fly to memory. Anything beyond those would require the book as reference, so there was no point in familiarizing myself with them extensively. My time was better spent trying to find something, anything, that would let me separate whatever bond the sword had created with my friend. He was connected to me, to my magic, and always would be. And that meant there might be a way to make the blade let go.

"What do you think I'll have to do?" Albert asked, the words bouncing around our nearly bare stone room.

"I doubt it will be anything strenuous," I told him. "They'll just want you to use the sword, draw on its magic, and make sure there aren't any negative side effects. Maybe they'll put some bacon out for you to chop, and we can all have breakfast tacos."

"Why do we have to wait, then? I could do that now."

"It's not really breakfast if it's before sunrise." I partially closed my tome, keeping a single finger between the pages so I didn't lose my spot. "I'm sure it's because they want to test you with as little ambient magic around as possible. Sunrise and sunset both have a lot of power in terms of purging magic. It's why so many curses and spells center around when the sun is going up or down. Doing it at sunrise is just a safety precaution, giving you the best environment to test in."

I left out my other theory, which was that having daylight on hand could take Fred right out of a fight (he was already pretty useless, but only we knew that), and waiting until after sunrise would purge many of the preemptive spells Amy and I could lay on ourselves. If that Arch guy was planning to do something that might make us fight, he'd have an easier task on his hands by waiting just these few hours. Albert didn't need to know that, however. Those were my concerns to deal with.

"That makes sense," Albert said. "I feel like I should be doing something though. Like training, or preparing mentally, the stuff they always do in action movies before a big fight."

"Since you're not actually going to fight anyone, why don't we play cards instead?" I dug through my small satchel (a gift from Amy that held more space inside than outside) and pulled out a deck of cards. Amy had been adamant that every mage worth his or her salt should have mundane playing cards on them at all times (also, curiously, salt). She'd yet to tell me why, but I'd seen enough of her power and knowledge to trust her instructions implicitly.

"It could be a fight," Albert pointed out. He got down off his cot and sat on the floor, setting the blade down nearby. I could sense the threads of magic still connecting the two, even without them physically touching. They were small, but powerful. I'd never gotten to see a magic quite like it before. Reluctantly, I took my hand out of my tome and got down on the floor with Albert. I could hunt for a solution after one game, especially if it helped take his mind off what was ahead.

"How would they make you fight someone? The whole purpose of the test is to make sure you won't accidently hurt yourself or someone else. Doesn't make sense to put another person in harm's way before they've figured that out." I pulled the cards free and began to shuffle, an exercise that immediately made my brain calm down and my breathing shift. Amy liked to make me shuffle cards as a meditation technique for clearing my mind. After so many months doing it, the effects kicked in even when I wasn't intending them to. Plus, I could now shuffle really well. "Want to play War?"

"Sounds good," Albert agreed. "I hope you're right, about the fighting thing. I really didn't want them to try and make me hurt someone. I don't know if I could have done that."

I did know, and the answer was that he couldn't. Albert wasn't a fighter, but he wasn't a coward like Fred; he was just too soft-hearted. It was one of the things I admired the most about him. I was, on my best day, morally gray and decent. I mean, even raising Albert hadn't been a purely altruistic endeavor; I'd done it because I couldn't bear to be without my friend, not because I thought he'd be happier as a zombie.

That was the thing I worried and wondered the most about: was Albert happy that I'd raised him? He certainly seemed cheerful, but that was his default, so it told me nothing. I wondered if he wished I'd left him at peace. If, under all the smiles and cheer and fun . . . Albert resented me for forcing him back into this world.

"I think they're shuffled," Albert said, drawing me out of my reverie.

"Huh? Oh, sorry." I quickly began dealing the cards, making small piles in front of each of us.

"Neil, there's something I've been wondering, but no one seems to be talking to me about it," Albert said, watching his stack of cards grow. "What happens after this test? I mean, if the sword doesn't hurt me or other people or anything . . . what am I supposed to do if I can actually wield it?"

"So long as it's lawful, I suspect you can do whatever you want." I finished dealing and picked up my pile, pushing the errant corners into a single neat stack.

"I get that no one is going to make me do stuff, but that doesn't tell me what I *should* be doing." Albert glanced at the sheathed sword as he collected his own cards. "Krystal said those things were weapons of destiny, that they pick their wielders for a reason. Mr. Arch said if it chose me, then I'd use it eventually, whether I wanted to or not. The thing is, I have no idea what to do with it. I guess it would be kind of a good letter opener for sorting Fred's mail, but honestly, I'm pretty sure the smaller one he already has works better; magical properties or not."

"Well, that's one thing you could do right off the bat," I said. "You could quit that assistant job and get something a little flashier. There's bound to be better career prospects for people who can wield weapons of destiny."

"But I'm a good assistant," Albert protested. "I've been studying a lot in my downtime, and Fred is even letting me help with some of the easier paperwork."

"I'm not saying you aren't good at the job, just that there are better jobs out there. Ones you might be able to fill." I flipped my first card over—a three. Albert laid his own down—a four—and then scooped both cards into the bottom of his deck.

"I don't want a new job. I like working for Fred. He's nice to me, and the work he does helps people."

I bit back a derisive snort, but only barely. While I'd have happily knocked that notion down if Fred had proposed it, Albert saying it meant he believed he was part of something that helped others, and I wasn't going to take that away from him.

"You might not have to take a new job," I reassured him. "Maybe this is something you can do part-time. Like when you worked at the gas station."

"If wielding the sword requires me to clean out the toilets truckers use, I'm leaving it here and never looking back."

Though Albert clearly meant it as a joke, I saw the threads of magic between him and the sword pulse ever so slightly. It didn't like the idea of being left behind. Not even in jest. Part of me wondered how exactly it would enforce its will. Destiny was highly theoretical magic; even Amy had given a shrug when asked how it worked. It was encountered very rarely, and understood even less frequently. The one thing everyone seemed to agree on was that it was strong.

"Albert, no matter what happens today, just remember that you don't owe anyone anything. Not that sword, not the Agency, not Fred, and not me. This is your life. You live it the way that feels right to you, not in the way you think you're supposed to."

Albert looked up at me and tilted his head. "Neil . . . that's crazy. I owe so much to so many people. You brought me back to life. Fred gave me a job. Bubba is teaching me to shoot pool. Amy made me that balm to keep my skin looking healthy. Krystal and the Agency keep us safe. And that's just one for each person; I could keep going on for a while."

"And the sword? What has that done to put you in some perceived debt?"

"Well . . ." Albert bit his lip softly, then looked over at the blade in question. "It's hard to explain. I guess it hasn't done anything yet, aside from cause me trouble, but I have this really strong feeling that it's *going* to be a big help. If that makes any sense."

It didn't, not logically, but magic and logic didn't always see eye to eye.

"Just promise me that you won't let anyone force you into things you don't want. Sword or no sword, you're a free, independent parahuman, and you have the right to live the life you want."

Albert nodded, a new smile on his face, and flipped over another card. "I promise. Actually, as much as I've worried about all of this, I'm also a little excited. It's sort of neat, not knowing what's coming next. And to be selected by something like The Blade of the Unlikely Champion . . . I've never been selected or special before."

"You've always been special, Albert," I told him. "All that sword did was see what everyone else already knew was there."

He nodded again, but I could tell he didn't really be-lieve me. That was Albert, willing to believe in anything except himself. It was okay, though. I had enough belief for the both of us. He could be worried, and I would be pragmatic. No matter what happened at sunrise, I would keep Albert safe. I wouldn't let anyone or anything take him.

I was not going to lose my best friend again.

5.

NOTE: WE'LL NOW RETURN TO MY RE-COUNTING OF THE TALE. THOUGH I'D LIKE TO THANK NEIL FOR HIS CONTRIBUTION, EVEN IF SOME PARTS DID SEEM UNNECESSARILY HURTFUL.**

I wasn't too surprised to find that Amy and Bubba were still awake. As a therian, Bubba's natural resilience meant he could push himself for days at a time if needed; a trick that made doing long trucking hauls far easier.

Add in his enhanced strength and stamina for the loading aspect, and it was no wonder that so many men and women hauling goods around our nation could shift into some sort of animal. Amy, on the other hand, had taken so many pills and potions that it was hard to say if her brain even needed sleep anymore (or to prove that she wasn't somehow sleeping while she talked to you).

"Figured you'd be 'round sooner or later," Bubba said. He was laying on one of the cots—it's meager frame struggling to accommodate his substantial size—with a small book of poetry cracked open.

"Yeah, can't sleep unless the sun is out."

"Even if it were shining directly overhead, I doubt you'd be able to get so much as a wink," Bubba clarified. "You're too worried about Albert."

"Aren't we all? No one knows what will happen when he uses that sword. He could get really hurt."

"Highly unlikely." Amy had been sitting on her own cot, digging through a bag for some misplaced object. She kept burrowing through her belongings as she spoke, not bothering to look up. "Though zombies may not have wielded a Weapon of Destiny before, there have been enough cases of vampires and Ghoul Lords doing so to make it unlikely that the sword's magic would react badly to being in undead hands. Zombies are different, it's true, but not so different that we should expect to see some giant reaction."

"Oh. The way Arch and Krystal have been treating it . . . I just sort of assumed . . ."

"Krystal and Arch are agents, and neither of them have the knack for weaving magic," Amy said, face still half-buried in her bag. I wondered if I'd be able to make out her words so clearly without my vampiric senses. "They see magic as some big, unwieldy beast. They know it can be useful, but they also know it can suddenly go wild and turn on them. Every time they encounter some new aspect of it, they're immediately wary, which isn't necessarily the wrong reaction for people tasked with ensuring others' safety. But it means they tend to make mountains out of basilisk hills. If they'd bother to read the higher theories on necromantic displacement and theoretic—aha!"

Amy pulled a small stone—dark in color, with a clearly etched rune in place—from the depths of her bag. She deposited it into one of the many pockets on her strange jacket (which looked like a mix between a lab coat and a patchwork quilt), and snapped the bag shut. She looked at me for a moment, then to Bubba, then back to me, then finally around the whole room, before speaking.

"Sorry, what were we talking about?"

"You were tellin' Fred why Albert will prolly be fine from using the sword," Bubba reminded her.

"Really? I have the faint sensation that I was about to dive into some truly complex and meaty magical theory."

"No, Bubba is right, definitely just assuring me that Albert will be fine." Amy was a lovely woman in her own right, but she could go off on technical tangents that may as well have been in another language, for all the understanding we took from them.

"If you're both sure . . ." Amy squinted her eyes for a moment, clearly trying to redirect that odd brain of hers toward the function of memory. After a few seconds, she gave a small shrug and abandoned the endeavor. "Anyway, the odds are that Albert won't have any negative reaction to wielding the sword. That it chose him at all practically serves as proof."

"Personally, I'm more worried about what's waitin' for him after the test," Bubba said.

"You know about that?" I asked.

Bubba shot me a strange glance. "Course I know about it. I grew up with it. I'm a little surprised that you do, though."

"You're talking about different things," Amy chimed in, producing a water bottle that I was fairly certain she'd taken from the plane and sprinkling in some strange powder.

"Are we? I was talking about how Krystal thinks Arch is going to try and recruit Albert into the Agency."

"I think we all saw that coming," Bubba said. "I was more talking about what life will be like for Albert after he's free and clear to be a Weapon Bearer. It's a hard thing, getting a lot of power and duty dumped in your lap like that. We have to run whole counseling programs just for newly turned therians to help them cope with the change."

"Albert already handled dying pretty well," I pointed out.

"That's different. This is him being handed a mess of power, a sense of obligation, and no direction. Turning therian isn't a perfect metaphor, but it runs close. We get incredible bodies, but also a tangled snarl of culture, etiquette, and obedience," Bubba said. "Albert's a good kid with his head on right, but that can be a real sticker bush for anyone to push through."

"It's curious to me how all of you are worrying in the wrong direction," Amy said. She'd finished her sprinkling and taken a few sips of water. "But that might be due to the fact that I can't remember how much I know versus how much you do. Either way, trust me: you don't have to worry about Albert."

"You say that, but you still seem a bit wound up yourself," Bubba pointed out.

"Of course I'm wound up; I'm all kinds of worried," Amy replied, her expression somewhere between confused and aghast. She added a few more sprinkles of powder to the bottle before twisting the cap back on tightly.

"I have to admit, I expected to see Neil in here with you, trying to find some way to get the sword to let go,"

I said, trying to steer the conversation into waters where Amy made a bit more sense.

"He's headstrong as a drunken bull, but Neil knows the right thing to do when it matters," Bubba said. "My money says he's over in their room doing all he can to make sure Albert feels calm going into the trial."

"Should we go over and help?"

"No," Amy said, voice strong and word quick. "Leave them be. This is important. Their bond needs to be as strong as possible."

Though I had no idea what she was talking about, I trusted Amy's judgment, especially when it came to her apprentice. She'd turned an overly ambitious sociopath into a tamed student, and from what I saw, she'd done it mostly with kind words and careful discipline. If she thought they were best served by being alone, then I wouldn't be the one to break them apart.

"So, do we just sit around until it's time for the trial?"

"Welcome to 'hurry up and wait,' the basis for every form of combat since the first caveman realized he could stake out a watering hole," Bubba said. "It's why I always keep a book on me, and I got a hunch it's why Amy likes to have cards on hand."

I had neither of those things, but I was carrying a smartphone preloaded with various apps and games. Though getting a signal in a place like this was laughable, I could still manage to whittle the time away with the things already on the phone. I pulled out my device and checked the battery.

"Over eighty percent," I noted. "Well, hopefully that will last me through an hour."

"That's what I admire about you, Fred," Bubba told me as he reopened his book. "You're a damned hopeless optimist."

6.

BY THE TIME ARCH CAME TO GET US,
Krystal had woken up and wandered over, with Albert
and Neil joining us about fifteen minutes later. We were
in the middle of a spirited game of Hearts when I first
picked up the scent of his cigarettes wafting down the
hall. When he finally arrived, we'd put the cards away
and were on our feet, waiting for him.

Arch lifted one of his eyebrows carefully when he
saw our united front. "You all thinking of jumping me?"

"What?" (It is my unfortunate burden to admit that
I may have yelped that word just a touch. My already

healthy fear of agents had been compounded by Krystal's assessment of Arch's abilities.)

"You're all up, looking like you're ready to throw down." Arch took a long drag of his cigarette as he eyed each of us. "Of course, you'd have had to take out Agent Jenkins first, and at least one of you would have been smart enough to ambush me when I came through the door. Wouldn't have worked, obviously, but it would have been the smart play."

"Enough," Krystal said, using the voice she generally reserved for dealing with people she was arresting—and cable companies. "Everyone is playing along real nice, Arch. Don't push it."

"Sorry, just thought I'd try to lighten the mood. All right, Weapon Bearer Albert, you're coming with me. Technically, the contract holder and the necromancer have the right to oversee this, so Agent Jenkins can lead them to the observation area."

"As the necromancer's master, I am permitted to follow him anywhere I deem my presence to be needed," Amy said. I wasn't sure what she'd taken in the last hour or so, but her hair was shining like long strands of tinsel and there was a soft purple glow around her eyes.

"And Bubba's coming too," Krystal added.

"What rule are you invoking for that one?" Arch asked.

"Section fifteen, paragraph twelve. It's the one titled 'fuck you; it's happening because I say so.' Surprised you didn't know that one, Arch. Most agents invoke it all the time."

I could actually see Arch consider pushing back on Krystal, but evidently, he decided he had better ways to spend his energy than slamming it against the brick wall known as arguing with my girlfriend. My regard for his intelligence rose a few more notches.

"Fine, screw it, the whole gang can come." Arch stubbed out his cigarette and dropped it into the bag at his side, immediately producing a new one. Whatever brand of parahuman he was, I hoped it was one that didn't make much use of their lungs. "No sense in taking you out of the room to explain things then. Albert, I'm going to lead you down into the testing arena, where you'll be wielding that sword of yours for a bit. We've got it set up with various inanimate objects for you to break, so you'll have time to get used to the thing. Given that it's a Weapon of Destiny, you shouldn't need more than a couple of swings. Once all of those are broken, you're going to fight a small chimera."

"You're making him fight something?" Neil interrupted.

"Not sure how else you thought we'd see how the magic affects creatures that aren't Albert," Arch said.

"Besides, he won't be in any real danger. We had the thing de-clawed and de-fanged before bringing it over."

"I . . . I don't know how I feel about killing something that's helpless," Albert said.

"Respectable, but chimeras like this are happier dead," Arch told him. "They're creatures formed by mages, bound together from all sorts of animals. If it's done right, you get some pretty incredible beings. If it's done wrong, like the one waiting for you was, it just becomes a mass of fear, hunger, and most of all, pain. Weaving flesh isn't easy. Do it poorly, and you create something that lives in constant agony."

Albert looked at Neil, who gave a small nod.

"That's pretty much exactly what Amy taught me about chimeras. It's also why she doesn't make them."

"Still . . . isn't there some way to help it?"

"If there were, we wouldn't be doing this," Arch said. "Thing's not even truly sentient, just a mass of instincts. And if that doesn't put you at ease, know that we picked this thing up for a reason. I did mention that they were made of pain *and* hunger."

"Oh," Albert said, comprehension dawning.

"Like I said, this thing needs to die no matter what, and it will. While you do all the sword swinging ,we'll have some Agency mages watching you with their fancy vision, making sure the magic is flowing well. Once everything is done, assuming there are no problems, we'll talk about the results and you'll be free to go. Got it? Good. Now keep up."

I found myself doubting the last part of Arch's speech, but whether it was something in his tone or just suspicion aroused by Krystal's theory would be impossible to say. At the moment, my greater concern was for Albert, who still looked quite nervous. As Arch walked out of the room, motioning for us to follow, I made my way over to my dear assistant.

"Holding up okay?" I didn't try to whisper (pulling that off while following Arch through the stone hallway would have been a fool's errand), however I did try to keep the discussion as quiet as possible.

Albert looked at me and managed a genuine smile, the sort of thing only he could do in a situation like this. "I'm kind of just ready for it to be over. But I guess it never really will be, will it?"

He rested his hand on the sheath of the sword, and I wondered just how heavy it had already become. I could only imagine the weight it would accumulate as time went on. Perhaps it would have been kinder to lie to him, to ease his burden just a bit, but it wouldn't have been right. And at that moment, Albert needed clarity about what lay ahead, not words full of hollow comfort.

"No, Albert. It probably will never be over, not how you mean it. For better or worse, drawing that sword changed things, and they'll never go back to the way they were."

"I've been afraid of that." Albert's ever-present cheer seemed to slowly—finally—evaporate.

"Don't get the wrong idea, Albert. I'm saying things won't be the same anymore, but that isn't the same thing as saying they'll be bad." I let out a sigh and tried not to wince at the subtle irony of my being the one to say what I was about to. "Life, and unlife for that matter, is constantly changing. Sometimes it's going to be bad, but sometimes it's going to be good. I understand wanting things to stay the same—I spent the majority of my time alive trying to keep everything stable, balanced, and unchanging—but, Albert, changes comes regardless of what we do. Without change, I never would have been killed getting groceries, and as terrible as that was, it led to me meeting Krystal, and Bubba, and Amy, and you. The place in time you want to go back to didn't always exist; it came about because of change. Things won't stay the same, but you may just have some incredible experiences waiting for you over the horizon."

"Thanks, Fred," Albert said, looking at me with a strange spark in his eyes. "I needed that."

"Just the speech I wish someone had given me before I spent most of my twenties being a shut-in," I told him.

"This is where we part," Arch announced from up ahead. The stone hallway split off in three directions, and

Krystal was already standing in front of one of them. "Albert comes with me, the rest of you go with Agent Jenkins."

"Good luck," I whispered to Albert as he began heading toward Arch. He gave me a nod, then stopped in front of Neil. For a moment, the two seemed unsure of what to do, but Albert pushed forward and embraced his best friend in a firm hug. I truly hoped he didn't do any damage to the young necromancer; zombie strength is nothing to sneeze at. When they finally released the embrace, Albert made his way past the rest of his friends, getting a handshake from Bubba and hugs from Krystal and Amy.

I sidled up to Krystal as Arch and Albert began walking down their hall and slipped my hand around hers. I could still hear them talking as they walked, even if my vampire ears could only barely pick up Arch's steps.

"You seem pretty composed for someone going into a trial like this," Arch told him. From the tone of his voice, I felt reasonably sure he meant it as a compliment.

"I'm really scared," Albert admitted immediately. "It's all I can do to keep walking right now. But I don't want to let being afraid stop me. I want to be like my hero."

He tossed a quick glance over his shoulder, to where Krystal and I were standing. I could hardly fault Albert's taste in role-models—Krystal was a very impressive person in every regard. She was a great hero for him to have, though I was certainly glad he hadn't taken that as cause to emulate her more aggressive personality traits.

"Come on, let's get up there and cheer Albert on," Krystal said, giving my hand a quick squeeze.

"Damn right," Bubba agreed.

Neil was clearly too nervous to talk, and Amy seemed to be mentally preoccupied. That wasn't strange in itself, in fact, it was closer to the norm. What struck me as odd was the subject of her preoccupation. While the rest of us had been focused almost entirely on Albert, she'd had a different concentration point.

For some reason, Amy had scarcely taken her eyes off Neil.

7.

THOUGH I'D ONLY SEEN GLADIATORIAL
arenas in movies and documentaries, I immediately recognized Albert's testing area as one. True, it was carved
of stone like the rest of the underground base (as was the
viewing platform we stood on fifty feet above him), and
all the light came from those same cheap yellow bulbs
instead of from the sun, but it was an arena all the same.
Round and wide, with a floor composed of loose dirt
atop what was likely more stone, each end held a single
gated entrance. Albert came in from what I took to be

the southern one, based solely on my viewing position. The northern one still had its gate down, though I could hear sounds of strained movement coming from the shadows behind it. I tried to ignore such disconcerting noises as I watched Albert wander through the arena.

Around him were various minor obstacles—small stacks of boards, a few panes of glass, and even a metal rod or two. I was reasonably certain that no normal sword or wielder could be expected to slice through metal; however, given Albert's undead strength and the presumed power of a Weapon of Destiny, it might actually be a manageable, if difficult, challenge.

Albert seemed at a loss for what to do, merely wandering around and inspecting each of the different things he seemed expected to cut. A pair of what I presumed to be mages sat on either side of the viewing arena, opposite from our group's position, watching without comment as he stood around. Clearly, their job was simply to witness, not instruct.

"What's he doing?" I whispered to Krystal.

"Probably waiting for some kind of signal," she said, not bothering to whisper in the slightest. "I'd bet Arch is doing a quick tour to make sure there's no one near Albert, and then getting clear himself. Safety first, and all that shit."

"I wish they'd just get on with it," Neil muttered, staring down at his friend. Amy reached over and rested a comforting hand on her apprentice's shoulder.

For once, Neil and I were on the same page. Albert looked so small, so lonely down there all by himself. Our group had been through some rough situations before, but we'd always been together. Albert having to face a challenge like this alone just seemed . . . wrong.

"Everyone is now clear. Whenever you're ready, Weapon Bearer." Arch's voice boomed through the stone coliseum as he jogged up behind us, emerging from the entrance tunnel. To have dropped off Albert and then run back up to meet us was no mean feat, yet Arch didn't even seem to be out of breath. In fact, he pulled out a new cigarette as soon as he came to a stop. I found myself wondering once more what on earth Arch was. He didn't seem to have the mystical appearance mages favored, he lacked the bulk and presence of a therian, and he was too well-tanned to be an undead. My best bet was that he was like Krystal, hiding a supernatural power that only manifested under certain conditions. Curious as he was, I quickly turned my attention back where it belonged—on Albert.

In spite of the fifty foot difference, I could still hear the ringing echo as Albert unsheathed The Blade of the Unlikely Champion. From the looks on the others' faces, I doubted it had anything to do with my enhanced hearing either. There was something magical about that note, as if the sword wanted everyone nearby to know that it was out, and that they should beware.

The stacks of boards were the first objects that fell victim to Albert's new weapon. He approached one tentatively, holding the sword away from his body like he was afraid it might suddenly light him on fire, which was actually a fair concern since he was testing for unexpected magical reactions. Lifting it all the way over his head, Albert brought the blade down in a deliberate arc that focused on precision rather than power. Whether it was the sword, the zombie strength, or a combination of the two, the steel slid easily through each plank in succession, tumbling off their perches into the dust below.

"That's one sharp pig-sticker," Bubba noted as Albert turned to another stack and repeated his trick.

"The Blade of the Unlikely Champion is more than just sharp," Arch told him. "It's damn near woven entirely out of magic. Makes it incredibly powerful, and just as finicky. Most weapons find wielders every couple of decades or so, but that one hasn't left its scabbard for over a century."

Another clattering filled the air as more wood fell to the ground. This time, instead of attacking another stack of boards, Albert turned his attention the panes of glass that had been hung in the air. Sticking the sword out, tilted on its side, he slowly moved it over until it made contact with the edge of the glass. If the clear material put up any resistance, we couldn't see it, as the blade moved easily through the glass without causing so much as a single crack. The sheared off section fell into the dirt, breaking into several pieces as it did.

"Interesting," Arch muttered, eyes fixed on the shards embedded in the dirt.

"Don't be an ass, Arch. If you know something, then share it with the rest of the class," Krystal demanded.

"My apologies. It's just impressive, is all. The last Weapon Bearer to hold that sword would have shattered the glass as soon as it made contact."

"Wait, so Albert's a better swordsman than the last guy?" Neil asked.

"Not at all, or at least, not yet. The Blade of the Unlikely Champion responds to the soul of the person wielding it, and its capabilities change based on that. Its last owner was a temperamental man who preferred to solve situations with swift aggression. That made the blade's destructive power shoot way up, to the point that simply touching it to most materials would cause them to crack and break."

"You seem to know a lot about someone who lived over a century ago," I said.

"I damn well ought to. I helped train him," Arch replied.

A new ringing filled the arena, different than the sound of the sword being drawn and resulting from Albert easily chopping through one of the metal pipes that had been set up for him. With each broken object, his confidence was growing. Already, he held the blade with far more certainty and comfort. Arch was clearly right; it had taken little effort to acclimate to wielding a Weapon of Destiny. And, best of all, no unexpected reactions had occurred so far. If Albert could make it through his battle with the chimera, he would be home free, and we'd all be able to leave.

The last of the obstacles were taken down quickly, as the speed of Albert's strikes increased. Though he was growing faster, he seemed to be losing nothing in the way of precision. It made me wonder if he was even aware he was picking up speed, or if, to him, it all seemed as slow and controlled as it had with the first overhead blow.

"Weapon Bearer, the time has come for your final trial," Arch announced. "Slay the chimera, put it out of its misery, and let us test the effect of your sword on creatures nearby."

Albert gave a nod, visible even from where we were standing, and Arch turned toward one of the mages.

"Tell them to open the gate," Arch ordered.

The mage made no reaction, but almost immediately, the squeaking of ancient hinges grated against our ears as the gate slowly began to rise.

"There's something I've been meaning to ask," I said. "How is this supposed to test the effect Albert and sword have on nearby creatures? Isn't he just going to kill it with the first swing?"

"Chimeras don't go down that easy," Bubba told me. "Damn things can heal quicker than a therian. Even with a magic sword and zombie strength, it's going to take him several blows to put it down for good."

"If they heal that fast, then how did you take away its fangs and claws?" I asked, turning to Arch.

"Healing doesn't replace what's lost. That requires regeneration, and only certain chimeras have that. Specifically, ones with lizard spliced in." The squeaking of the gate was getting louder, and I could hear the creature behind it snapping and stomping in excitement. "The one Albert is facing is a mix of panther, boar, and scorpion, so it shouldn't have any kind of regenerative magic."

"Well . . . if you're sure," I said, my hesitation apparent. It seemed like a big risk to take, but he was a professional, after all. Surely they had ways of detecting what sort of animals a chimera was composed of.

"I'm dead sure," Arch assured me. The gate finally stopped squeaking when it reach its apex, and heavy footsteps thudded from within the shadows as the creature inside drew closer to the front. "And honestly, it's not like it matters, anyway," he continued.

"Why is th—" My words escaped me as the creature came into view. It was massive, easily as big as Richard in his lion form, and Richard was an alpha, the largest type of therian. It was sleek and black, with the large, feline head of a panther, though the pair of large tusks sticking out its mouth spoke to its boar genetics, as did the hooves on its feet. The scorpion aspect shone through in the chitinous armor along its back and the massive, stinger-tipped tail extending from its rear. The chimera let out a mighty roar, showing us the inside of its mouth—a mouth filled with rows of bright white, glistening sharp teeth.

"Because I was lying about it being harmless in the first place," Arch said, graciously answering the question I'd been unable to finish.

8.

ARCH HAD BARELY GOTTEN HIS WORDS OUT before the chimera charged, barreling toward Albert as it let out a series of sounds that were like a roar mixed with a grunt. My assistant was, thankfully, quick to adapt to the unexpected situation. He leapt out of the way in a motion more graceful than I'd have suspected Albert being capable of. In fact, I very much wondered if it was his zombie capabilities that let him dodge so well, or some sort of assistance from the sword. Either way, while I was watching Albert frantically scurry about, Neil was having a very different reaction to Arch's announcement.

"You son of a bitch!" The young man, who, in all fairness, was similar to Arch in both appearance and stature, pulled back his right fist and took a swing at the agent. Arch's reaction was so fast that even I had trouble following it. He easily moved his head out of range, grabbed Neil's arm, and tossed the amateur mage over his shoulder, where he landed in a heap.

"I'll let that slide due to circumstances, but if you attack an agent again, you need to be ready to kill or be killed."

"Who says I'm not?" Neil spat, pulling himself up from the ground. Before he could get close enough to attack Arch again, Amy was standing between them. I don't think any of us, even Krystal, could have made Neil back down the way Amy did. She said nothing, merely staring at her apprentice until he lowered his fists. The glowering stare refused to come off his face, however. Evidently, it was enough for Amy, as she turned to face Arch.

"What's the meaning of this?" Despite her still shiny hair, Amy had an aura of dominance I'd rarely seen on her. I realized that, probably for the first time, I was seeing Amy Wells, master mage and alchemist, angry. Given what I knew about her intellect, and that an ancient dragon held her skills in esteem, I found myself hoping that either Arch minded his tongue or the rest of us had time to clear the blast radius.

"He won't get that's sword's full power out unless he's in a life or death situation," Arch replied, not a single trace of apology in his tone. If anything, he sounded vaguely annoyed by our reaction. "It's nothing personal, just part of doing a thorough test."

"You could have told him the truth; given him adequate time to prepare," Amy said.

"With new Weapon Bearers, it's more about intuition than practice or skill. The less prepared he was, the more likely he'd be able to use the sword."

"Likely?" Neil said, eyes somehow narrowing even more than before. "As in, he might not be able to do it?"

"Weapons of destiny are smart, but not omnipotent. It wouldn't be the first time a new wielder has gotten taken apart early on."

Neil looked like he was going to try and charge Arch, Amy or no Amy, but a sound from inside the arena tore his attention away from the antagonizing agent. It was Albert, letting out a yelp that sounded as if he were in pain.

We all looked back into the arena to find Albert hobbling away from the chimera. Given the dark stains on the right leg of his jeans, along with the visible tears in the fabric, it looked like one of the tusks had managed to tear a chunk out of him during the charge. Albert was at no risk of dying from blood loss (you needed to separate the head from the body to bring down a zombie), but the wound was clearly slowing him down. If he didn't take the offensive soon, it was only a matter of time before the chimera tore him into so many shreds even Neil wouldn't be able to put him back together.

"I have to go help him." Neil was staring into the arena with an expression unlike any I'd ever seen on him before. His eyes were wide, his hands clenched, and his jaw set. Neil was always a bit impulsive and quick to react with aggression, like his swing at Arch before. But this was different. This wasn't Neil flying off half-cocked. This Neil looked like he was ready to go to war.

"Can't allow that. Albert has to be tested on his own. Adding in another magic-wielder invalidates the test," Arch replied.

"Then I won't use magic!" Neil spun around, clearly torn about taking his eyes off Albert. "Without Amy nearby, I can't use it anyway. That should preserve your precious test."

"Even if you're not wielding it, you exude the stuff. You've been training as a mage long enough to know that. You going in there changes the magical composition. End of story."

While they bickered, I watched as Albert narrowly escaped another charge. This time, however, the stinger-tail managed to spear him in his lower back. He let out a muffled yelp and pulled away, losing a fair bit of flesh in the process. I was reasonably certain that zombies didn't have to worry about venom, but when dealing with magic, nothing was ever cut and dry. I glanced back over to find that Neil had heard the cry and seen the blow. His face darkened as he turned to Arch with new resolve.

"I am exercising my right as the creator of that magical being to intervene for his safety. He is my creation, and I have the right to tend to him when injured, so long as he has not broken any laws. If you try to stop me, you're in violation of the Mage Treaty, and I will spend the rest of my life bringing down every manner of bureaucratic hell I can find on top of you. And I don't think you're the kind of guy who likes dealing with red tape and sanctions."

"Now that was a good threat," Arch said, knocking some ash off his cigarette. "The only problem is that you aren't really a mage, so you can't exercise that right. You've still got your training collar on, which makes you a bound apprentice. Those don't have the rights of mages, so I'm free and clear as far as the treaty goes." He let out a long breath of smoke. "I might hate all that shit, but I've been around long enough to know the ins and outs of it. Better luck next time."

Neil's face fell as what he'd likely considered his trump card failed to faze Arch even the slightest bit. He turned to look back at Albert, who had just used The Blade of the Unlikely Champion to block a tusk that would have gored him through the stomach, and found Amy had moved around to meet his gaze.

"Apprentice," she said, the purple glow in her eyes suddenly darkening. "This is a test of your master, and there will be consequences for failure. No matter what you think you should say, you will answer my question honestly. Why do you wish to save your creation? Why are you set on keeping Albert safe?"

"I'm supposed to protect . . ." Neil's first burst of words fell away as his face grew calmer. "He needs . . ." Neil stopped again, and a small vein bulged near the top of his forehead. The young man took a long, deep breath, then looked his teacher, his master, dead in her temporarily oddly-colored eyes.

"Because I need Albert. As much as I pretend I'm the one looking after him, the truth is that I was lost when he was gone. He's the one who props me up, who lets me feel okay enough with who I am to still function. I know mages are supposed to be bastions of internal strength, that's how we wield the arcane forces of the world, but the honest truth is that I'm not strong enough to lose him. I wasn't then, and I'm not now. He's my best friend. He's all I've got."

"You're wrong on several accounts, Apprentice," Amy said. "Internal strength does not come from existing without weakness. It comes from facing our weaknesses head on, by admitting they exist and refusing to let them rule us." She paused for a moment, a slight smile breaking through her serious expression. "And, more importantly, you are wrong about being alone save for Albert. You have much more than him. You have many people who care for you in this world."

Neil gave a small nod, but said nothing.

"Still, I don't think that's any reason to let one of them slip away." Amy reached into her coat and produced the small stone I'd seen her digging around for earlier. She whispered some words that I couldn't understand, but that made me shiver all the same. The stone began to glow. With exceptional care, she touched it to the front of Neil's collar, which immediately parted at a previously invisible seam and fell to the floor.

"Congratulations, Journeyman," Amy said, putting the rock back in her pocket. "Though you still have much study under my tutelage left ahead, you are now a true mage, and entitled to the rights provided to all of our kind." She turned to face Arch, all kindness flowing off her face like rain through a gutter. "I assume there's no problem anymore?"

"There's a hell of a problem, actually," Arch shot back. "Are you fucking nuts? Do you realize what you're saddling that kid with if you let him go down there?"

"His presence in the trial means that, for all intents and purposes, he is bonded to Albert so long as Albert wields The Blade of the Unlikely Champion. Because their magics were tested together, they are required to be together for the duration of Albert's tenure as a Weapon

Bearer. Yes, *Agent*, I am very aware of what happens if my student enters the arena." She turned to Neil. "Is any of that a problem for you?"

"Hell no."

"Didn't imagine it would be."

"There's still the—" Arch was cut off as Krystal stepped in front of him, the expression on her face leaving no question about whose side her allegiances fell on.

"Quit stalling. They outplayed you. Get over it. Now shut the fuck up and just watch." She turned to Amy and Neil. "You should hurry, Albert's getting slower."

Neil glanced down and realized that Albert had sustained two more wounds while he was dealing with Arch and Amy. "Shit! I'll never be able to run down there in time."

"Neil, the first lesson any mage should know is this: we never bother with the meandering path when there's an express lane open." She pulled out the water bottle I'd seen her sprinkling powder into earlier. It had a slight blue tint to it now, though I had no idea what that signified. "This will let you take the direct route. Now hurry."

"Thank you," Neil said, unscrewing the cap from the bottle. "For . . . for just everything. Thank you, Teacher." With that, he knocked back the bottle and drained the entire contents in mere seconds. He dropped the water bottle to the ground, took off running, and leapt—

—directly over the edge, with a floor that was fifty feet below.

9.

DESPITE WHAT EVEN A CURSORY UNDERSTANDING of gravity would lead you to believe, Neil did not immediately plummet downward toward inevitable injury, if not death. Rather, he drifted down lazily, like a leaf swept off a tree heading toward the ground at its own leisurely pace. It was then that it all clicked into place for me: the water bottle, Amy's odd behavior, her question to Neil, all of it.

"You knew this would happen." I glanced over at her, just in time to see her knock back a small vial of orange liquid. When she lowered her head, her eyes had changed color to match the same hue as the liquid she'd just swallowed. " When we were sitting on the cots, you already knew Albert would be in danger and Neil would have to jump in and save him."

"Actually, I've known something like was coming since meeting Neil and Albert," Amy replied. She walked to the edge and stared at her student's slow descent—he was nearly halfway there. Neither Albert nor the chimera had noticed him yet, but that wouldn't last much longer.

"How could you have possibly known a thing like that?"

"Because Albert shouldn't exist," Amy said, her voice a bit softer than before. "Raising a zombie takes tremendous magic, the sort that no one, not even a prodigy, could manage just by picking up a spellbook. The bond they share would account for some increase in power, but to pull back a soul as fully-functional as Albert's would take a veteran necromancer with ages of experience. Thus, I was forced to conclude that some other magic property had given Neil's ritual a bit of a nudge."

I very much wanted to ask her for clarification, though obviously, there was an explanation that stood out as having the most potential; however, before I could ask her, another voice tore through the arena. It belonged to Neil, and it was packed full of concern, desperation, and fear.

As well as a tremendous amount of magic.

"*Mortus Aurellius!*" Neil lighted to the ground with his hands raised, gesturing to Albert, who was barely getting away from a stab of the chimera's tale.

"Neil?" He jerked his head over in shock, a lucky move that actually made it so a rogue swipe of tusk missed taking his noggin off. "What are you doing here?"

"Duh. I'm helping you kick this thing's ass." Neil took a brief moment to catch his breath, then began waving his hands and letting out another spell. "*Merricort Stravinci!*"

I wasn't sure what this one did, but I could already see the effects of the first—they'd been apparent as soon as he cast it. Albert's flesh was knitting back together at an accelerated rate, his wounds closing over like they'd never existed. Vampires have exceptional regenerative capabilities, and Albert was healing far faster than I could have managed, even with a fresh swig of blood.

The chimera had turned around and was eyeing both Albert and Neil, clearly deciding which of them to take out first. Both were stringy and small, though the one with the sword had obviously annoyed it by dodging about. Of course, the fact that Albert could dodge made Neil seem like a more tempting target. The soft voice of my inner predator, the instincts that came with being a vampire, whispered insight into how this creature, formed of pain and magic, was thinking. It was, to say the least, very disconcerting.

"You shouldn't be down here!" Albert yelled, splitting his attention between the chimera and his friend. "It's dangerous."

"Which is exactly *why* I'm down here. You've been letting that thing treat you like a chew toy. Did you really think I wouldn't intervene?"

"This is my problem to deal with. I'm the one who drew the sword; I'm the only one who has to get hurt." Albert was practically pleading now, though I wasn't sure what good he thought his words would do. Even if Neil changed his mind at that exact moment, he'd still be just as stuck in the pit.

"Albert—and I mean this with love—fuck that, and fuck you for saying it!" Neil turned his attention completely away from the chimera, staring at his friend across the small distance between them. "Your problem? I'm the one who has to pick up the pieces and go on living without you. I'm the one who has to try and cope with a world that doesn't have my only damned friend. I won't do that, Albert, not ever again. Like it or not, your problems are my problems, and if you're in deep shit, then so I am. We're in this life, battle, sword, all this fucking craziness, we're in it together."

It was a heartfelt, if unnecessarily crass speech, and it would have been moving to all of us, if not for something else that was already moving. When Neil had turned away, the chimera had made its decision, and was bearing down on him from across the arena. It moved more silently than I might have expected, the dirt muffling its hooved footsteps as it barreled toward the young necromancer.

"Move, you dumb shit!" Krystal screamed, hands cupped to her mouth in a desperate attempt to mimic a megaphone. Despite the distance, her words reached their target, and Neil suddenly snapped to his surroundings. It was enough to get him mobile, but unfortunately not enough to let him dodge entirely.

A tusk tore through his side, a few inches below his ribs, sending blood spurting into the dirt and Neil tumbling to the ground. Finally given a chance to do some real damage, the chimera didn't hesitate. It leapt atop the young mage, a dark tornado of snapping jaws and pounding hooves. Neil managed to get his arms up in a feeble defense, but it would only take seconds for them to be shredded into uselessness. Fortunately for Neil, the chimera didn't have seconds.

There was no scream of warning or anger, which was the sort of thing that might have given the chimera time to react. Instead, it was suddenly seized by strong hands—ones that looked as though they might be gripping its very spine—lifted off Neil, and hurled across the arena, where it slammed into the stone wall with enough force to leave several small cracks. It was clearly still alive as it limped back to a standing position, but it obviously realized it no longer had easy game to attack.

Albert, tufts of fur still clinging to his hand, stood between his friend and the monster, looking at it with the sort of expression I'd never have thought my cheerful assistant capable of. He swung the sword once, then gripped it with both hands as he locked eyes with the beast.

"Holy shit," Bubba muttered. "Are zombies always that strong?"

"Not usually." Amy shook her head. "Neil's first spell was to regenerate Albert's flesh; the second was to increase his speed and strength."

"I didn't realize necromancers could do that." Given how little I knew about magic in general, I had no qualms admitting my dearth of knowledge.

"It's much harder with other undead, but with a zombie they've created, it's different. The two share a bond, they're connected. It's like Neil is casting on a piece of himself."

"That's the thing about zombies," Krystal added. "On their own, they're basically no trouble at all to put down. But you pair them with a necromancer, especially one who cares about their creation, and they can be some of the toughest bastards this side of Hell."

"Looks like he'll get to see for himself." Arch was still watching the fight carefully, with his same neutral expression. I wondered, just for a moment, how much of this he'd guessed would happen. Then I heard movement, and my attention was drawn back to the fight below.

The chimera was circling, trying to find a way to get at the injured Neil, but Albert was keeping pace with it every step of the way. His hands tightened on the sword's hilt, and it may have been my imagination, but it seemed to me the blade was glowing a bit brighter than before.

"I don't want to hurt you," Albert said, his voice still gentle, even as he stared at the blood of his friend on the chimera's lips. "I really don't. I don't like hurting anyone. But if you try to touch my friend again, I'll do it."

Either the chimera didn't understand him, or it didn't believe him, because it grew tired of circling and finally opted to take the initiative. Backing up a few steps, the chimera charged, its hooves pounding up a cloud of dirt as it tried to mow Albert down to get at the young man he was defending.

"I'm sorry," Albert said, digging his feet in. From the outset, it was clear; he didn't intend to dodge this time. He readied the sword and kept his eyes on the hungry monster bearing down on him. As it drew near, I feared for a moment that Albert had suddenly frozen in terror, as he stayed put even when the tusks were only inches away from his newly healed flesh. Then, in a motion so quick a single flick of the eye would have missed it,

Albert swung sword with all his might, catching the chimera directly in the head.

There was a blinding flash of a light, and I mean that quite literally. All of us were momentarily rendered incapable of sight, rubbing at our eyes and the spots that refused to clear. When they finally faded, we looked down, expecting to see a scene of gore and death.

What we actually found was quite different, and exceedingly unexpected.

"Well, I'll be damned," Arch said, peering into the arena. "Never seen that one before."

"Ditto," Krystal agreed. Bubba and Amy nodded their agreement, while I just stared in confusion.

Down in the arena were a still bleeding Neil, a very confused Albert, and technically no sign of the chimera. It had vanished, almost entirely. The "almost" was a necessary addition to the descriptor because, while the chimera was certainly gone, there were three new things in its place.

Nestled in the dirt and apparently sleeping was a panther cub, a baby boar, and what I greatly suspected to be a scorpion egg.

10.

"HE CUT THE MAGIC?"

"That's a very, *very* simplified way of phrasing it, but yes, Fred, you've got the gist," Amy told me. She was hovering near Neil, who'd been bandaged and brought up as soon as the fight was over. Despite how bad the wounds had seemed when he was attacked, Neil was already back on his feet and appearing unbothered by the chunks taken out of his flesh. Either mages had greater physical resistance than I was aware of, or someone in the facility had given him more than gauze and antiseptics.

"I actually liked Fred's phrasing," Bubba said. "Your whole 'unmaking the enchantment while simultaneously appropriating the base components' explanation gave me a headache. It's a sword. It cut the magic. That's the sort of shit I can wrap my head 'round."

"Technically, it was a theory, not an explanation," Amy replied. She pulled another bottle from her coat and took a small sip. As she did, the orange glow in her eyes faded to a soft white, and a far more placid expression eased over her face. "I'm just guessing, after all. What Albert did, I've never heard of before."

"Arch said there had been other wielders. Shouldn't they have been able to do the same thing?" I asked.

"Don't you ever pay attention?" Neil said. "Arch told us that the sword responds to the soul of the person wielding it. Albert didn't want to hurt that chimera, but he had to swing the blade anyway. The sword adapted, giving him a way to end the fight without shedding blood. Though Amy is right, it is strange. I've been studying constantly, and that's the first I've heard of such an incident."

"There's a few legends handed down through the packs, but nothing . . ." Bubba trailed off as the sound of approaching footsteps caught his attention.

The four of us were back in Bubba and Amy's room, while we waited for Arch and Albert to finish getting the results from the watching mages. Krystal had tagged along at her own insistence, since, at this point ,none of us trusted Arch as far as we could throw . . . actually, several of us could throw Arch rather far, given the proper motivation. Suffice it to say, we did not trust him enough to leave Albert in his care without at least one of us there as escort.

Bubba and I both perked up as we heard the sound of footsteps echoing through the hallway. Neil and Amy took a bit longer to notice the impending people, but as soon as they did, the injured necromancer was on his feet. It was probably a good thing he'd been getting treated when Albert had to leave, otherwise, he'd have a pitched a hell of a fit about coming along. His actions in the last hour had left me with a newfound respect, but that didn't change the fact that we weren't home yet and still needed to play nice.

Krystal stepped into view first, followed closely by Arch and Albert. We didn't even need to ask about the results—the Cheshire grin Krystal was sporting, coupled with the look of sheer relief on Albert's face, made it abundantly clear before a single word was uttered. Still, it was nice to hear Krystal loudly announce what we'd all been hoping to hear.

"He's all clear! No magical side effects, no reason he can't use the sword."

There were sighs of relief, smiles, and even a whoop from Bubba as we rushed over to give Albert handshakes and hugs. It took a few moments for the clatter of happiness to die down, but as soon as it did, Arch reminded us that he was, unfortunately, still in the room.

"Congratulations, Weapon Bearer. As a representative of the Agency, I wish you all the best on whatever path your new weapon leads you down, and remind you that, so long as you're adhering to the laws and upholding the treaties, you can always look to us for assistance."

"Um, thank you," Albert said. It was an impressive amount of politeness, given that most of us just glared at Arch. To his credit, he did pick up the hint.

"You're welcome, Albert. To the rest of you, I know I'm not your favorite person right now, but my actions were out of necessity, not malice. If I'd given Albert a half-hearted trial, we might never have seen him swing the sword's real magic, not until it happened in a place without proper safeguards. Hate me as you need to, just understand that, because of my test, Albert can now go on with his life, having no fear that wielding the blade will cause inadvertent harm to those around him."

"We don't hate you, Arch," Krystal said. She chanced a quick look at us, no doubt taking in the hard eyes on Bubba and the unmasked glare that Neil was sporting. "Well, most of us probably don't. I know why you did what you did, but I also know there were better ways to go about it."

"We'll have to agree to disagree," Arch told her. "Before I take my leave of you all and send you back to Winslow, there is one more matter to discuss." He turned to Albert, whose face scrunched up in renewed fear. "Albert, that sword of yours is very powerful, and to unmake a creature formed of magic the way it did is a gift I'm not certain it's ever possessed. Whatever other abilities it might hold are bound to be special as well. Wielding that power is no small responsibility, so, if you'd like, the Agency would be willing to help train you on how to do it."

Neil grit his teeth, Albert's eyes went wide, and I felt my back tense. In all the excitement of the chimera, I'd nearly forgotten that this might happen. My eyes were stuck to Albert, who seemed to be having trouble finding the right words for his response.

"I . . . that would . . . could . . . what would that entail?"

"You'd be transferred to an Agency training facility immediately, and would begin learning how to wield your new weapon, eventually becoming an Agent who protects the parahuman world. Given what I've seen today, I would undertake your training personally. While I know you dislike me, even Agent Jenkins will vouch for my skill and capabilities as an instructor."

"Much as I hate to admit it right now, getting personally trained by Arch is a fairly prestigious thing," Krystal muttered.

"So . . . I'd have to leave everyone?" Albert looked at us with a panicked expression.

"You don't have to," I said quickly. "This is your choice, Albert. No one is going to make you do anything."

"He's right," Arch said. "It's your choice: learn to use your sword in a way that helps the world, or tuck it away and ignore the responsibility you've been charged with."

"Fuck your guilt trips," Neil spat, wrapping an arm around Albert's shoulder. "He can make up his own mind."

Arch crossed his arms. "And what you're all doing isn't guilting him into staying around and wasting his potential, to say nothing of the sword's?"

Albert mumbled something under his breath, so soft that not even I could hear it over the steadily rising voices of people arguing. He shuffled awkwardly and stared at the ground, motions I knew all too well meant he had something to say, but was scared to speak. It was the same body language he'd had when he admitted to accidentally shredding three days' worth of filing work.

Neil was reaching a fevered pitch. "Why don't you take that—"

"Why don't we all quiet down and listen to what Albert actually has to say." Much as I loathed raising my voice, I knew it was a far easier task for me to accomplish than Albert. He gave me a grateful look, then turned to face everyone.

"Mr. Arch is right. This sword does come with responsibility. I can tell every time I draw it. There are things I'm supposed to do. I don't know what. Just . . . things."

Neil began speaking, but Albert stopped him with a hard stare.

"That said, it's just a sword," Albert continued. "I'm my own person. I get to choose what I do. Drawing the sword is no different than being turned into a vampire: I still get to decide what kind of person I am. So, no, Mr. Arch, I won't go with you. I'm going to keep working as Fred's assistant, keep hanging out with Bubba and Krystal and Amy, and keep spending my time with my best friend. If you really think what I can do is so important, then you can come to Winslow and teach me there."

"What if I say this offer is non-negotiable? You either come with me, or you get nothing." Arch's face was placid as always, hiding whatever true sentiment he felt. The man knew how to play things close to the vest, I had to give him that. It was an excellent skill, but against someone as straightforward as Albert, it was entirely wasted.

"Well, then I would have say—" Albert's eyes darted over to me, then to Krystal, and then to me again. "I would have to ask you to, pretty please, if at all possible . . . go fuck yourself."

The room was quiet as death. We all stared at Albert, some of us with mouths agape, shocked at his reply.

Albert almost never cursed, and cursing in a way that told someone to piss off . . . that was completely unheard of. I sincerely don't know how long we would have stood like that if another noise hadn't broken the spell. It was unfamiliar at first, almost alien in nature. In fact, it was only after looking around and finding the source that I realized what it was.

Arch was laughing.

Not doubled over or anything, just small bubbles of mirth escaping his mouth, clearly unbidden. It didn't last long, and once he realized, he resumed the usual hard-faced expression. But it was too late. The mask had slipped, and for just a moment, we'd seen past the stony-walled exterior of Agent Arch.

"I like you, Albert. If nothing else, you've got some serious brass ones on you. I'll think over your counter-offer and be in touch. For now, all of you get out of here and go home. I've got paperwork to do."

With that, Arch turned and walked out of the room, leaving us alone.

"It might not have seemed like it, but I'm pretty sure that was him agreeing to your conditions," Krystal said. "Arch isn't one to mull things over, and when he takes interest in something, it's hell getting him to let go. My money says he's booked a hotel room before we even land." As she spoke, Krystal urged us forward, back into the halls that would hopefully be the start of our journey home.

"I hope I did the right thing," Albert said, absent-mindedly touching the hilt of his sword.

"You did the best you could." Bubba added a slap on Albert's back for encouragement. "That's all any of us can do. Right or wrong, just keep doin' your best and things will be okay."

"Bubba's absolutely right," I said. "You stood your ground and decided on the terms you were okay with changing your life for. That took a lot of courage."

Albert stared up at me, and at last, his usual cheerful grin fixed itself back in place. "You really think so?"

"I truly do, Albert. Now, let's go home and rest. You've earned it."

A LAWYER IN THE MANOR

1.

WHEN I WAS FIRST TURNED INTO A VAMPIRE, I'd known immediately that my employment options had suddenly become vastly more limited. Certainly, there were (and are) jobs out there that have to take place in darkness; however, most of them are either criminal in some nature or simply use a different skill set than what I possessed. Even if I could have talked my way into a night janitor position or dock-working job (which would have been a hard sell given my very apparent lack of muscle), I wouldn't have been happy. For all its faults,

I have always loved being an accountant, and what's more, I consider myself to be quite adept at it.

In a way, being turned undead was one of the greatest blessings of my professional life, because it forced me to take a step I would never have found the courage to do without sheer necessity: I started my own business. I'll admit, the first year was a rough one. Not everyone was comfortable dealing with an accountant who kept the sort of hours that precluded daytime meetings and preferred to work through a messenger service. Luckily, a combination of teleconferencing, and rates so low I feel cheap even recalling them, allowed me to get my feet in enough doors to build a reputation. One of the few upsides of being a vampire, or at least, one of the few that comes in handy given my peaceful nature, is that sleep becomes optional. We can only do it during the day, and that's only if we're so inclined. With twice as much working time as regular accountants, and a healthy drive to see my fledgling company succeed, I was able to put out quality work in fractions of the time.

After a while, my reputation grew to the point where I had consistent work whenever I needed it, and of course, becoming a CPPA opened a whole new avenue of clients, many of whom were aching for the services I offered. Still, even at the point I had reached after Albert's sword debacle, there was no getting around the fact that some of the bigger client's required more wooing than

I could deliver via phone, text, and mail. To quote one of Bubba's favorite sayings: "If you want the biggest fish in the pond, you have to be willing to wade out and get your feet muddy."

It was that reason which had me on the outskirts of my town of Winslow, Colorado, staring up at a large, pristinely kept building. The architecture was immaculate and clearly Victorian inspired, with three stories and a generous size. Once, it had been home to someone of affluence, but now it served as a bed and breakfast, though I had no intention of availing myself of either of those services. I was here for a dinner meeting with Mr. Price, one of the three partners at Price, Wordsworth, and Stern, a local investment firm notorious for using multiple outside accounting sources to ensure accuracy and compliance. Getting in with them represented a huge amount of well-paying business, and openings came along rarely.

I walked carefully up the steps of the building, my briefcase clutched firmly in hand. It was fortunate that vampires didn't sweat, as for once, I was able to go into a situation like this without looking like I'd just been caught in a light shower. At my old firm, Torvald & Torvald, I'd been respected for my acumen with numbers, but was never permitted to meet with actual clients. It was a policy I'd neither objected to nor found particularly offensive.

As I neared the front door, I noticed a bronze plac-ard resting just above the frame. In elegant script were scrawled two words: "Charlotte Manor." Perhaps this would have been comforting, assuring me I'd come to the right place, if there had been any other building within the last two miles that might have qualified as a B&B. The outskirts of Winslow were nowhere near as vibrant as the downtown scene, and I couldn't imagine a place like this saw very much business, quaint charm and all. Heaven only knew why Mr. Price had chosen this as the place for our meeting, but after all the effort I'd put into getting this far in the interview process, I would be damned if I missed out over a thirty-minute drive.

As I stepped through the door, a small bell tinkled overhead. The sound echoed off the wooden walls, stop-ping only when it hit one of the many plush carpets running the length of the halls. To my right was a wel-come desk with cubby holes set behind it, a cash register that easily dated back to the turn of the century, and an old woman with a warm smile. I'd scarcely made it two steps in when she greeted me.

"Good evening, young man. Are you here to take a room or for the dinner party?" Once upon a time, I might have described her voice as ancient; however, meeting beings who counted their lifespans in centuries had removed such wanton hyperbole from my thinking. Her voice was merely appropriately old for the number of years she'd evidently been alive, yet it was still friendly and welcoming. This place wasn't all superficial charm, it seemed.

"The dinner party, I believe. I assume that's the one being held by Mr. Price?"

She nodded, an action far more time consuming than it might have been for a younger person. "You'll be eating in our dining room. We don't usually rent that out in respect to the other guests, but you managed to get lucky and catch us when we were empty."

Though the words were delivered in the same cheery manner as earlier, I found myself questioning their truthfulness. Somehow, I highly doubted that it was very hard to find this place without many guests. Of course, having been raised with half a modicum of decency, I kept such notions to myself.

"I can't imagine why, your home is perfectly lovely." That part was certainly true; everything from the molding to the paintings on the walls looked vintage and hand-crafted. "Would you be so kind as to point me to the dining room?"

"Well, aren't you a polite one." The old woman gave me a larger smile, this one appearing more genuine than what she kept on for guests. "Just go down the hall. The doors should be open and on your left. You can't miss it."

"Thank you very much." I began my trek down the lengthy hallway and within ten steps, I knew exactly where

I was heading. Despite usually keeping my vampiric hearing under control, it still tuned to ear-catchingly loud noises on its own. Mr. Price's robust voice certainly qualified as such a sound, his booming tones racing through the air to all who might be within reasonable vicinity.

"Now, none of that," I heard him say. "We'll talk shop when everyone gets here, and not a moment before. Get yourself a drink and relax. This is the social part of the evening."

Then, having tuned into the conversation, I overheard a new voice. This one was softer and more controlled than Mr. Price's, though achieving either of those things was hardly a mean feat. Despite its delicate nature, the sound of that voice froze me in my place. I stood, halfway between steps, as it spoke.

"We certainly understand, Mr. Price, I just wanted to answer any lingering questions you might have while we've got this opportunity."

I knew that voice. It belonged to a woman who'd led several meetings a month during my tenure at Torvald & Torvald, one of the top minds in the legal department. She was one half of the best closing team the company had to offer, paired with an accountant who was all wavy hair and white teeth instead of actual numbers knowledge. Almost on cue, I heard his voice.

"Besides, we can save you the trouble of spending dinner with the second-stringers. At Torvald & Torvald, we're dedicated to being the best. Our reputation speaks for itself."

And there it was, the old dynamic duo still in action: Asha Patel and Troy Warner. This made matters far more complicated. Not only did they represent some incredibly stiff competition, but they represented an issue I hadn't really dealt with since reconnecting with Krystal: talking to someone who'd known me when I was alive.

I'll admit it: I briefly considered turning tail and racing out of there. By this point in my memoirs, I can't imagine that bit of information will shock or amaze you. However, I am proud to say that I fought that urge down and instead, continued my trek forward. I'd known going in that this wouldn't be an easy client to win, and I refused to give up before even trying. I might have been a useless coward in most matters of life (as well as the supernatural), but by God, I was a good accountant, and on that single battleground, I refused to concede.

With a quick adjustment of the tie I'd worn over my pressed button-down shirt, I finished walking down the hallway and stepped into the dining room. As far as heroic charges went, I doubt it would make anyone's top ten, but for me, it was enough.

2.

"GOOD EVENING, MR. PRICE." I WALKED briskly through the door and took the large man's hand in a careful handshake. Despite him being several inches taller and wider than me, I had to be careful not to injure him as our hands interlocked. That would surely torpedo my chances at the account, as well as leave me with a fair amount of explaining to do.

"Ah, Fredrick Fletcher. Nice to finally meet you in person." Mr. Price gave my arm a hearty pumping, which I endured with a smile. My prospective employer wore one as well, a wide grin that peered through his bushy beard. He was a large man, though he didn't hold a candle to people like Bubba or Richard. Still, he possessed broad shoulders and thick arms. They'd been slimmed by age, the mass moving southward to his stomach, but he'd still managed to maintain an athletic shape despite the advancing years. I'd have said I wanted to look as good as he when I reached that age; however, I already knew perfectly well what I would look like in another thirty years. Vampires didn't age, after all.

"The pleasure is all mine." Our hands released, and I turned to face the other guests in the room. Asha looked much as I'd remembered her: tall, lean, and with skin the color of slightly burned caramel. She was quite pretty, though in that regard, I found her a bit diminished. Asha was too put together, and while I'd once enjoyed such a feature, my tastes had turned to the type of woman who kept a gun in her boot and a knife by the bed. Troy was so similar to when I'd last seen him that it was eerie; I suspected he was even wearing the same tie. There was no true warmth in the bleached-white smile resting beneath his dark eyes and wavy blond hair; it was simply an accoutrement he wore, no different than cufflinks, or a tie-pin.

"A pleasure to see you both again." I reached into the breast pocket of my shirt and produced a small, faux-silver case, out of which I plucked a pair of business cards. I handed one to each of my former coworkers, curious to see if they'd even remember our association. In life, I'd been substantially heavier, as well as painfully shy. I wouldn't begrudge them at all if my name rang no bells. In fact, in a situation like this, I'd rather prefer it.

"'Fletcher Accounting Services. Our numbers never miss their mark.'" Troy read the card out loud, turning it over a few times, no doubt inspecting the quality of the stock and print. "President: Fredrick Frankford Fletcher." He looked up, taking note of my face again. "I know who you are."

"Oh?" My nerves tensed, but I refused to let my discomfort show on my face.

"Yeah, you're the guy who stole the Engleman account from us a few weeks back. How did you manage to lure him away, anyhow? He'd been with us for twenty years." Troy managed to keep his plastic smile plastered on as he spoke, making the whole discussion seem like lighthearted trash-talk. The anger in his eyes, however, he was less successful in masking.

"I simply offered Mr. Engleman a level of service that your company was unable to match. If you watch closely, I believe you'll see me do the same for Mr. Price tonight." The truth of the matter was that Mr. Engleman was a mage who needed an accountant capable of deducting his ritual components on his taxes, but I saw no reason not to shake Troy's confidence a touch before the meeting started.

"All right boys, put them away, there's a lady present," Asha said. She popped open her purse—a small black clutch—and dropped my business card into it before turning to me with an expression of familiarity. I should have known she'd remember me; the woman's attention to detail and level of recall was legendary. "Besides, you already know Fred. He worked at Torvald & Torvald until about two years ago." She greeted me with an actual warm expression. "Tell me, Fred, how have you been? You look great."

"Proper diet and rigorous exercise," I said. "I've been doing quite well. Striking out on my own has been a wonderful adventure. How are things at the old company?"

"Oh, you know, there's ups and—"

"Wait." Troy snapped his fingers and pointed at me. "You're *that* Fred? Big guy, really quiet, ate lunch by himself at his desk?"

"Some of us were too busy to go off for hours in the middle of the day." Okay, I'll admit it: I was being petty, but I really didn't enjoy being reminded of my old life. Especially not from someone who'd only made it less enjoyable.

"Nothing wrong with a man who works hard," Mr. Price added. He turned over his sizable hand to check his watch. "Looks like our last guest is running low on time. I have no tolerance for those who lack punctuality. Mark that well, all of you. If he doesn't make it by eight, it will just be the two of you in the running."

"All the easier to narrow down your selection, then," Troy said.

Unbeknownst to the others, I heard the soft jingle of the door at the front, as well as frantic footsteps scurrying across the floor. Despite the fact that this newcomer would represent competition, I still found myself hoping they made it. Even aside from enjoying anything that disappointed Troy, I disliked the idea of winning things by default. This was my only battleground, and I wanted to prove I was truly the best for the job.

"I'm sure our final guest is on their way right now. I have no doubt at all that they'll make it."

Troy opened his mouth, no doubt to say something spurious and distasteful, but before he had the opportunity, our final dinner guest dashed through the door. He was a middle-aged man in a semi-rumpled suit, sweat dripping off his bald head and onto the carpet. We all looked at him in shock, this was not at all appropriate attire for such a meeting, but as he panted heavily, it became clear he needed to catch his breath before an explanation could be offered.

"Car . . . broke down . . ." he said at last, pulling himself to a standing position and wiping his forehead with an already damp sleeve. "About two miles back . . . ran all the way here . . ."

"Now *that* is the type of dedication I like to see," Mr. Price announced, walking over and gripping the man's sweaty hand. "Cliff Puckett, welcome to the final interview."

"Thank you . . . sir." Cliff managed to hold on through Price's rigorous handshake, which was no small accomplishment given their size difference and Cliff's clearly weary status. Once he was finally released, he began making the rounds to introduce himself. I was marginally closer, so that made me the first stop on his tour.

"Cliff Puckett, Puckett Account Management." He handed me one of his cards, and I gave him one of mine, the accounting version of the handshake. "Fredrick Fletcher, Fletcher Accounting Services."

Cliff made his way over to Asha and Troy, but I allowed my attention in their conversation to lapse as I took notice of the employees entering the room. They were male, all tall and dressed in crisp black tuxedos. As they walked, they rolled carts of silverware, dishes, and glasses, which they began to set atop the starched white linen adorning the spacious table. In truth, it was largely unremarkable, but the poise and coordination with which they moved drew me in. It was imperfect enough to be human, yet graceful enough to make me wonder.

"Spectacular, aren't they?" Mr. Price said from behind me. "Everything here is incredible. The food, the service, the decor, it's one of the best kept secrets in Winslow. At least . . . for now."

"Dare I wonder what that means?"

"In due time, Mr. Fletcher. We're going to talk about business over dinner, and not a moment before." Mr. Price hesitated for a moment, then added, "But since I brought it up, I suppose I can give you a hint. Part of the reason we're taking on new account services is that our firm is looking to do some serious expansion of Winslow as a whole, really putting our town on the map. That's all you get until the appetizers arrive."

Mr. Price walked away from me, clapping his hands together to get the others' attention and directing them to the dinner table. I watched him go, wondering exactly what he had in store. Winslow was already a vibrant town with ample corporations headquartered there. Heck, it was big enough to have the King of the West living amidst its citizens, though that was likely due to Richard and Sally more than his own preference. I rather liked my city; I'd chosen to move there, after all.

As I headed to the dinner table, it was with a new worry gnawing at my stomach. Now I had to wonder not only if I could even get the account, but if it was something I wanted in the first place.

3.

THOUGH MY DIGESTIVE SYSTEM TREATS ALL food and drink that isn't blood the same way a human's treats gum or the wood pulp additive found in many grains, I was still perfectly capable of enjoying the flavors in well-prepared cuisine. By the third course, it was clear that the chef at Charlotte Manor intended to delight my still active taste buds through every step of the meal. The bisque was sublime, the stuffed quail moist yet flavorful, and the fish seared perfectly.

Personally, I was content to enjoy the artfully prepared meal and let Mr. Price drone on about his latest fishing trip with the other partners (a tale which, surprisingly, involved no accounts of giant catches, as he admitted to hooking nothing the entire outing). The others, particularly Troy, were a bit more eager to see the show get on the road. I was surprised at his presumptiveness, though I supposed the right employers could see his attempts to steer things in a business direction as aggressiveness. As a salesman and representative, it was surely a desirable trait, but I personally believed accountants best served our craft by being conscientious and deliberate.

"—and that's just one of the exclusive services you'll find at Torvald & Torvald." Troy slid his half-eaten fish plate onto the cart as the waiter walked by. The rest of us had cleaned the moderate portions without hesitation, but he'd been too busy talking to pay it proper attention.

"I'm sure Mr. Price is already aware," Asha said. She'd been doing her best to keep him reined in; no doubt that was part of the very reason they were assigned to work as a team. Of course, having both a lawyer and an accountant to speak to all sides of the business was also a strong move, as was using an aesthetically pleasing male and female. No matter the client or situation, they had the deck stacked in their favor.

"It's fine, I was planning to hit the main topic over the steak course anyway." Mr. Price added his own plate to the cart, and the waiter moved soundlessly into the kitchen. Something about him—about all of the staff—was still off, but for the life of me, I couldn't place what it was. To be fair, I wasn't trying terribly hard. Tonight was not about parahuman weirdness; it was about business, pure and simple.

"Let's start with why I'm looking to expand our current accounting partners. I already gave Mr. Fletcher a bit of a hint, but I think we've reached the point where I can lay things on the table." As Mr. Price paused to drink his wine, Troy shot me a glare of unmasked anger and Asha eyed me with suspicion. Even Cliff seemed to be giving me a sideways glance, as though I'd been working with a secret leg-up instead of some cryptic clue.

"Our investment company has decided it's time to start rebranding Winslow, Colorado. Time to take it into the new century. Sure, our downtown is nice, and we've got more than a few companies with major offices here, but that's small potatoes. I'm talking about busting through the burbs, building a true metropolis to rival New York and LA."

"You think we can do that in Winslow?" Cliff asked. I was glad he'd voiced the skepticism that I also felt, but was too reticent to speak out loud.

"Not easily, no," Mr. Price said. "It's going to take a lot of money, a bit of time, and a fair amount of . . . let's call it 'economic landscaping' for now. Winslow has a good climate, and a nice proximity to lots of major attractions; our biggest weakness is how stuck in the past we are. For example, this whole neighborhood used to belong to a small farming community. Now, the only thing that matters for miles in any direction is this bed and breakfast. That's loads of property waiting to be bought up and turned into something worthwhile."

"And what would you propose doing with it, sir?" Had Troy been wearing a checkered sports coat and tried to sell me a "mint" Cadillac off the lot, he couldn't have come off as more slimy. Sadly, Mr. Price either didn't share my assessment or didn't care, as he went right on talking.

"First and foremost, we cut the history out of this town: gut the good stuff and repackage it into a modern brand. No one cares about old bed and breakfasts anymore, or about the historical windmills to the south, or our old churches scattered through downtown. We're not New Orleans; we don't have enough salacious history to turn it into a marketable aspect. Best to torch it all and turn ourselves into a sleek, modern destination. Take this place for example; there's a reason I brought you here."

Mr. Price raised his hands, nearly clipping one of the waiters who were setting down fresh steak knives in preparation for the next course. They moved so silently, it was hard to blame him; even I had scarcely noticed their return to the room. Again, something in the depths of my mind tried to rise to the surface, but I was too busy listening to Mr. Price's plan to pay it any heed.

"This whole place is fantastic; the service is perfect, the food is amazing, and whoever runs it gets every detail right. Been coming here off and on for years; it's one of the best kept secrets in Winslow. Why? Because there's no reason anyone else would come here, not unless they were dragged by an ex-wife for a 'romantic' weekend like I was. Yet, the whole thing is wonderful. If it was a little more updated and centrally located, it could be a top-tier hotel. In fact, I love this place so much that I did a little digging into who owns it."

One of the waiters fumbled slightly, nearly dropping a knife in Asha's lap. Before she even had time to gasp, the young man's hand snapped out and grabbed the blade, setting it gently down on the place setting in front of her. I braced myself, waiting for the scent of blood to invade my nostrils and try to steal my attention, but it never came. Somehow, that waiter had grabbed a sharp knife in mid-air and managed to avoid even a scratch. The nagging suspicion in the back of my head suddenly became much more difficult to ignore.

"Turns out, it's owned by some fourth cousin of the original owner's grandson. No luck running him down yet, but someone keeps mailing in taxes on the place every year. Just an envelope full of cash; shows up at the tax office at the same time annually. I've tried talking to the staff, but none of them are keen on telling me about the owner or who runs the place. I've got a few of our people working on sussing it out, though. Once I find the owner, I'll make him a great offer and turn this place into a prime example of what we plan to do."

The waiters were coming out of the kitchen again, this time wheeling a cart with what appeared to be delectable pieces of tenderloin on each plate. Unlike before, however, they seemed less graceful and removed. Now, they were all watching Mr. Price from the corner of their eyes, clearly hanging on every word he had to say. At the thought of them listening, the spark of insight that had been clamoring about the back of my brain finally leapt to the forefront, making me realize what my subconscious had noticed since I first saw them.

None of the waiters, not a single one, had a heartbeat. Though I dislike admitting it, I am usually keenly aware of the sound of blood pumping through a living person's veins, something I've used selective attention to willfully tune out. Once I was listening, it was, unfortunately, unmistakable. Whoever these men were, they certainly weren't alive.

"When we own the place, we take all the stuff that makes it special: the cook, the staff, the general manager, everybody who turns this musty old building into a nice place to stay. Then we set them up with a proper establishment downtown, tear this place to the ground, and buy up the surrounding property to use for one of the expansion projects. Nothing is wasted, and we make our town just a little bit more exceptional."

"Mr. Price, I dearly wish you hadn't just said that." The voice came from one of the waiters, speaking as he stepped around to the end of the table opposite Mr. Price. Despite the fact that it was the first words any of them had uttered, there was something about his voice that struck me as just a touch familiar. "I've enjoyed having you here over the years, and greatly appreciated the dinner parties you threw. It livened things up."

"Don't worry, son. Like I said, the staff makes this place incredible. You'll all be moving on to better facilities with a nice bump in pay."

"Unfortunately, that proposal is unacceptable." As he spoke, the other waiters kept moving, setting the food down in front of us. "I cannot allow anyone to take ownership of this house, nor will I permit anything to happen to it. This means, much as it saddens me, that your plans must die here, tonight."

"Look, kid, I get that you're upset—" Mr. Price's words cut off as another waiter grabbed his chair and thrust it forward, jamming the edge of the table into his diaphragm.

"I am not a kid. In truth, I've been alive far longer than any of you, and I have no desire to meet my end quite yet. You have my dearest apologies, Mr. Price, but I've gotten to know you too well after all your years visiting here. You're a stubborn man, so no amount of things I could do to you or promises I might extract would stop you from doing whatever you wanted once you were outside these walls."

"What are you saying?" I asked.

The doors to the dining room slammed themselves shut just as the lights flickered out, leaving us trapped in darkness.

"I am saying that Theodore Price is never leaving this house."

4.

IT IS WITH CONSIDERABLE SHAME THAT, when the lights burned away into the darkness and the doors shut on their own, my first thoughts were not ones of safety for those around me. Nor were they, I can say with a touch more pride, fear for my own safety. To be completely frank, as we sat there, steaks growing cold on our plates and fear blooming in the heart of my human companions, I only had one simple thought:

Not again.

If this seems callous, try to remember that the para-human side of my life was one I had neither asked for, nor intentionally pursued, yet it had invaded all the same. While I accepted the weirdness and occasional bit of danger as a price for the friends I held dear, I also enjoyed keeping some parts of my life sectioned off from it. True, I undertook some risk of the unnatural with my parahuman clients, but such was not the case with Mr. Price. What had happened to us was more than just a threat; it was the supernatural invading a new territory of my fragile world, one I was not keen to give up easily.

"I won't be unreasonable about this," the waiter said. The others had vanished in the chaos of the door closing and lights flickering away, though I was likely the only one who could see that. There was enough light spilling through the windows that their eyes would adjust eventually, but mine needed no such accommodation. If anything, my senses were better in the dark.

"Locking us in seems pretty damn unreasonable," Mr. Price choked out, finally getting his wind back after the shove.

"A detestable, but necessary, precaution. What I meant was that there's no need for me to hold everyone here. Only you pose a threat, Mr. Price. Only you need stay."

"You mean you'll let us go as long as he stays?" Troy asked. The fear in his voice might have been the most genuine thing I'd heard from him all night.

"So you can go alert others and try to mount a rescue? Certainly not. But if Mr. Price is willing to permanently silence himself, to save me the trouble, then I see no reason to detain the rest of you."

Asha stood up, her eyes scanning the dark for the waiter's location. "You're out of your mind. You can't honestly expect him to kill himself over a few parlor tricks and a lame threat. There's no way your entire staff will go along with this, and even if they do, we'll still find a way to take them."

"A very brave, but perfectly incorrect statement. There is only one of me, my dear guest, but I am so much bigger than the rest of you. Take your time and consider the offer. I'd rather not take matters upon myself, but if you wait too long . . . forgive me, I've kept you from your fourth course. Please, enjoy."

The lights flared back on, blinding all of us. When our eyes readjusted, the waiter was gone, as if he'd never been there in the first place. Everyone else rose from their seats, save for myself and Cliff. He seemed to be overwhelmed by the situation, whilst I was merely trying a bit of the steak while it was still warm. I already had a plan for what to do; it started and ended with calling Krystal. A few nibbles of well-prepared meat wouldn't affect the outcome of whatever siege she laid to the place.

"Windows are locked," Asha called, pulling against the wooden-framed panes of glass as hard as she could. "It's actually more like they're painted shut or something; I can't even get a wiggle."

"Same for the kitchen." Troy pushed against the door with all his might, which, in fairness, was muscular and considerable, yet it had no effect.

"Hall doors too," Mr. Price confirmed. "I don't how that kid is doing this, but it's a hell of a trick. Someone must have gotten wind of the deal and set all this up." He walked back over to the table, shaking his bearded head. "I really didn't think the staff would object so much to raises and better facilities."

"People can grow very fond of the familiar, even when change would be objectively better for them," I said, setting down my utensils. "I loathe being the one to suggest wanton destruction, but since those who usually would aren't with me today, I'll take the burden. Perhaps we should try breaking one of the windows."

"Hate to say it, but I'm with Fred." Troy picked up the chair he'd been sitting in—a wooden piece with considerable heft—and headed toward the nearest windows. "These assholes think they're going to trap Troy Warner that easy? They've got another thing coming!"

He reared back, then swung over his shoulder, slamming the chair into the clear pane of glass with considerable force. Unfortunately, that force sent him tumbling to the ground when the chair bounced off the window and twisted back over his shoulder. Both Troy and the chair hit the floor in a heap, though the chair seemed relatively unscathed by comparison.

"Fuck!" Troy was grabbing his left shoulder, rocking on the carpet from side to side. "Goddamnit, I think I tore something."

"How the hell did they do that?" Cliff muttered next to me. "Are the windows plastic?"

"It seems they prepared for us more thoroughly than we anticipated." I patted his shoulder for comfort, though I myself had very little. This didn't strike me as premeditated at all, if anything, it seemed to have come about in hurried response to Mr. Price's proposal. I highly doubted those windows were made of anything besides glass, which made their imperviousness to damage all the more impressive. By wild conjecture, I guessed that we were dealing with a spirit of some kind, a type of parahuman that I knew precious little about. Luckily, there was a way to change that.

As casually as I could, I removed my cell phone from my pocket and looked for Krystal's number. Before I'd even finished selecting her from the list of contacts, I realized my efforts were for naught. The icon at the top of my phone indicated that I had no service whatsoever. Still, I finished the attempt just in the case, but I wasn't surprised to find that the call was unable to connect.

"Does anyone have a signal?" Asha asked. Glancing up, I saw that she had produced her own phone as well, apparently meeting with similar results. Cliff, Troy, and Mr. Price all tried theirs, and not a one of us had so much as a single bar.

"Doesn't make sense," Mr. Price said. "I've stayed here lots of times and never had a problem getting a signal."

"They must have bought a cell-phone jammer," Troy suggested.

"This is getting a little ridiculous." Mr. Price walked back over to the table and retook his seat. "Indestructible windows, cell-phone jamming technology, automatic lights and doors . . . if someone had the kind of money and skill to turn this quaint place into a deathtrap, why wouldn't they just decline my offer? It's a free country; I couldn't have made the guy sell."

"If I were to wager a guess, I would say that the person keeping us locked up and the person who actually owns this property are entirely different people," I said. "In fact, I daresay that if you finally found the technical owner, he'd have no idea such a place even existed or was tied to his name."

It seemed prudent to keep them from probing too deeply into how all of this was being accomplished, so supplying some threads of reason, no matter how tenuous, would hopefully keep their ignorance aloft until we could get out of there. It helped that I really did believe my theory to be true; I was just leaving out the part about how I thought the bed and breakfast was being run by ghosts.

"I get it, you think this place is a front for some cartel or something," Troy said. He and Asha walked back over to the table as well. "Like they put on this show for guests, but in the basement they're cooking meth and dealing hookers. That's why the place can be locked down like this."

"Yes, I suppose, something along those lines." Had I really been as gullible as these people before I was turned? Obviously, the answer was yes, but it was still strange to see the way they clung to the most absurd explanations in order to avoid the obvious ones right in front of them.

"Then why are they letting us live?" Cliff's voice was growing slowly more erratic, the fear worming its way through him. I felt for the man; truly, I did. Had Krystal not gotten me acclimated to the unusual, or were the threats leveled at me instead of Mr. Price, I might very easily have been in his emotional state as well.

"I don't know . . . it doesn't make any sense," Asha said. Her eyes had a distant gleam in them, her mind clearly far away from what was in front of her. "One body is easier to dispose of than five, but having witnesses would be much more trouble to deal with. If they were going to kill us, why not just do it? What point does asking Mr. Price to kill himself serve? None of this is adding up."

"To be fair, you're trying to ascribe sanity to the actions of a man who takes five innocent people prisoner in a booby-trapped house," I pointed out. "A lack of logic might be something we have to make peace with."

"Maybe . . ." Asha clearly wasn't convinced, but since she didn't have any better leads, she seemed content to concede the point to me.

"So, what we supposed to do?" Troy was staring down at his plate, the now lukewarm steak looking back up at him.

"For the moment, it seems like our best bet is to follow instructions," I said. "The waiter mentioned the fourth course, so perhaps we should finish our dinner."

"If I eat anything, I'm going to puke." From the look on Cliff's face, it seemed that might be a possibility whether he took a bite or not.

"Agreed," Mr. Price said. "I don't want to touch any more of this stuff. You hear that, whoever you are?" He tilted his head back and raised his voice, looking as though he were quite perturbed with the ceiling. "We're done with dinner! Take it all 'cause we aren't eating another bite!"

The slight sound of a door whispering open came from behind him, and the empty cart rolled out along the carpet. There was no one steering it, yet it moved with immaculate precision. As it circled the table, our plates, napkins, and silverware floated away from us and onto the cart, as if being scooped up by an invisible hand. The others watched in slack-jawed shock, an expression I quickly mirrored as soon as I realized the need.

As the cart finished its circle and began heading back toward the kitchen, Troy was struck with some sort of realization. He bolted up from the table and made a run for the kitchen door, no doubt assuming it was unlocked to let the cart through. Troy scarcely made it a single step before something gave way beneath his feet and he was sent crashing to the floor. By the time he recovered, the cart was gone and the kitchen door firmly shut.

Before we had the chance to comment on the strange occurrence, the waiter's voice echoed out from an unseen location, bouncing off the walls at too many angles to trace.

"Now that dinner is done, please feel free to relax in our other facilities before bed. Mr. Price, the clock is ticking."

Then the voice was gone, and we were plunged into a short-lived silence. It was broken by the least likely sound any of us had expected: one of our barriers being lifted. The dining room doors slid gently open, revealing the hallway we'd entered through.

Dinner was clearly over, though we had no idea what next lay in store.

5.

EVERYONE ELSE MADE A MAD DASH FOR THE hallway, but I forced myself to hang back. Despite seeing how Troy's attempt at bashing through the window had yielded him nothing more than injury, I was curious to take my own crack at it. My vampire strength had cost me no less than six keyboards when I was first turned and before I learned to keep it under control. Tonight, it might be good for something other than tipping up the fridge when I swept my floors. The catch was that, unfortunately, I couldn't very well go showing it off in front of my very human co-captives.

I'd been searching through my brain, trying to think of a method I could use to get them to leave me alone long enough to see if I could open us a door to freedom. As it turned out, I needn't have bothered with the effort. Asha, the last of the bunch save for me, had no sooner crossed the door's threshold when they slammed back together, separating me from the rest of the group.

"I can't imagine this is a good sign," I muttered softly. My eyes swept the room several times, coming up with nothing. Then, as suddenly as before, the waiter was simply there, standing in front of me with his hands raised.

"I'm glad you hung back. I was going to grab you so we could talk, anyway," the waiter said. Unlike before, the dominance had slipped out of his voice. It was a strange effect, like speaking to an actor when he has just walked off stage and slipped out of his persona.

"Why? What could we have to talk about?"

"First off, I wanted to apologize. This really isn't the sort of service standard I try to set here. Secondly, I wanted to let you go." He gestured to the window, which opened soundlessly. When I thought about it, there didn't seem to be any sound coming from outside the room either. Strange, I'd have expected the others to at least make a ruckus and bang on the door.

"Not that I don't appreciate the gesture, but would you mind telling me why I get a pass?"

He stared at me for a few moments, brow furrowed and head tilted just a few degrees off center. "Because I obviously have a lot on my plate tonight, and I'd really rather not deal with an angry vampire on top of it. I love a supernatural throw down as much as anyone else, just not this evening."

"Ah, right. Of course. We vampires are a fearsome, terrifying lot." That was true in the sense that vampires as a whole were respected in the parahuman community, even if I didn't precisely fit the expected mold. "Though I confess, I'm not sure how I'd even hurt a ghost."

"A ghost? You haven't been at this for very long, have you?"

"Turned only a couple of years ago," I admitted.

"But still holding down a human job like accounting. That's . . . interesting." He shot me another curious look, then walked over to the dinner table. As he drew near, a chair pulled itself out and he took a seat. "They said you're name was Fred, wasn't it?"

"Fredrick Frankford Fletcher, though yes, most people do call me Fred." I walked to the table and sat down across from him, keeping us eye to eye. I wasn't entirely sure what was going on, but it seemed that the longer we talked, the less chance he had to be threatening and killing my associates.

"Nice to meet you, Fred. I'm Charlotte."

"Interesting. Should I assume there's a reason behind the feminine name when you're clearly male?"

He looked confused for a moment, then glanced down at himself and let out a small chuckle. "This? This is just a form I use for dinner service." His whole body began to ripple, and when it ended, I was staring at the kindly old woman who'd greeted me at the entrance. Another ripple, and this time Charlotte was a lovely young woman wearing a conservative dress that looked to be from the turn of the century. "All just images I create to facilitate guest service. The truth is I don't have a gender, Fred, because I'm not a ghost. I still have my body, and you're in it right now."

My mind flashed back to the sign I'd seen when entering, the placard that read "Charlotte Manor."

"You're a house?" I'd like to say that, after all I'd seen, I was able to keep my voice calm and show no signs of surprise, but I was unable to do any such thing. Even in the loose terms of what I associated with "normal," this was stretching things.

"That community Mr. Price talked about, the ones that used to live here, it was a cult of mages," Charlotte told me. "Animating a domicile isn't easy, but they had the time and persistence to keep trying until they got it right. Wanted a safe-house that would be impenetrable, a shelter in case things went awry. Thus, me." Charlotte stretched out her . . . his . . . its . . . let's just stick with her, since the house's form was currently female. She stretched out her arms in a *ta-da* motion, and flashed on oversized grin. "Anyway, once they died off, it was just me, so I decided to use the magic they'd laid in me—the ability to create food, control of my interior, that stuff—to create a bed and breakfast. Nice, useful, and no one ever tries to tear them down . . . usually."

"I see. May I ask what happened to those who animated you?" I didn't want to pry, but finding out a cauldron (which is the proper term for a group of mages; I know, I was surprised too) had lived and died on the edge of my town provoked more than a touch of curiosity and concern.

Charlotte leaned her head back and looked up at the ceiling. "What do you think happened to a bunch of mages that lived apart from society, practiced crazy weird magic, and felt the need for a magical safe-house?"

"Agents?"

"Agents." Charlotte nodded and looked back down at me. "Don't get me wrong, I hear everything within my walls, and I'm glad the agents stepped in. Those folks were not planning anything pleasant. Still, it left me stranded here. I've been able to cover up the fact that the house was uninhabited all these years, but if Mr. Price finds the owner, he'll sell in a heartbeat. You understand, don't you? This is self-defense. I don't want to be torn down."

"I do understand." As I spoke, I rose from the table, carefully pushing my chair back as I moved. "But, Charlotte, there must be another way. Mr. Price and the others are innocent of any malice; they had no way of knowing that destroying a building would cause a living thing harm. I'm sure there's a reasonable, non-killing solution we can reach."

"Like what? Tell them that I'm an animated house, oh and that the supernatural is all completely real? Even if they bought it, which would be a stretch for Mr. Price, it would open up a whole new can of issues. I realize that what I'm doing isn't a permanent solution, but it buys me time." Charlotte rose from her seat as well, the hem of her dress nearly dragging on the floor. "I'm sorry about the job opportunity and getting you involved in this. Maybe one day I can make it up to you. But for better or worse, I've set my course. Please leave, so I can see things through."

"You are very kind to offer me freedom." I stared at the open window, imagining myself leaping out of it. Once free, I could contact Krystal and the others, get the sort of help I knew could handle these problems. Of course, Charlotte had been built specifically to be a fortress and keep people out. While I was certain Krystal could find a way in, I was far less sure about whether the others would still be alive by the time she did. Maybe we'd be able to save some, but not all.

There was no excuse that let me skirt the simple truth of the situation: if I took my leave, people were going to die. Even knowing that, I was still deeply tempted to fool myself and accept Charlotte's offer. After all, my being there didn't guarantee their safety. I wasn't Krystal; I didn't know how to stop something like Charlotte. All hanging in would do was put me in danger as well. What would that possibly accomplish?

"As much as I appreciate your gesture, I have to decline it." I stared at Charlotte, whose face was steadily darkening. "While I don't mean to make war with you, I also can't just leave these people alone. Maybe if I'm here, if I talk to them, we can find a solution that saves everyone."

"You're a nice man, Fred, but you really haven't been a parahuman for very long." Charlotte motioned to the doors behind me, which slid open to reveal an empty hallway. "Sooner or later, we all end up in a situation where our only choices are to kill or be killed. It's unavoidable, and if you don't face the reality of that before your time comes, then you'll find yourself dead in the permanent fashion. You can't save everyone, Fred. You'll be lucky if you can even save yourself."

Then she was gone, and I was alone. Except I wasn't, not really. Everywhere I went, Charlotte would be watching me. I was, after all, treading around inside of her. Which meant I needed to find the others as soon as possible.

Scarce as time was, I still stopped to grab my briefcase from the floor where I'd set it. I had the barest inkling of an idea, and it would require my laptop to execute. Of course, first I'd have to try and make sure everyone was still alive.

I dearly missed the days when changes to the tax code were the most stressful parts of my job.

6.

THE HALLWAY WAS EMPTY, THOUGH I DID notice the carpet in front of the door was slightly bunched up, as if a lot of movement had occurred in a short period of time. Maybe they'd tried to break the door down once I was cut off from them. Or perhaps they'd merely beaten a hasty retreat to safer grounds. We were associates, not friends, after all.

A quick glance to the foyer of the house told me that they weren't there, though I did notice one of the tables that held vases had been moved. Probably another attempt at using force to procure an exit; one that had met with obvious failure. With the foyer and main hall ruled out, that left me several areas on the ground floor to search, to say nothing of the expanse of rooms over my head. True, I could dart about frantically, bouncing from room to room until I hit something, but that seemed like a risky strategy. With so much space to work in, Charlotte could easily keep shuffling them to different areas as I searched, like a magician slipping cards up her sleeve.

Sound was obviously a possibility; however, the way she'd managed to muffle my companions the moment the doors closed hinted to the fact that either the rooms were magically soundproof or Charlotte could make them so; either scenario rendered my hearing useless.

I did have one more trick up my sleeve, though it was one I was loathe to use. All vampires, at least so far as I knew, have a sense of smell as keen as a bloodhound. Though I actively blocked it out the vast majority of the time, I too possessed that skill. What's more, the thing I was searching for was what the primal part of my undead brain was wired to track: humans. It would have been easier if one of them had cut themselves—the scent of blood sang out so fiercely that it took all my willpower not to be overwhelmed if I was close to it. Still, vampires hunted plenty of non-bleeding humans, so I should be able to follow their trails.

My eyes closed as I tried to extend my sense of smell. The last time I had attempted any real tracking was several months back, when we thought Amy was kidnapped and were trying to find her. Ultimately, that hadn't been the case at all, but it had still given me the chance to practice a bit under Richard's guidance. Therians could track far better than vampires at anything save for blood, so it was a worthwhile learning experience. Short though his tutelage was, I still remembered the basics. I mentally combed through the scents of the house, searching for one I recognized.

The first one I located was, unfortunately, the worst of the lot. Cliff Puckett, the determined man who had run two miles after his car broke down, was still leaving a musty, sweaty trail of scent wherever he went. As soon as I found it, I nearly gagged, then wondered how on earth I'd missed the thing in the first place. My selective attention was better than I gave it credit for.

Following Cliff's scent was effortless in terms of tracking, but required significant willpower in that I had to force myself not to try and lose the lingering odor. I trailed it down the hall, to where Cliff had entered and exited the dining room, back to the foyer where it hovered near the front door. From there, it trailed around through the parlor room and began ascending a staircase.

As my pursuit continued, I tightened my hold on the briefcase clutched in my hand. The longer they were away from me, the higher a chance Charlotte would attack. I might have let my worry turn to panic, if not for the simple fact that I'd yet to catch the scent of any blood. Powerful as Cliff's funk was, not even it could overcome the red flags my brain would throw if I caught scent of the life-essential liquid. No blood meant, hopefully, that no one was dead yet. There were certainly bloodless ways to kill, but I doubted an animated house would have access to them. Or perhaps I should say I hoped she wouldn't, as I really had no idea what Charlotte was capable of. My knowledge of the parahuman world came from tax codes and movies, neither of which was especially helpful in this situation.

After several minutes of carefully following the odorous smell of Cliff Puckett, it at last came to an end. I found myself standing in front of an oak door with a golden knob, which I will admit did go well with the red carpet and trim adorning the upstairs hall. It was closed, and I heard not so much as a peep from inside, but the sweat trail Cliff had left behind didn't lie. This was where at least some of the others were.

I grabbed the knob and tried to turn it, finding so little give it seemed as though the thing had been welded into place. I tried again, giving it some of the undead *oomph*, and found I could move it ever-so-slightly. So, Charlotte's stopping power could be overcome by brute force, just not the sort that any human could generate.

It was good to know; however, I preferred to avoid such tactics whenever possible.

"Charlotte," I said, keeping my voice down just in case she decided to start broadcasting my words to the other side of the door. "I would very much like to go see the others, but your door seems to be jammed. I wonder if you'd be so kind as to open it up for me."

Another twist of the knob, another failure.

"Let's be reasonable here. I'm being polite, and despite the fact that we both know I could knock down the door, I really don't want to. It's a lovely piece, excellent craftsmanship. I realize you don't think I'll find a compromise, but the least you could do is let me try. Please."

There was a slight sound from the door, and this time when I tried, it opened so easily it seemed like the hinges had been greased. I pulled back the oak barrier to find myself looking into a sizable and lavish bedroom. It had white carpeting, gold trim, a hand-crafted writing desk, and a four-poster bed that looked downright elegant. If not for the threat of violence, I might have enjoyed this establishment's accommodations enough to book an evening for Krystal and me.

"Fred? You're alive?" Asha rose from her seat, racing across the room and giving me an enthusiastic hug. "We thought you'd been killed!"

"Ah, no, just a little extra fear thrown my way," I replied, carefully extricating myself from her grip. I understood emotions were running high, but propriety was still propriety, and I was spoken for. "Glad to see the rest of you are doing okay."

"That's one way to put it," Troy grumbled. He and Cliff were sitting on the ground near a stone fireplace, his hand gripping his injured shoulder.

"After we tried to bust you out, then failed to break the front door down, we finally decided to start exploring up here to see if we could find anything useful. We stayed together, so when the door slammed shut, we all got stuck here as a unit," Mr. Price informed me. "By the way, so far we've found all of jack-shit."

"Whoever these people are, they really built themselves a hell of deathtrap," Troy noted.

"Impossibly so," Asha added, walking back to the middle of the room. "I mean that literally; some of the stuff they've been doing seems basically impossible."

"With sufficient technology, anything can be done, or at least, appear to be done. Obviously, they threw a lot of money into special effects," I told her. As I stepped in, I expected to hear the door slam shut behind me, but no such noise emanated. Evidently, Charlotte was content to let us leave this room now that I'd broken the proverbial seal. "Speaking of, I might have an idea that could get us out of this."

"You do?" Cliff Puckett looked at me like I'd just promised him immortality along with a free puppy.

"This ought to be good," Troy said, clearly less impressed than Cliff.

"Simply put, the, er . . . person posing as a ghost seems to be primarily concerned with Mr. Price taking ownership of this house. If we draft a document that legally binds him from ever doing so, or permitting one of his associates to do so, the threat is removed and there is no more reason to keep us here."

"Except that the people pulling these strings have now threatened, imprisoned, and attacked us," Troy pointed out. "These guys are pros. Even if we swore up and down that we wouldn't go to the cops, and we meant it, they still wouldn't take the chance on letting us go."

"Troy is right." Mr. Price rose from his seat on the bed and walked to the middle of the room. "Fred, your idea is outside the box, and I like that, but the only way it could have worked is if we were dealing with an actual ghost. Since that's obviously ridiculous, our only hope is to find some way out of this place before the people pulling the strings get bored and try to kill us."

"I really feel like they would be content with just the contract not to try and buy the place," I protested. But even as I spoke, I could see my words falling on deaf ears. The others, not knowing what I did about parahumans or the laws they lived by, were stuck facing the ridiculous assumption that there were real people behind what we were experiencing. Without knowing the truth, they would never agree to my plan, and for very logical reasons. The only way I might bring them around was to tell them what we were really facing.

Of course, even if I wanted to out the supernatural to them, there was no guarantee they'd believe me. Humans were very stuck in their belief that there was nothing hiding in the darkness, even as those very things slipped up beside them and asked to borrow a cigarette.

"Lads and lady, I think we're past the point of trying to stick together," Mr. Price said. "Right now, our only hope is to cover enough ground to find a way out of this place. That means we're better off working in teams. Since I'm the main target, I'll go alone."

"No way. You're the main target, so the minute you're alone is when you're in the most danger." Asha thrust her finger over to Troy, whose brow immediately furrowed as he sensed his partner about to volunteer him for something. "Troy might be one arm down, but he's still a big guy. If we're going to split up, we'll do it smart. Take Troy along. Between the two of you, I bet you can handle a lot of challenges."

"You up for that?" Mr. Price asked Troy.

"At this point, I'd rather be on a team of two ass-kickers than watching over the small folks," Troy said, pulling himself off the ground. "No offense, you guys."

"None taken," I replied curtly.

"Fred, Cliff, and I will form the other team," Asha said.

"Actually, I think I'll be fine on my own," I said. Despite my initial hurry to get to them, it had become clear that if I wanted to stop Charlotte, I was going to have to get some work done. With them gone, I could talk to her, ideally buying myself a little time, and then knock out the paperwork. If she refused . . . well, I'd just have to work fast.

"Fred, we just got you back," Asha pointed out.

"Which is why I think I'll be fine. If these . . . people . . . wanted to kill me, they already had the perfect opportunity. Obviously, I'm not high on the priority list, so I should be all right. Plus, more teams means we can cover more ground."

Asha's stare had elevated from curious to downright scouring as she searched my face for some signal of what was going on in my head. The woman was too observant for my own good; the longer she stuck around, the harder it would be to deal with the secret side of our predicament. At long last, she gave a small nod and turned to Cliff.

"You ready?"

Cliff responded by rising from his seat and trudging over to her—the walk of a man who has already accepted his fate and is just plodding down the path to meet it.

"Mr. Price and Troy can take the third floor; Cliff and I will finish looking over what we didn't check on the first. Fred can finish out the second floor, since we barely got anything explored before getting snared in this room. We'll meet back here after an hour to share findings. Everyone good?" Asha looked around the room, waiting for questions. When none came, she tapped Cliff on the shoulder, and the two headed out the door. Mr. Price and Troy were only a few steps behind.

I made a show of checking over the rest of the room, then, when they were gone, I carefully pulled the door shut.

"Charlotte, would you be so kind as to manifest? I'd like to have a discussion with you."

"Sure, Fred. Since you asked nicely." Charlotte was sitting on the bed, still wearing the image of the young brunette woman in the early-century dress. She gave me a polite smile as she watched me jump a bit in surprise. "Didn't go the way you expected it to, did it?"

"Things could have gone better," I admitted. "But I maintain that there is still a way to keep you safe without hurting anyone."

"Your contract idea? That was cute, but I've listened to Theodore Price talk business too many times to believe he wouldn't find a way out of it, even if you could find a trick to make him sign."

"I didn't expect such a contract to succeed. It was just a ruse to get them to stay close while I worked. I really do think I have an idea, but it's going to require some time for research. Would you be so kind as to delay the execution for a few hours? Also, if you wouldn't mind allowing me access to my phone so I can use the internet, that would help as well."

"An outside line and time to work in?" Charlotte let out a soft tinkle of a giggle. "You must really think me foolish. If I gave you that, I'd have a nest of vampires swarming through my halls in no time."

"I promise, I'd only use it for research. No outgoing calls." I adjusted my glasses slightly, a touch worried that my next statement would give too much away. At the point Charlotte and I had reached, it was a necessary risk to tell her something of the truth; I just didn't want to destroy my imaginary leverage. "Besides, I don't associate with any other vampires. I was turned and left, and when I did meet my sire, he was . . . well, he was not a pleasant person. I won't call anyone: accountant's honor."

Charlotte looked at me for some time before speaking, her dark eyes searching my face for signs of falsehood. "All right, Fred. You seem earnest, and you've conducted yourself like a proper guest since arriving. I'll give you one hour of safety for the others, and *very* limited use of your phone, which I'll be watching closely. There is one thing you should know, however."

"What's that?"

"The clock starts now, and any time you spend explaining to her comes out of your hour." Charlotte pointed behind me, which caused me to spin quickly around.

Standing there, with the door cracked halfway open, was the dumbstruck face of Asha Patel.

7.

"FRED . . . WHAT THE HELL WERE YOU talking about with that girl?" Asha pushed the door the rest of the way open and stepped tentatively into the room. "And where did she go?"

A darting glance back showed me that Asha was right, Charlotte had indeed vanished into nothingness once more. Bad as the situation was, I also made sure to check my watch. The last thing I wanted was to get someone killed because I went a few minutes over time.

"Where's Cliff?" I asked.

"Waiting outside a restroom where I gave him the slip," Asha replied. The wonderment on her face was slowly being replaced by aggressiveness. Clearly, she didn't like being kept in the dark. "I knew you were hiding something, so I decided to double back and see what you were up to. Though I didn't expect to find you chatting it up with some lady about vampires."

I winced, just the teensiest bit, at the mention of the V-word. Part of me had hoped she'd missed that part of the conversation. "Let's start from the beginning: how much did you hear?"

"That is not the beginning, Fred. The beginning is you telling me what the fuck is going on, not trying to keep as much of this to yourself as possible."

I took my briefcase over to the writing desk and set it down, then popped open the clasps and pulled out my laptop. This was done both because it was necessary, and to buy myself a few seconds with which I might consider my situation. Asha was here, she was tipped off to things not being what they seemed, and she wasn't the type to let all this go. I could either tell her the truth, lie, or try and physically force her out the door. Given my degree of discomfort with confrontation, the last choice was already off the table, which only left trying to lie or telling her the truth.

"Do you really want to know?" My voice came out lower than I meant it to. I was just trying to convey the seriousness of the question, but it almost sounded threatening in the context. "Asha, what you're asking about . . . you can't ever unlearn it. Right now, you're still on the other side. With enough time and mental distance, you'll be able to rationalize all of this away. Once you cross the gap, there's no going back. It's hard, knowing the truth, even for me. For you, I can't even imagine. So, please, think hard before you answer. Do you really want to know?"

I didn't look at Asha as I set up my laptop, the slender silver marvel that I had probably spent too much on, but adored nonetheless. It took her until after I'd run the power cord and was halfway through syncing it to my phone's internet connection (which had begun working again, thanks to Charlotte) for her to decide.

"Yes. I want to know what's going on." Her voice was softer than before, but there was no hesitation in it. She'd thought it through and come to a decision. Sad as I was about the one she'd reached, I was selfishly a bit glad as well. With less than an hour left to work in, every bit of help I could get would make a difference.

"The very, very, *very* short version is that Charlotte, the woman you saw, is actually a manifestation of the house we're standing in. She was created by mages and enchanted to be alive, so the idea of Mr. Price tearing her down has her somewhat concerned."

"What about you?"

"Ah, yes. That." I turned around to face her, if for no other reason than it felt like the sort of news I should really deliver while looking someone in the eyes. "I'm a vampire, though you don't have anything to fear. I buy my blood; I neither have the inclination nor skill to harm a living person. I'm sure this opens up a new avenue of questions, but as you heard, we're working on a deadline, so please limit them to the truly essential."

"This is why you left the firm." Asha walked over to the bed and perched on the edge, eyes wide and vacant as her mind raced to assemble a puzzle she hadn't even realized was there. "It's why you started your own accounting practice. The Fred I knew would never have had the guts to do that on a whim, it had to be out of necessity."

"A nine-to-five puts me in the path of too much sunshine than is good for my health. For the record, zero sunshine is my ideal amount." I began pulling up files I'd thankfully saved to my hard drive, while also bringing up a browser window and opening a few tabs. I kept everything accounting related on the drive, since some parahumans lived outside cell and wi-fi coverage, but this situation reached beyond the tax code. I was going to need additional resources.

"Wow. So vampires are real. And living houses, evidently. Anything else?"

"Near as I can tell, almost everything else, in some form or fashion." I clicked open a bookmark to a familiar site and scanned the page for what I needed. "Therians, who are what you'd call werewolves, though they come in many different breeds of animal, as well as zombies, mages, dragons, and devils; all of them are mixed in with the humans of the world."

"You've seen all those things?" Asha's voice was tipped on the knife-edge between wonderment and suspicion. She was taking the news well—far better than I had when I woke up as undead—but a healthy amount of doubt was perfectly forgivable. Given the situation, it was actually the most rational response a person could have.

"Truthfully, that was just a list of people in my social circle," I said. "Anyway, the point is that we don't exist in some lawless anarchy. Parahumans, that's what we call ourselves, have laws and rights just like human citizens. We even have our own breaks in the tax code, to say nothing of the various laws that govern us. That's what I'm looking for at the moment."

Asha rose from her seat at the edge of the bed. "Let's pump the brakes for a minute: you're saying your kind, parahumans, have rights and laws, as in the things that are written in the constitution and ruled on by judges? How would a thing like that even be possible?"

"Remember, you're getting the abridged version here, but parahumans were intrinsic in America's founding. We helped create the nation, so it became a place where we were protected citizens, not monsters to be hunted."

"My parents really weren't kidding about it being a melting pot," Asha muttered, running a hand through her thick hair. "Okay, assuming all of this is true, and I'm cutting you a *lot* of slack with that one, why haven't I ever run across any laws referencing parahumans? I'm good at my job, and I would have noticed something like that."

"Obviously, we have to keep our laws and codes separately," I said. "I don't how they did it in the old days, but for the last forty years or so, they've hidden them right in plain sight." I tapped on my screen, pointing to the site I was currently downloading several .PDF files from.

Asha leaned in over my shoulder, her eyes going wide and a derisive snort slipping through her lips. "*Swords, Spells, and Stealth: Modern Justice.* You're fucking with me. An entire secret part of our society, composed of several different breeds of supernatural creatures, has their law books in a tabletop role-playing game?"

"Law books, tax books, even a few historical accounts," I replied. "It's the perfect system, when you think about it. New editions come out periodically as things change, the documents can reference any type of parahuman needed without arousing suspicion, and the actual books are so boring that almost no role-player would actually bother reading them. A few people wonder how the company stays in business, but rumors of an eccentric billionaire who loves the game keep them fairly quelled."

"This . . . this is a lot to take in," Asha said. "I mean, seriously. Tonight has been weird, but I'm not sure I'm quite ready to hop aboard the crazy train you're piloting just yet. Can you prove literally any of this?"

"You mean, aside from the magically closing doors, disappearing people, and unbreakable windows?" I turned upward, putting my face only a foot or so away from Asha's, and opened my mouth. My fangs aren't just on display for the world to see all the time; that would be unspeakably embarrassing. They usually only come out when I'm feeding, or when I'm riled up by a strong emotion. As I've gotten more accustomed to being undead, however, I've made a point of learning to do a few things. Marshaling my senses was one of them; controlling the extension of my fangs another.

"Holy shit!" Asha backpedaled away, nearly tripping over her feet in the hurry to get away as she watched my canines lengthen and shift into the iconic fangs associated with my people. I tried not to take the reaction personally. It had been a hard night, after all.

"You're a vampire." Her voice was scarcely above a whisper.

"Yes, and I don't drink from people. We covered this already." I didn't enjoy being brusque, but I really did have only so long to work with. My teeth shrank back to their regular size as I turned to my computer. Only a little bit left to go on the first download.

"Right . . . but that was just . . . talk." Asha shook her head once, tumbles of straight dark hair flying about in every direction. "Right. You're a vampire, we're stuck in a pissed-off magical house, and you think you have a way to stop it?"

"Its name is Charlotte," I told her. "And yes, maybe. I remember a deduction that applies to ghosts who have exercised certain legal precedent. Unfortunately, my side of things only told me about how this action functioned financially and after it was used. Based on what I do know, however, it's possible that the law could work for Charlotte's situation as well. I just have to find it and wrangle through the legalese."

"Sounds like a lot of 'ifs' and 'maybes' to me." Asha crossed the room slowly, her eyes not wavering from me as she drew close. It seemed she was willing to take me at my word for the moment, but trust that I didn't view her as a meal would come over time.

"Welcome to my world." I clicked on the first document that finished downloading, bringing up the file. "This is all I can do, though. I'm not a good fighter, I don't know magic, and I'm not nearly as foolhardily courageous as some of my friends. All I've got is a head for numbers and a willingness to slog through files and forms."

"But you don't know much about law," Asha pointed out.

"Outside of the financial side of things, no, I don't."

"Well then, put the laptop a little more center so I can see it too." Asha leaned forward, and as she did, I heard her heartbeat pick up. She was still scared, possibly more of me than of Charlotte, but she refused to let it stop her. I found myself reminded of why I had admired this woman from afar, back when we shared a building.

"Done and done," I said, sliding the laptop over. "Now, all that's left is to save the day with paperwork."

"Shhh. Be quiet, Fred. I'm reading."

8.

"SHOOT STRAIGHT WITH ME HERE: WHAT are the odds this actually works?" Asha asked. We were walking down the stairs, back to the dining room where the evening had originally gone so spectacularly off the rails. If Charlotte had kept her word, the others would be joining us shortly, still alive and healthy. If she'd lied . . . well, I didn't really have a great Plan B for that.

"By my guess, maybe fifty-fifty. It mostly hinges on Charlotte, but Mr. Price could mess things up if he refuses to go along with it."

"You seem oddly calm for going in with only a fifty percent shot at getting us out of here," Asha said.

I gave a small shrug. "Vampires don't sweat. Otherwise, you'd see a lovely sheen of nervousness on my forehead. As for why I haven't gone into full panic-attack mode, well, much as it pains me to admit this, fifty percent is actually pretty good odds compared to whatever trouble I'm usually stuck in." I pointedly left out mentioning that the reason I'd pulled through on those other occasions was because of my friends; there was no reason to worry her right before showtime.

Asha stared at me for a moment, and then shook her head. "You know, in all of the weirdness of tonight—vampires, magic houses, supernatural laws, the whole bundle—I think you're still the strangest part."

We crossed the last step, settling into the foyer and moving toward the hallway. "What do you mean?"

"Fred, you were the quietest, meekest, least socially skilled person in a room full of people who preferred numbers over people. The only reason I knew who you were is because you had a reputation for being super accurate and speedy. Now, you're rolling with being stuck in a possessed house like it's a rough day at the office and planning a way to fight back all the while. Not to mention you've managed to hold a conversation with me, a woman who has no issue saying she knows she's good-looking, without getting flustered even once. Being a vampire sure changed you."

"No, it really didn't," I said. "Most of that, especially the last part, has all come from the people I've met after becoming a vampire. My girlfriend has a . . . unique . . . job; one that constantly puts me in situations outside my comfort zone. I suppose, after all that I've been through, and the friends I've made, a little basic socializing just doesn't rate the terror it once did."

"Girlfriend, huh? Is she . . . like you?"

I allowed myself to laugh at that insinuation, light chuckles rolling forth as Asha looked at me with increasing curiosity. "Not in the slightest," I said at last. "Neither in terms of vampirism, nor personality, nor really anything. Krystal is Krystal. She's one of a kind."

"Sounds like an interesting lady." Asha halted as we arrived at the closed dining room doors. We exchanged a short glance, and I tightened my grip on the briefcase with my laptop (and quite possibly our salvation), inside. "You ready?"

"Heavens no, but that's never going to happen, so we might as well press on." I raised my voice slightly and called into the empty hallway. "Charlotte, we're going to enter now. If you'd be so kind as to make sure the doors are unlocked, I would greatly appreciate it."

Asha grabbed the handle and pulled, easily sliding the door aside and revealing a dining room and the rest of our companions. Troy and Cliff were over in a corner, while Mr. Price had retaken his seat at the head of the table. They all looked at us as we stepped through, minds reeling at what had to be yet another surprise. Sadly, they were in for a few more of those before the night was through.

"Asha!" Troy yelped, rushing over to her. He made it three steps before a small hole opened in the floor, causing his foot to go through and sending him sprawling on the ground.

"Tut tut, no running toward open doors. Your friend went through a lot of pleading to convince me to hold this meeting. Don't waste his effort." Charlotte had appeared in the seat across from Mr. Price, the one that had sat empty during our dinner. She was once again wearing the illusion of the waiter, though now I noticed some of the female features from her dress-wearing form in his face. "Hurry in, you two."

Asha and I finished our entrance, the door forcefully sliding closed as soon as we were through. She went over to check on Troy, while I made a beeline for the table and set my briefcase down.

"Glad to see you're all right," Mr. Price said. "We were exploring the upstairs when the floor opened up under us and sent us all the way down here. Damn near a miracle we didn't break anything."

"Yes, that was my fault," I told him. I didn't bother to look at the confused face he was no doubt showing me. Instead, I focused on getting my laptop pulled up. "A meeting was in order, and Charlotte was kind enough to accommodate my request of gathering everyone together."

It had actually taken quite a bit of convincing to get her to send everyone to the dining room, especially since it went past the hour deadline, but I'd been adamant that it would be worthwhile. The upside was that it meant she'd kept Mr. Price alive that much longer; unfortunately, the downside was that, if she didn't go for my proposal, she was likely to be fed up and would kill him on the spot.

"Charlotte?" Mr. Price asked.

"We'll get to that in a few moments." I finished setting up the laptop and looked over at Asha, who had pulled Troy back to his feet. From the way he favored one of his legs, it seemed he had twisted something on the way down. Even though I disliked Troy, I felt for him. The poor man was not having the best of nights, getting abused both mentally and physically. "If everyone could take a seat, we can get started."

The others made their way to the table and retook their same chairs, with one exception. Asha plopped down next to me before Cliff could, leaving the rumpled man to take the vacant spot by Troy. As everyone stared at me, I pulled a bundle of papers from my briefcase, generous amounts of script adorning each one.

"Today, you are all gathered here to serve as witnesses to Charlotte Manor's acquisition of its own deed and ownership." I handed the documents to Asha, who began passing them out to their recipients. "This being done under subsection four-c-eleven of the Disembodied Spirit Property Repossession Act, which states that any dwelling can be seized by its inhabitant if it is the original owner and the papers are filed within two months of passing, or if the dwelling has remained unoccupied for two consecutive years, save for the spirit in forced residence."

"I'm not a ghost. We already went over this." Charlotte's fingers drummed on the table, making a muted knocking sound despite the fact that they were only illusionary.

"We're getting to that," I said, keeping my voice as calm and patient as possible. I'd once read that showing certain emotions will make others inclined to replicate them. For all our sakes—and especially Mr. Price's—I hoped that worked. "Asha, if you would."

"Based on the precedents set by *Cherie vs. Derkin's Impound Lot*, animated objects with sentience are considered disembodied spirits for purposes of the rights and treaties they are obliged to," Asha said. If she felt at all silly about citing a case where an animated car sued for parts of its engine back, she didn't show it. The woman was a professional, regardless of the circumstances. "This means that Charlotte Manor, who is referred to in the contracts I wrote up as Party A, is entitled to exercise the Disembodied Spirit Repossession Act just as any formerly human entity would be."

I handed Charlotte her copy of the contract, which she immediately began reading. I chose to take that as a good sign, since she wouldn't have bothered if she thought I was completely full of it. It was going about as well as I could have hoped, which was, of course, the thought in my mind right as Troy piped up.

"What the hell are you two talking about? Disembodied spirit acts? Are you trying to make a joke out of all this?"

"I must admit, I'm confused as well," Mr. Price said. "These are very exhaustive and creative fake contracts, but I fail to see what you two are trying to accomplish with this pretense."

Charlotte sat up like a bolt and locked eyes with me. "*Fake* contracts?"

I confess, in the sudden, unexpected turn of the situation's momentum, my mind froze and speech failed me. Luckily, Asha was more experienced at high-stakes negotiation, and she was hardly the type to choke when it counted.

"The contracts are very real, I wrote them up myself." She flexed her hand, which was no doubt cramping after all the writing she'd had to do in only an hour. "Mr. Price just doesn't understand the laws we're referencing, because he's . . . do you all have a word for someone who doesn't know about all of this?"

"Human," Charlotte replied. Her tone was frosty, but her eyes went back to the page as she continued reading.

"Asha is quite correct," I said, my tongue finally obeying signals to move once more. "Everything here is thorough and genuine. Once the papers are filed, you will take possession of this home in a legal and binding manner. The man who currently holds it will receive a reasonable percentage of income generated through its use for the next twenty years as compensation, but will otherwise have no claim on the property or rights to sell it."

"You're saying that I would be the one who owned me." Charlotte glanced up from the contract, eyes still narrowed, but with a slight twinkle of hope behind them. "That's not something you should promise if you can't deliver. I won't take it lightly."

"By every statute and law we could find, it holds up," I told her. "Additionally, everyone here will be signing documents that serve to show us as witnesses to the transaction, and gag orders about what happened here."

"You want to me sign what?" Troy said, half-rising out of his chair. It scooted forward, catching him behind the knees and sending him right back down. From the way he winced on landing, I suspected he might now have added a bruised tailbone to his list of injuries.

"A non-disclosure," Asha snapped at him. "Tonight's deal is being done in confidence, which means unless you're being called on in your capacity as a witness, no one is allowed to talk about the things we've seen or experienced since setting foot in this mansion."

"And honestly, would you really want to?" I added. "Think about how absurd this series of events will seem to someone who wasn't here to experience it firsthand. It sounds like a lie in the best case, deranged ravings in the worst."

Mr. Price had been about to speak, but my words sealed his mouth and turned his attention back to the contract. He might not know what to believe about the things happenings to him; however, he did understand that he was in danger and this might get him out of it.

"This all sounds too good to be true," Charlotte interrupted. "What's the catch, Fred?"

"The catch is that these people, *all* of them, are the witnesses to your ownership," I told her. "It's written in your contract, and neither Asha nor I will change it. If you want us to file the papers—if you really want to be in control of your own body—then you have to let everyone leave here alive."

"How do I know you won't tear up the contracts as soon as you leave my walls?" Charlotte asked.

"Because in your stack of papers is one hiring Fletcher Accounting Services as your de facto representative for various accounting and filing matters, since you obviously aren't able to leave the premises. If you sign, you become one of my clients, and I have not built my business on the back of broken deals."

"Is it me, or does he seem way too comfortable with how impossible all of this is?" Cliff whispered to Troy. I ignored the question, largely because I didn't want to consider the implications. I was somewhat exposing my secret to them by doing this—there was no way to seal the deal without that risk—but hopefully I could think of a viable lie once we were all safely outside.

"You're asking me for a lot of trust, Fred. I like you, and you talked a good game, but once you're out the door, I've got no guarantees."

"Can I say something?" Mr. Price asked, looking up from the papers he'd been combing through. When no one objected, he took that as permission and continued. "I'll confess that I don't entirely understand what's going on here. In fact, I'm starting to wonder if I got food poisoning from the first course and this whole thing is just a bad dream, but I do know something about Fletcher Accounting Services. I researched this man's company thoroughly before I even considered working with him, and I couldn't find a single spot on his record. Far as I was able to tell, he's prompt, accurate, and has zero instances of broken contracts. If you're going to trust someone here, you could do worse than Fredrick Fletcher."

"The endorsement is a little hard to take as earnest when he's advocating for your life," Charlotte replied.

"Maybe so, but before all this started, I was seriously considering doing business with the man; that's why he was here in the first place. I've been coming here for years, and you said earlier that you knew me well. So, think about this, would I really have invited someone who didn't run a clean, tight ship to a final interview?"

Charlotte stared at the large, bearded man for several seconds before her gaze turned to me. She was almost there, so close I could practically see her reaching for a pen. All she needed was one more small push.

"Charlotte, I promise, I'm going to take care of you. After all, we're of a kind, and we have to look out for each other."

Excruciatingly slowly, Charlotte began to nod. "All right, Fred. If everyone here signs the contracts, then I'll let you all go. I'm trusting you, one of us to another."

"You won't regret it," I promised her.

"I don't know what the fuck you all are talking about, but there is no way I'm sign—" Troy's great attempt at defying the course of the conversation was halted as Asha kicked him in the shin under the table. I could have heard the impact even without my vampire senses, and I noted Troy's eyes watering just a touch at the edges.

"Don't worry about him. He'll be happy to sign," Asha assured us.

Charlotte held out her hand to me. "Well, Fred, let's pass out the pens and be done with this night."

9.

AS MR. PRICE DROVE OFF IN HIS CAR—
Cliff riding shotgun since his own vehicle was temporarily ornamental—I kept a firm grip on the briefcase
holding everyone's contracts. Of course, we'd taken pho-
tographs of them as soon as they were signed, both to
provide copies to the signers and to serve as back-ups,
but things could get murky if the originals were lost.
Since Charlotte was a new client, I would hate to set a
poor precedent by making things more complicated for
her. That was, after all, the opposite of what a good accountant should do.

Asha finished helping Troy into the car they'd shared over, setting him upright and helping him buckle the seatbelt. My guess was that his next stop would be a nearby hospital. He didn't seem to have broken anything, but he was no doubt in need of getting a few things x-rayed and hopefully receiving some painkillers.

With Troy settled, Asha walked back over to me, a half-smile curving across her face as she looked at the house that had held her captive for much of the evening. Charlotte stood on the porch, once more in the appearance of a woman wearing a century old style of dress. Despite her technically genderless nature, somewhere along the line, I'd begun thinking of Charlotte as a "her." That might not have been proper, but she'd yet to correct me, and referring to a client as "it" felt wrong on multiple levels. Especially for a parahuman.

"Be honest with me: am I going to wake up tomorrow and be able to pretend this was all a bad dream?" Asha asked.

"Honestly, I'm not sure. Lots of people do, but you went in pretty deep. If you try, really try with all your might, then you might one day be able to lie yourself into believing it was something other than it was."

"I figured you'd say something like that," Asha replied. "Thing is: I am terrible at lying to myself."

"Then you might be good and well stuck on this side of the curtain."

"It could be worse. At least I know the monster under the bed has certain laws he has to follow. Who knows, maybe when I get home, I'll go buy a copy of that role-playing book and see exactly what those rules are."

"Shouldn't you get some sleep instead?"

It was Asha's turn to laugh, and she did so freely, letting out a half-frantic giggle that was probably a mixture of relief at being free and terror at the truths she'd learned about the world. "No, Fred. I don't see myself getting any decent sleep for a long time."

"In that case, go to the book's website. There are free .PDFs you can download. Should keep your brain occupied until sunrise."

"Good to know." Asha's mad bubbles of laughter subsided, and she looked at the imposing silhouette of Charlotte Manor against the moonlight flooding down on us. "How do you do it, Fred? How do you live every day knowing that there are all sorts of terrible, horrifying things that really could be waiting in the shadows? How do you even get out of bed?"

"It helps that I've met a lot of those 'things,' and most of them are just like regular people. They work, they worry, and they do their best to survive. Even Charlotte, for all the craziness she put us through, was just afraid of being killed. But, at the end of the day, I suppose I have a source of comfort you don't: I am one of those terrible, horrifying things."

"I didn't mean it like . . . I'm sorry." Asha jingled the keys in her hand as she turned away from me. "It's been a long night. I need to go home, decompress, and try to make sense of all this."

"I find a good merlot helps tremendously," I told her.

"Not a bad idea." Asha glanced back at me over her shoulder. "Good luck with everything, Fred. Maybe I'll see you around some time."

"For all our sakes, let's hope next time is a bit tamer."

Asha gave a curt nod, and then headed to her car. She slid in, pointedly ignoring whatever Troy was talking to her about, and revved the engine. Moments later, they were gone, little more than fading tail lights on the half-deserted concrete road.

"Credit where it's due: she took that better than most people," Charlotte said from the porch. "The mages used to initiate new recruits in my basement, and a lot of them just broke down after learning about the supernatural world."

"Hard to blame them." I walked up the steps and took a seat on one of the antique rocking chairs set out on the porch. "Truthfully, it took me about a week to leave my bed after I'd made the transition, and I was arguably far better off for it."

"You seem to be coping well these days." Charlotte sat down next to me and extended her hand. "Though, I bet a drink would help. You said merlot, right?"

"Yes, I—" A quick glance showed me that there was now a wine glass filled with red liquid on the table next to me, where previously there had been only empty space. "How do you do that?"

"Built-in magic, remember? After all, I was meant to be a fortress, and running out of supplies is a big concern during a siege. One of my more useful tricks, too. It's not like I can set up contracts with vendors for outside food or anything."

"Actually, you can." I took a deep breath of the wine and found it enticingly complex. The first sip hit my tongue and left me appreciative of Charlotte's tastes in vintages. "Or, rather, I can on your behalf. I can also arrange upgrades for you as well, if you'd like. Internet, new fixtures, whatever you'd like; assuming you can finance it."

"Money isn't an issue. Those mages left a couple tons of gold squirreled away in one of the hidden rooms in my basement."

I snorted very unbecomingly into my wine glass. "Did you say *tons* of gold?"

"They weren't building a sanctuary and hiding from the law without good reason," Charlotte replied.

"If you have all that money, and the ability to keep yourself repaired, then why open a bed and breakfast in the first place?"

"Same reason everyone reaches out, I guess. I was lonely." Charlotte ran a hand along the armrest of her hand-carved chair. "When the mages were gone, I was all by myself. That's no way to live, not even for something like me. I could have been a haunted house that scared people away, but I wanted company. So I became a place where people would enjoy themselves, make fond memories, and come back to visit. I know, kind of crazy given how big of a secret I was keeping."

"No, Charlotte. I don't think that's crazy at all. I'll do my best to keep you running and get people to visit. I know how it feels to be lonely, and I wouldn't wish that on anyone, let alone a new friend."

Charlotte smiled, and a glass of wine appeared in her hand as well. She raised it up and tilted it slightly toward me. "I'll cheers to that."

We clinked glasses, despite one of them being illusionary, and took our drinks. It didn't matter that hers was fake, or that the image she was putting in front of my eyes was equally illusory. The sentiment was real, and that was far more important than a silly thing like corporeality.

A DRAGON IN THE OFFICE

1.

DESPITE MY ADMITTEDLY FORMAL MANNER OF dress, I was not practiced in the art of the bow tie. It had never been a skill that required cultivation, as I'd always gone with a classic tie knotted in a full Windsor for work and formal occasions in my youth. (It certainly didn't help that the few occasions which might have necessitated such a fashion accessory were ones that required a passable level of social ability to attend—such as prom, or a friend's wedding.) Therefore, I found myself faced with the increasingly frustrating task of trying to weave a proper bow tie from the single piece of fabric wound around my neck and failing spectacularly at it.

There was a knock on my bedroom door, followed immediately by the sound of it opening. It invalidated the entire point of the knock, but I was thankful for the gesture. Krystal could be indelicate at times; that was her way of at least giving me some warning.

She was a vision of loveliness, to the point where I found my old shyness creeping back the longer I looked at her. Krystal, the girl perpetually in jeans, had donned a form-fitting red dress that crossed in the back, leaving much of her skin exposed. Her hair had been curled ever so slightly, and then piled atop her head in a way that somehow managed to be messy, yet simultaneously elegant. She'd even put on a little extra makeup, accentuating her already striking features. Those same features twisted into a spontaneous bout of laughter as she took in my situation and the frustration evident on my face.

"No luck so far?" She was keeping her giggles down, but it took obvious effort.

"That infernal internet video made it look so simple. But every time I try, it comes out lopsided. At best." Despite the growing desire to stamp my foot like a petulant child, I held my calm. I'd been out of place or felt silly before; another night of it wouldn't kill me.

"Does this mean the proud, mighty vampire is finally willing to accept the help of my dainty woman hands?" Krystal asked, moving a few steps closer to me.

"I never said anything like that. I just said the others would likely need more help than I would."

"You weren't wrong there; Albert had his cummerbund on backwards, Neil tried to show up in formal necromancer robes, and Amy spilled a potion that made her dress keep shifting colors. It finally settled on periwinkle, which doesn't match her shoes, but at this point, I'm taking what I can get."

"At least it sounds like Bubba didn't give you any trouble," I pointed out.

Krystal shook her head, using such force that I was momentarily concerned her hair would come out of its carefully constructed shape. "Bubba was the worst of the lot. Yes, he knows how to put on a tuxedo, but he wouldn't stop bitching about it the entire time. I had to bribe him with a case of beer just to get him down to grumbling. If this were an event by anyone but Richard, I think he'd have bailed."

Thinking about it, if any of us were less inclined toward formal wear than Krystal, it was Bubba. I scarcely ever saw him outside of his worn clothes and beaten baseball caps. It would have been strange to see him in something as formal as a sport coat; a tuxedo might just blow people's minds.

"Since you have managed to wrangle the rest of our friends into presentable shape, I humbly request your expert intervention." I pulled on both ends of what was supposed to be a bow tie, bringing the fabric taught. "Please tie this damned thing for me. I'm quickly running out of patience, and I'm afraid I might accidentally rip it soon."

"We can't have that. These things are rentals, after all." Krystal turned me toward the mirror as she stood behind me. She pressed herself against my back—certainly closer than was necessary—but I didn't object. Much as I could be reticent about affection, her playful enthusiasm and penchant for embarrassing me had grown to be a counterbalance. It was one of the many things I adored about her, and from the nimble way her hands worked, it seemed I would have to be adding competency with bow ties to the list.

"Are you nervous?" Her mouth was so close that I could feel her breath run across the back of my ear.

"Certainly not, we're just walking into a room full of parahumans who are all of such power and importance that Richard invited them into his home for a formal occasion. What possible thing could I have to fear in a situation like that?"

"You'll be fine; there are rules to these things. Besides, it's not like everyone is a heavy-hitter. Some of the guests are just like you and Amy, people he has business relationships with. And there are some that are attending out of form, like inviting me because I'm an agent or Albert and Neil because they're tied to a Weapon of Destiny."

"Those latter examples are a zombie wielding a weapon of tremendous power, the necromancer who multiplies his strength, and an agent, one of the most feared beings in the parahuman world," I pointed out. "Not exactly a strong case for most of the guests being 'not heavy-hitters,' as you said."

"You think most people in my league have time to go to a party celebrating two therian packs finally finishing a peaceful merger? My point is that Albert, Neil, and I are going for the same reason as you and Amy: because we like Richard as a person. The vast majority of the guests will be therians, and while they aren't super keen on vampires, no one would try to hurt one of the other guests. It would be an insult to Richard as a host." Krystal finished weaving the formerly shapeless fabric into an exquisite bow tie, symmetrical and crisp in every measurable capacity. "Besides, if worse ever came to worse, Gideon is there, and I think he sees you as more useful alive than permanently dead."

"I fear you may overestimate his affection for me," I said. With my bow tie on, I reached over to a nearby hanger and slid my jacket, the final piece of my ensemble, across my narrow shoulders.

"You saved Richard a lot of money. Dragons love gold, that isn't just myth, and anyone who brings more of it into their proximity can't be all bad. Hell, that might be as close as they get to having friends." Krystal stepped back, admiring me now that I was fully adorned in the required wear of the evening. "You know, you clean up pretty nice."

"I would take more comfort in that notion if I weren't so keenly aware of the fact that I'm going to be walking in with the absolute definition of beauty. How well I clean up is unimportant; no one will even realize I'm there once they see you."

Krystal stared at me for a moment, then did something I was completely unprepared for. She blushed. Only a touch in the cheeks and for no more than a few seconds, but it was unmistakable. The rising of blood is not the sort of thing my vampire senses were likely to overlook. Then, as quickly as it was there, it was gone, hidden in a flurry of movement as she stepped closer and kissed me firmly on the lips. By the time I pulled free, there was no trace of those red cheeks. Instead, she wore her usual half-wild grin.

"Keep up the sweet talk, and I'll end up making us late for this thing."

"Wonderful as that sounds, I would be too embarrassed to leave this room if the others heard us . . . being affectionate. Which would be unavoidable, since at least two of them have enhanced hearing, possibly three depending on which potions Amy has taken so far today."

"Actually, I sent the kids off to school," Krystal replied, gently teasing one of the buttons on my pressed, white tuxedo shirt. "I thought it might be nice if we went over together, just the two of us. It's been awhile since we managed a real date, and since I've got an out-of-town gig coming up, we probably won't pull one off for another week or so."

"I'll have to plan something special for your return, then." I gently ran my hand across Krystal's cheek, perhaps unconsciously trying to sense the heat that had been there only minutes before.

"Please do. I like hanging out with the gang as much as anyone else, but even I like some romance from time to time. Just . . . you know the deal."

"No reservations that can't be canceled," I said.

She nodded and took a step back, finally breaking the half-embrace we'd locked ourselves in since she fixed my bow tie. "Yeah. I hate that we have to make that a rule, but I never know when a call is going to come."

"You don't ever need to feel bad for doing your job. We came into this with open eyes. I knew who I was committing to. Sometimes, I have to let plans fall away due to your more pressing matters; sometimes, you have to watch movies that don't have slapstick or explosions with me. We've all got our burdens to bear."

"It could be worse," Krystal conceded. "At least you clean up nice. Just don't get too comfy in that tux."

"I daresay it would take a mage of legendary caliber to make such a thing viable, so I doubt it will be an issue."

"Good, because Albert is staying with Neil tonight, which means we've got the apartment all to ourselves." She threw me a glance that, even on my least socially adept day, I could have correctly interpreted. After having been with her for so many months, I knew its meaning in an instant.

"Ah, um, right. Yes." I would love to report that I'd reached a point where I was finally less bumbling when it came to discussing intimate matters; however, such was simply not the case, as my swarthy dialogue proves.

"Whoa there. Put a leash on it, you wild animal. We've got to get through a party first." Krystal shifted gears from sultry to playful, trading her telling leer for a flirty wink before I'd even finished recovering.

"I believe, when tuxedos are involved, it's called a gala," I said.

"Fred, I've been to a few 'galas,' and trust me on this: no one will ever call a therian party a gala, no matter how fancy they make the guests dress. Now, shake that cute ass. If you're late to these things, all the good food is gone."

Krystal slipped her arm through mine, pulled open the bedroom door, and the two of us headed out, en route to what was supposed to be a lovely party surrounded by a few friends and a myriad of potentially deadly strangers.

I only found it mildly disconcerting how normal that situation seemed at the time.

2.

IT HAD TAKEN ME BY SURPRISE TO LEARN that, despite the kidnapping attempt some months prior, negotiations between the two tribes of therians had continued. When I voiced this sentiment, Bubba kindly reminded me that, just because their leader was a dick, it didn't remove the displaced tribe's need for shelter and homes. A new leader had been chosen, this one with a very firm stance against stealing little girls, and the negotiations had resumed.

Part of me still wanted to know what could drive an entire tribe of therians from their home, but every time I came near the subject, Krystal's face took on the serious demeanor I'd begun to recognize as a sign that I was about to hear something disturbing. Never let it be said that I was beyond learning, as I halted those conversations as soon as I caught sight of that look. I had quite enough to worry about and be afraid of, thank you; there was no need to pile a few more nightmares onto my plate.

We arrived at the party in Krystal's pickup truck, as she steadfastly refused to be seen getting out of my hybrid, and I was struck by the change in Richard's building. It was a tall one, in the heart of downtown—not quite a skyscraper, though definitely a skyneighbor—but only the top few floors were used by him. The rest were rented out to various corporations, with the bottom being owned by a club that played music I would generously refer to as the dying screeches of a speaker that was dumped in the ocean. Tonight, however, there was no sign of the usual customers hosting multi-colored hair and abundant piercings. Instead, tuxedoed staff waited at the entrance, politely greeting each guest as they made their way up the concrete walkway to the steel-and-glass doors. From the size of the men, I had no doubt they were therians, though they barely stood out amidst the crowd of lumbering guests filing through the entrance. Somewhere in the nation, a tuxedo rental chain must have been completely out of all sizes over extra-large.

The small line of vehicles in front of us quickly dissipated as a series of swift, efficient valets delicately removed guests from their automobiles. From arrival to the moment a sizable hand pulled open the door next to me, it couldn't have been longer than two minutes—no mean feat given the number of cars they were working through.

"Impressive," I told Krystal, as she slid her arm through mine and I watched her truck being swiftly driven away. "This is more coordination than I usually see from Richard's people."

"They're trying to make a good impression," Krystal told me. "Both on their new tribe members and on the bigwigs in attendance. It's a subtle thing, but showing strong teamwork in mundane activities will make people more hesitant to take you on in battle. After all, if that's how good they are at parking cars, you can only imagine what they'd be like at spilling blood."

We continued forward in silence as we drew near the entrance. There was a small line as the security team confirmed each person was indeed a guest—though what madman would try to break into *this* party, I couldn't imagine. As we waited, I caught sight of a few symbols drawn above the doorways. My eyes followed them, noting the way they wove down the sides and even across the ground in small sections. I'd only been to Richard's building a few times in our association, but I felt reasonably certain I'd have noticed those if they were present before.

"Are those supposed to be decoration?" I asked, nodding slightly at the symbols over the door.

Krystal looked at me with a fleeting touch of surprise and shook her head. "I didn't expect you to see those, but it makes sense, given whose blood you drank. They're draconic runes, part of a spell that Gideon set up over the building."

"Dare I ask what it will do?"

"It's a suppression charm, meant to bring the guests a little closer to human than para. You'll find them at lots of gatherings like this, though most places have to use mages instead of a dragon. They're handy for keeping the peace and making sure that, if any scuffles do break out, they don't take down an entire building."

"Should I be concerned? After all, a vampire without magic is, well . . . just a corpse."

"Give me a little credit; I wouldn't have brought you along if the things were that powerful. There's no magic that can just turn off what a parahuman is. This is nothing more than a dampener. You'll be fine. Honestly, I'm not even sure they'll affect you." Krystal patted my arm with her free hand, letting it linger there as she spoke. I wanted to hear why she had such a theory, but at that moment the guests in front of us were cleared to enter, and it was our turn to talk with security.

The exchange was brief and polite. Krystal gave them both our names, and after one checked a list while another talked on the radio to an unseen guard, we were permitted entrance. Had I still breathed out of anything but habit, I likely would have held my breath as we stepped through the threshold. Krystal's firm grip permitted no such theatricality though, as she pulled me through the door and into the lobby. I thought I felt a slight tingle run across my skin, but it easily could have been my imagination. Either way, I neither dropped dead nor suddenly turned human, so it seemed Krystal was right about the undead not being at risk.

With my fear assuaged, I allowed myself to take in the scene before me. A long, deep maroon carpet ran from the building's entrance to a set of large white stairs. White balloons adorned the railing, along with swaths of matching fabric hung with such delicacy that I immediately knew Richard had outsourced the decorating. I could already hear the soft strands of string music—too lively and imperfect to be recorded—floating down from several floors up. Much as I respected Krystal's opinions, at that moment, I had to disagree with her: therians most certainly could throw a gala.

We ascended the stairs slowly, savoring the peaceful journey together. I'd expected her to be off-balance in heels, but Krystal moved as easily as she did in a pair of sneakers. I wondered if that was part of her agent training, the devil-magic inside her, or simply a practiced skill acquired during the decade when we hadn't spoken to one another. Ultimately, it was irrelevant; she was simply graceful as we walked up the stairs, and I was enraptured with her, the moment, and the entire experience.

Sadly, that peaceful bliss was broken as soon as we stepped off the final stair, putting us in view of the party. The open doors before us showed a vast ballroom, already filled with dancing guests, a small orchestra, and a sizable buffet station loaded with food. The last part was easily the most crowded, as therians tended to have large appetites, gala or no. None of that was disturbing, however. In fact, it added to the moment—seeing a gorgeous destination at the end of our happy journey. No, what took us out of the fantasy was a voice that I'd hoped not to hear again for some time.

"Evening, Agent Jenkins, Fredrick Fletcher." Arch was standing nearby, arms perched on a railing that looked down over the lobby, where new guests were still coming in. He looked exactly as he had at Albert's trial, save only for the fact that he'd traded his utilitarian clothing for an old-fashioned tuxedo and wasn't surrounded by the usual cloud of cigarette smoke. (Richard's building had very firm no smoking policies.)

"I'm off duty, Arch. It's just Krystal tonight." She left my arm and walked over to her fellow agent, giving him a light hug that lasted for less than a second.

"We're never really off duty," Arch replied. If he was bothered by the slightness of her embrace, it didn't show.

"Tonight, I am. You do what you want."

I made my way over as she spoke, trading a polite handshake with Arch. "So, how do you know Richard?"

"Never met the man," Arch replied. "I was in town apartment hunting, somehow he caught wind of it, and I wound up with an invite."

"Apartment hunting?" I worked as hard as I could to keep my tone placid, but from the look on Arch's face, it seemed I was unsuccessful.

"Looking for a place to live," he clarified. "Since your assistant handed me that ultimatum about not leaving, I didn't have much choice in the matter."

I bit back the retort on my tongue that wanted to point out he'd had the option of not coming at all. It was in poor taste to be so impolite, especially at a function as elegant as this one. Besides, Arch as not my priority. I needed to warn Albert, lest he be taken by surprise.

"Well, I wish you the best of luck at that," I told him. "If you'll excuse us, we have to meet our friends inside."

"I'll come with. Might as well let Albert know he got his wish, after all."

I looked at Krystal, who gave her head the slightest shake. The message was clear: now was not the time to fight this battle. We linked arms once more and headed into the proper area of the party.

Once inside, I was able to take in details I'd missed before: the small tables set up at irregular intervals where people could rest their food, the bar in the back corner that I suspected stocked a quality of beer not normally found at tuxedo functions, and a small podium at the far end of the room. On that podium was Richard, another man I didn't recognize, and Gideon, each dressed in a fine tuxedo. It was strange to see the King of the West without Sally present, but Krystal had told me that Richard's daughter had taken ill in the last week.

As my gaze went over them, I caught Richard's eye for a moment, and he gave a slight smile in my direction. It was nice to be recognized, even in such a small manner, by a being of such prestige. Perhaps that was why I chanced a direct glance at Gideon; maybe I was curious to see if what we'd been through had sown any familiarity for me in the dragon's heart. It took a few moments, but eventually, we locked eyes. It was only for a second, yet it changed the outcome of the entire night.

I could feel the pressure as soon as he looked at me; that terrifying aura that I'd always felt around him came surging back. It thundered through my veins, freezing my muscles and tripping every panic impulse hard-wired into my vampire brain. It sliced through me, tearing apart all manner of reason. I thought for certain that I'd end up a catatonic, drooling mess, but this time, it didn't happen.

This time, the aura hit something within me, some small piece of power that I hadn't been conscious of, and that piece fought the panic back. It screamed against the foreign presence, driving it out with a sentiment that I could only describe as fury. Slowly, ever so slowly, my brain began to function again and my body returned to my control. As soon I regained some semblance of reason, I understood what had saved me: Gideon's blood. The power of a dragon still lived inside me, and it was the only thing that had brought me salvation. Unfortunately, I also knew—in a way that I would never be able to articulate—that the power inside me and the one that had been fought off belonged to two entirely different beings.

"Fred, you okay?" Krystal snapped a finger in front of my eyes, and I realized I must have frozen up for a bit after all. "You've been staring at Gideon for like a solid minute."

With great effort, I moved my tongue, forming what might have been the most terrifying words I'd ever spoken, in life or after.

"That isn't Gideon."

3.

THE WORDS HAD SCARCELY LEFT MY MOUTH before I felt the hard prick of metal pressed against my ribs. Though he'd managed to conceal it from onlookers, Arch had a small blade wedged against my jacket. Strange as it was given the circumstances, my first concern was that he might have put a hole in the shirt and jacket, both of which were rentals. Only after I'd had a second to process did I realize all the terrible implications his action might carry.

"Not a word more," Arch whispered. Despite the harshness in his voice, he was still looking as placid as he had moments prior. Krystal, on the other hand, seemed as though she were rounding the bend of confused and was now on a direct track toward pissed off.

"Arch, get your fucking hands off my boyfriend."

"Apologies." Just like that, the blade was gone, stashed somewhere in the old-fashioned coat he wore. I hadn't even thought about it at the time, but no one had bothered frisking us for weapons when we came in. It made a certain amount of sense, though. Bullets and knives were less effective than most parahumans' natural abilities—unless they were made of silver, of course. The flaw in that strategy was that it was akin to having a deadly shellfish allergy and carrying around a shrimp bomb: it invited unnecessary danger upon one's self.

"We need to speak somewhere with more privacy." Arch was still calm and detached; honestly, he struck me as closer to bored than anything else. I didn't know what sort of parahuman he was, but I'd begun to suspect it wasn't something I was familiar with. Not when even a situation like this didn't make him panic.

"Let's go back out to the stairway. Meet on the left," Krystal suggested. She still didn't seem happy, but it was evident that she was going along with whatever Arch wanted for the moment.

Arch nodded, pulling out a cell phone and pressing it to his ear. He jammed a finger in the other, muttered some words as he scowled at the band, and then hurried out of the room. It happened so quickly, I barely had time to register that he'd faked getting a call and needing to find a place with silence. Arch definitely thought on his feet, I had to give him that.

"We'll have to wait a few moments." Krystal whispered this directly in my ear, a feat she accomplished by unabashedly pressing herself against me in a way that almost certainly would have made most onlookers uncomfortable. Given the very public place we were in, it would have made me uncomfortable too, if not for the still fading sense of terror that was soaked into my system.

I nodded, my eyes sweeping the room as I killed time. I caught sight of Albert and Neil, both loading plates high with items from the buffet. Neil was cutting a swath through the shrimp skewers and crab quiches, while Albert had helped himself to more cake than any reasonable person would be able to put down. Moments later, I saw Amy and Bubba, both walking away from the bar. Bubba was holding three beers—two unopened in his left hand, the one he was already drinking in his right— while Amy had a tall glass filled with ice and purple liquid. There was perhaps a fifty percent chance that hers was a regular cocktail, and not something she'd added her own ingredients too. As I watched them, Bubba noticed me, giving a nod and rerouting Amy in our direction.

"Oh dear. Amy and Bubba are coming this way," I told Krystal.

"Guess it's time to move then." She leaned away from my ear and moved to my face, pulling me in for a kiss far more gratuitous than the situation called for. After a few moments, she pulled away, taking my hand with her and leading me back out toward the stairway entrance. To any observers, we no doubt appeared as if we were heading off to find a private spot and finish our moment. It was mortifying, but the situation was so dire, I only managed to be slightly embarrassed by the whole thing.

We emerged into the darker area of the landing at the top of the stairs. Krystal kept up the act as she pulled me around the side and toward an undecorated hallway to the left. Only when we were out of sight did the dramatic sex-kitten act fall away, revealing the serious face of an agent in an unexpected situation.

Arch was already there, leaning against a wall with his phone still at his ear. He was impossible to see from the stairwell, but if someone walked over and caught a glance of him, it would seem as if he were doing nothing more than trying to take a call. As soon as we arrived, he lowered the phone and turned to face me.

"How did you know?"

"It's hard to say." I didn't need to ask Arch for clarification—there was only one bit of information I had that he could possibly be interested in. "Something about his aura of fear. It felt different than the other times. And when he gave me his blood, it faded completely. Tonight, it was—"

"Hold. Gideon, the King of the West, allowed you to drink from him?" His eyebrows were slightly raised, and there was the barest of wrinkles in his forehead. It was the closest thing to shock I'd yet seen on Arch's face.

"Months ago, when Sally Alderson was kidnapped. He needed me to get her to safety, and I was catatonic from being near him, so he gave me a drop of his blood. When that happened, the fear stopped affecting me. Tonight, I felt the aura as strong as ever, only this time, it felt like something . . . I don't know . . . stopped it."

"Lovely." Arch leaned back against the wall and reached into his coat. He pulled out a cigarette and twirled it through his fingers. Given how many he'd gone through the last time I saw him, I could only imagine how badly he wished he could light the thing up.

"All right, Arch, what the fuck is going on?" Krystal asked. "News like this would get a reaction, even from you, if it were really news. Obviously, you knew something, so how about you spill?"

"There were concerns that, over the last few days, Gideon's behavior had become slightly different," Arch said. "Nothing erratic, or dangerous, just variant. Given his status, however, any potential issue must be considered, so I was sent in to see what I could find out. Thanks to Mr. Fletcher, I now know that he was captured, and another dragon has taken his place."

"Wait, *another* dragon?" My voice came out in a choked whisper as I tried to reconcile my need for secrecy with my desire to yelp.

"Gideon is old, and very powerful," Krystal said. "We know he wasn't killed, because slaying a parahuman as strong as he is would have sent out the sort of magical resonance that every mage in the state would pick up on. Plus, I seriously doubt he'd have gone down quietly. The only creature that could have contained him, set up the runes outside the building, and still projected a draconic aura is another dragon."

"Which leaves us dealing with a rogue dragon, and no idea where the King of the West is," Arch surmised.

"That's not entirely true," Amy said. I nearly leapt up to the ceiling in surprise, but Arch and Krystal seemed unfazed. Unlike me, it seemed, they'd been paying enough attention to our surroundings to notice her and Bubba approaching us.

Amy continued, politely ignoring my impromptu leap. "To seal a dragon like Gideon, this other fellow would have to stay close to the cage. Unless he's as powerful as another king, there's just no way he could maintain the spell over a distance."

"Highly unlikely," Arch replied. "If one of the major players suddenly vanished, we'd have noticed. How close would you say the faux-Gideon needs to be in order to keep the real one contained?"

"Ordinarily, I don't think he'd be able to get more than half a mile away from the cage." Amy pulled an eye-dropper from somewhere in her dress and added a few splashes of yellow liquid to her cocktail, which shimmered with a metallic sheen as she took a sip. "But with the whole building sealed off like this, they've basically created a distinct environment, separate from the outside world. Which means, as long as our dragon is in here, he or she is close enough to keep the mojo flowing. So the bad news is that Gideon could be anywhere in this building, but the good news is that he *has* to be somewhere in this building."

"All we need to do is track him down," Bubba said. "If we find something of his with scent, it should be no trouble at all."

"First off, this is a building full of therians, so if the dragon went to the trouble of caging Gideon, they almost certainly warded off his smell. Secondly, even if that weren't the case, I doubt you could do more than pick up a few fragrant notes here and there, seeing as the runes out front will have suppressed everyone's parahuman abilities." Arch twirled the cigarette faster through his fingers, it's dancing movement the only sign of the frustration he had to have been feeling.

"Not everyone's," Krystal said. "You and I should be fine, and Fred has Gideon's blood inside him. I thought it might keep him functioning when it was just Gideon's wards we were dealing with; against some imitator's attempt, I'm sure he's still at full vampire power."

"Is that true, Fred? How do you feel?" Arch asked, finally looking away from the spot on the wall he'd been staring at.

"Same as ever." I really didn't feel any different; my senses were still keen, my muscles strong, and obviously my undead body was still animated. "Well, same as since I died, I mean."

"Given how high he jumped when we came up, I'm guessing he's still pretty strong," Bubba noted, blatantly ignoring the unspoken agreement to let my brief moment of shameful shock pass unmentioned.

"Congratulations, Fred," Arch said. "As the only non-agent here who still possesses all of his abilities—and the only one with a blood connection to our missing parahuman—you have just been selected to lead the search for him. Agent Jenkins and I need to get back inside the party."

"The hell I do," Krystal snapped. "I'm with Fred."

"No, you're not." Arch didn't raise his voice or puff out his body. He did nothing more than put the cigarette back in his pocket, yet, as he spoke, it was with such authority that I couldn't even imagine saying no to him.

"You and I are agents, which means any identity-stealing dragons will keep an eye on us. Fred is a relative nobody; his presence won't be missed, which will ideally stop our hand from being tipped. The longer we can keep our opponent in the dark, the better."

I might have been ready to go along with anything Arch said, but Krystal was made of more stubborn stuff. She thrust a finger down into Arch's chest, the height difference between them making the exchange almost comical.

"You might have come here on a case, but I'm here as a guest, with my date, who I am damned sure not going to send skittering off into a therian's building on a wild dragon hunt. I am not your subordinate, and I won't take orders from you just because you've got more experience. Clear?"

"Like most of our younger personnel, Agent Jenkins, your emotions are getting the better of you." Arch pointed down the hall, toward the party. "Those people are the ones in danger. They are the ones in a room, their own abilities suppressed, within striking distance of a dragon we know nothing about, save for the fact that it's strong enough to capture the King of the West. I am sending your boyfriend away from the threat, but you and I have to stay put for the sake of the others. Should this facade turn bloody, we're likely to be the only defense they have."

"Krystal, it'll be fine." I gently put my hand on her shoulder and pulled her away from Arch. "It's just searching an empty building for Gideon. Even I won't mess it up."

"Fred, you don't get it. If someone went to all the trouble of capturing Gideon, they won't have left him undefended," Krystal said, turning around to face me. "I don't know if its guards, or magic, or what, but there will be something, probably something deadly, designed to keep you from reaching him."

"Which is why Fred isn't going alone," Bubba piped up from behind us. "Amy and I aren't big deals either. We can go with him and help."

"You two are closer to human than para at the moment," Arch pointed out. "It's more likely you'll get in the way."

"First off, fuck you," Amy said. "Secondly, we can still use our eyes and look for things. Thirdly, Bubba knows this building better than any of us, so he's the one who can point us toward the most likely spots to hold a dragon. Fourthly, all the runes in the world won't change the effects of the potions I brought along. And fifthly, fuck you again, just for good measure." She took a long swig of her metallic purple drink to punctuate the sentence.

"I still don't like this," Krystal said. Her hand was gripping mine tightly, so strongly in fact, that, for a moment, I wondered if her power were somehow leaking through.

"It's not how I wanted to spend the night either, but Arch is right. You two have to keep the others safe. I've got Bubba and Amy with me, and we're going away from the dragon. We'll be fine."

Krystal leaned forward and kissed me. This was nothing like the theatrical lip-smacking she'd laid on me when there was a room full of people to sell the act to. This was short, and tender, and fierce. Neither of us was good at talking about our feelings, but she managed to pack all the fear she had for my safety and the loneliness she'd experience without me into that single kiss. When we parted, she immediately looked away from me, turning to Arch.

"Let's get this fucking thing done."

4.

"THIS CAGE THAT COULD HOLD GIDEON, 'bout how big would it have to be?" Bubba had taken the napkin from Amy's cocktail and a pen from his pocket, and was proceeding to scribble down something I couldn't yet make out.

"For a dragon like Gideon, we'd be talking pretty damn huge," Amy replied. "Even in his current form, the amount of magic he has would take wards upon wards to hold back. We'd be looking at binding circles that would take up half of one of these floors, minimum."

"Do they have to be undisturbed?" I asked. "If so, then that should narrow it down. Most of the floors will have walls and furniture breaking up the space."

"That would be the case for most binding circles, but dragon magic can work a little . . . differently, depending on the caster." Amy shook her head. "We're better off not making any assumptions we don't have to."

"That still gives us something to go on," Bubba said. He held up the napkin, which had a numbered list of various locations. "There can't be that many floors in here where an entire half could just go unused and not draw attention."

"Not with real estate costs what they are and a location this prime," I agreed.

"Out of the floors Richard controls directly, there's the top three where he lives and does business, and then the basement. I seriously doubt Gideon is stashed on any of the top floors, since those have been full of therians dealing with the negotiations for the past few weeks. Richard mostly uses the basement for storage, which would make it the ideal spot to stash a bound dragon, except that it also doubles as an entryway for his private guests and the nocturnal visitors, meaning he has sweeps of it done regularly."

"Which all leads to the conclusion that our dragon thief wouldn't have put Gideon on any of the floors Richard controls directly," Amy said.

"He's most likely on one of the others. Maybe the dragon even rented a name under a fake business just to have a place to stash Gideon," I suggested.

"That seems a little involved." Bubba's skepticism was polite, but still present.

"Fred's on the right train of thinking," Amy said. "Binding Gideon would have taken months, maybe years, of magical preparation. Renting a floor would have been a minor task to undertake, relatively speaking."

"There's a security directory at every guard station in the building," Bubba told us. He folded his napkin and tucked it into the jacket pocket of his tuxedo, where I greatly hoped he would not forget to remove it before the return came due. "We can take a look at all the floors and their owners, see if anything jumps out at us."

"It's as good a plan as we're likely to come up with, under the circumstances," I said. Amy nodded her agreement, and the three of us were off.

Bubba's knowledge of the building might not have presented overt usefulness in helping us locate Gideon initially, but it immediately became indispensable as we made our way from the party and into the momentarily deserted depths of the structure. He took us through various hallways and concrete staircases, careful to keep us away from areas where we risked being noticed. While we may not have been missed from the party itself, there was a very good chance that being discovered prowling through Richard's domain would put us in a very uncomfortable position.

As we made our way through yet another identical hallway, I noticed a change in Bubba. Despite his sizable frame, the big man had always moved with a surprising amount of grace and energy. In all our time knowing one another, I could scarcely recall ever seeing him worn out, or even short of breath. This was, of course, due to the inherent physical gifts of being a therian. But as we walked briskly down the hall, I realized that I could hear Bubba breathing heavily. It was a small thing, completely unimportant in other circumstances, yet it stood out to me like a drop of blood on a white carpet. It was easy to forget that my friends, usually far more powerful than me, were weakened while in this building, which meant I'd have to do all I could to keep them safe.

We finally made it to one of the small, kiosk-like stations near an entrance, where, normally, security guards sat to scrutinize and direct each guest. It was immaculately clean, with no sign of any books, directory or otherwise, present on the desk. Amy and I looked at Bubba, who waved off our concern.

"They keep that stuff locked up, obviously. It's in the bottom drawer on the left." He leaned over, grasped the metal handle, and pulled. Moments later, when it failed to come free, Bubba stepped forward, braced his feet, and gave a much hardier tug. The metal drawer groaned and began to bulge, but otherwise held in place.

"Maybe we should let Fred try," Amy suggested softly.

Bubba looked like he wanted to fight the idea, but whatever discontent he had was swallowed as he released the handle and stepped away. He turned around, though not before we could see the sheen of sweat across his forehead. Bubba quickly wiped it off with the arm of his tuxedo jacket.

"We all know it's the dragon runes," I said, hoping to placate what I assumed was his wounded ego.

"Knowin' why doesn't change the fact that I'm weak, and I *hate* being weak." Bubba didn't turn around to talk with us; instead, he kept his eyes trained out the nearest doorway, looking into the night air. Less than thirty feet of distance, but once he crossed that threshold, Bubba would be whole again.

It had never occurred to me that the other para-humans I knew might be terrified at the idea of being weakened. I had always been weak—it was my default setting—so the idea of losing some of my power didn't rankle me in the slightest. But it was clear I was the oddity here, not them.

"I'd hardly call what you did to this drawer weak," I said, leaning over and grasping the handle. (It is worth noting that said handle had been slightly warped into the shape of Bubba's hand.) "It just needs one more solid tug to get it loose." I yanked, and the drawer gave way, flying open so quickly I nearly pulled it all the way out.

Bubba had been right; there was a security directory right there in the top of the drawer. Amy snatched it up and opened it on the desk, which finally drew Bubba's attention back to the task at hand. The three of us began reading the pages, trying to spot something, anything, that was out of place.

"I suppose it was too much to hope they'd use some sort of dragon pun in the company's name." I sighed as I skimmed through the list of various business names. From the look of the directory, there wasn't a single un-rented floor in the building, which spoke wonders about the Winslow economy, but also made our job all the more difficult.

"We're not dealing with a Bond villain," Bubba said. "Someone went through a lot of trouble to take Gideon's place; they're not going to make finding him that easy."

"If it's even on one of these floors," Amy reminded us. "Right now, we don't know anything for sure."

As my eyes ran through the list of names for what had to be the fifth time, I lingered on the moniker of a company on the eighth floor: Alcron Technical Industries. There was something off, something that didn't feel quite right. I read through the small entry written below its name, no doubt there to help the guards direct people who knew the purpose of the business, but had forgotten the name. By the time I'd finished, I knew what was wrong, and I had a good idea of where Gideon was.

"I think it's this one, on floor eight." I pointed to the Alcron entry and tapped it with my index finger. "The note says it's a startup business in communication technology."

"So?" Bubba asked.

"So, I make it a point to keep abreast of new, important companies in our area. It's sort of my business to get in early and offer services, after all. For a startup to need this much office space, they'd have to have accrued substantial staff and revenue, which means I should have at least heard of them. Granted, it's possible they're such a niche company that they slipped my notice, but it's the only one that seems off to me."

"At this point, a hunch is better than nothing," Amy said. "We can bring the directory with us, so we're better off moving, anyway."

"I trust Fred's judgment. If he thinks something is off, that's good enough for me." Bubba checked the floor number, then looked around the area. "As soon as I remember where the elevator is, we're going up to the eighth floor and hopefully busting out one pissed off dragon."

"I find it hard to picture circumstances where I would ever want to see Gideon truly enraged," I said.

Bubba paused, then gave a slight shrug of his shoulders. "Well then, you might want to close your eyes, because I don't see any other way of him taking this."

5.

THE FRONT DOOR OF ALCRON TECHNICAL Industries seemed almost excessively mundane. Usually, corporate offices tried to appear at least somewhat aesthetically pleasing on the outside, even if they were in a place that didn't attract visitors; it helped set the right tone for guests, clients, and investors. But Alcron had clearly gone with a different stylistic choice. No tastefully-stained glass or well-crafted logo adorned their exterior; instead, it was a large gray door with the name of the company in small print.

"Looks normal to me," Amy said. I often forgot that, as much as she knew about magic, Amy was woefully under-equipped with knowledge on the way things worked in a corporate office environment.

"Trust me, it isn't." I reached for the doorknob, only to be stopped when a large hand wrapped firmly around my wrist.

"If this is the place, they might have trapped the door," Bubba said. He released his grip on me slowly, as if afraid I might dart forward and try to grab the knob anyway, just for the heck of it.

"Which is precisely where I come in." Amy rummaged around in her purse, filling the nearby air with the sound of tinkling glass as bottles (far more than should have been able to fit in such as a small purse) bounced off one another. At last, she produced a small vial filled with an emerald-colored liquid. With a quick twist of the cap, Amy pulled off the top and downed its entire contents.

"Just out of curiosity, why did you bring so many potions to a simple dinner gala?" I asked.

Amy closed her eyes and shook her head vigorously from side to side. When she stopped and reopened her eyes, they glowed with the same color as the liquid that had been in the vial. "Because it's a party, which means it's a great chance for me to move some product. That's the key to successful business, Fred. Always be looking for opportunity."

"Ah, right." I often let it slip my mind that Amy's income as a mage came from her exceptional capability in designing potions strong enough to create reality-altering states for even the most powerful of parahumans. While, in my human days, I might have expected these to be used as a weapon or poison, I had since learned that the vast majority of her clients bought them for recreational use.

Amy moved between Bubba and me, shifting us slightly to the side as she examined the door. I had no idea what she was looking at, but it was certainly keeping her attention rapt. After several silent moments, she turned back to us.

"We're definitely at the right place." Amy jerked a thumb over her shoulder, gesturing to the door. "This thing is warded up and down. Luckily, the vast majority of the stuff is built around keeping things in—sound, magic, all the shit that might tip someone off to Gideon's existence. Focusing all that magic inwardly made it more or less impossible to ward against things getting in, similar to the way any good door with a lock only swings one way. Too bad for us, though, they did add a few spells to send out an alarm if the door gets opened."

"Meaning if we go in, we tip off the other dragon, whose only obstacle is a room full of weakened parahumans," I said.

"No, they're in a room full of weakened parahumans and two agents," Bubba corrected me. "I'd say we press on, even if it was just Krystal in there. With Arch around too . . . we don't need to worry about the other guests. We need to worry about Gideon."

"Is Arch really that powerful? Every sense I have keeps telling me he's human."

"Yeah, but I bet Krystal reads the same way." Bubba reached over and patted me on the shoulder. "Agents are their own kind of breed. Don't try to understand them, just trust that they can do their job. Because, since I'm powered down and Amy doesn't need to waste a strength potion on this, it's on you to bust down the door."

"I don't have any idea how to do that." I'd seen lots of movies where people ran through doors, but I had assumed that to be mere Hollywood license. Sure as Bubba seemed about the agents dealing with our rogue dragon, I didn't really want to dilly-dally about on the door once the alarm was tripped.

"With your strength, a single kick near the knob should do it," Amy said. "Enough force will either break the lock out of the wall or the door off the lock, and either one suits our purposes."

I walked up to the door and raised a single leg, focusing on staying balanced while also doing my best to aim; the last thing I needed was to ram my foot through the door and get stuck. Leaning back just a touch, I thrust my foot forward, landing the sole of my well-shined shoe a few inches above the knob. The door buckled, but remained in one piece—though it now possessed a large, shoe-shaped dent in it.

"Looks like they didn't skimp on materials," Bubba noted. "You're gonna have to get a real piece of that thing."

Rearing back again, I took aim and struck, targeting the same spot. Unlike before, I blocked out any fears of falling through, focusing instead on putting as much power as I could muster into the kick. Moments later, a loud cracking sound filled the air and the door swung open, tattered remnants of a deadbolt still wedged into the wall as the door moved freely.

"If I'm being perfectly honest, I think a part of me has always wanted to do that." I lowered my foot to the floor carefully, as though it might wildly lash out and destroy another piece of the building if not handled delicately.

"The first one is always the best," Bubba agreed. I was tempted to ask him exactly what he meant by that, but then we were through the door and into the proper offices of Alcron Technical Industries. Or, rather, what should have been offices.

There were no uncomfortable rolling chairs present— the hallmark of any good office environment—nor were there desks to sit at, computers to work on, or chest-high walls to divide the peons and curb unproductive chatter.

In fact, there was nothing remotely office-like at all. The whole area was completely bare, save for a single object.

A massive metal cube took up the vast majority of the floor, with perhaps five feet of space on any given side, save for the front. There were dozens of runes on it, similar to the ones I'd seen outside the building, only far more complex. I'd never really tried to imagine what sort of cage it would take to hold a dragon, but this seemed about right.

Amy let out a soft, low whistle as she stared at the gleaming monstrosity. "This is incredible. I mean, just glancing over the spellcraft on this thing, I can already get a sense of the depth someone put in. Whoever made this must have put in *years* on it."

"Got it, damn thing is a piece of art. Now, how do we bust it the hell up?" Bubba asked.

"I'm going to need a few minutes to figure that out." Amy walked slowly through the room, analyzing each rune carefully, and then following it to the next. As she moved, her hands dug in her purse, rooting aimlessly for a concoction I could only imagine the effects of.

"I hate to be the one to bring this up, but are you sure we'll be able to smash it?" I asked. "If this was made by a dragon, isn't there a chance that we aren't strong enough to break Gideon's cage?"

"Fred, with enough time and knowledge, a human could tear apart a prison built by a god," Amy said. "There is always a way, if you're willing to pay the price for it." Two potions came out of the purse and into Amy's hand. She opened them both and downed them simultaneously. It was a trick I'd only ever seen Bubba do with two beers, yet she pulled it off without spilling a drop.

"In about five minutes, I'm going to be comatose." Amy glanced over at us, clearly noting the obvious alarm in both of our faces. "I'll be fine after a day or so, but it means this is the last I'm going to be able to contribute tonight."

"Why would you drink something that does that?" (I will admit that I may have sounded a bit more frantic than the situation called for, but it was the surge of emotion I felt at the time.)

"Because during these next five minutes, I'm going to be the smartest mage in this and every other plane in existence." Amy looked back at the cube and took a long breath. "If there's a way to crack this bastard, I'll find it. You two just make sure nothing distracts me."

I was about to assure her that we would keep ourselves quiet, when I noticed the sound of heavy breathing and hurried steps coming from a few floors down. I looked at Bubba, who showed no signs of awareness, since his hearing was lessened along with the rest of him.

"That might prove difficult. It sounds like there are four, no, five people currently en route to our location, moving as fast as they can."

"Sounds like our dragon wasn't working alone," Bubba said. "I really hate dealing with smart opponents."

"What do we do?" I asked.

"You heard Amy. She needs time to work. That means there's only one thing we can do: hold the line. No matter what comes through that door, we don't let it near her."

I gave a nod and tried to ignore the way my stomach was doing cartwheels. Violence. It always seemed to come back to violence, an avenue I was so terribly ill-suited for. This time, however, there was no Krystal to protect us, no stronger friend to hide behind. I was currently the strongest of us, which meant the others would have to depend on me to keep them safe.

Not for the first time in my afterlife, I was very thankful that vampires couldn't throw up.

6.

THE FOOTSTEPS WERE STILL A WAYS DOWN the hall when I finally realized that I'd mis-analyzed our situation. It was the breathing that gave it away. The heavy breathing of our impending opponents led me to notice their quickened pulses—their hearts were racing after running up several flights of stairs. Except a mere effort like that should have been nothing for most parahumans.

"Oh, for the love of . . ." I resisted smacking myself in the head, but only barely. "Those wards affected everyone who came in the building, right? Even if it was someone who was in cahoots with the dragon?"

"Unless they had enough juice to be considered comparable, or were apparently carting around dragon blood," Bubba confirmed.

"Little less talking would be nice while I try to unravel the secrets of an ancient arcane lock." Amy had made it halfway around the cube, causing her voice to echo off the surrounding walls, tinny and distant.

"That means whoever these people are, they're probably close to human too."

"Right, but given your usual attitude toward spillin' blood, I can't imagine that will work too much in our favor," Bubba said.

"We don't have to fight them; we just have to stop them. And if they're almost human, then I know exactly how to do just that." I raced forward, all too aware of how close our enemy had drawn, and grabbed the door. I slammed it shut, then turned around and braced myself against the seam where it would have connected to the lock.

"This thing is reinforced. I'm betting they can't punch through it," I declared. "At least, not in five minutes."

"Down to four, actually," Amy called from somewhere on the other side of the cube.

Bubba stared at me for a moment, then rushed across the room, throwing his bulk against the door right before a huge force struck it from the other side. I was so taken by surprise that I bucked forward, my smooth-soled shoes slipping against the dull gray carpet beneath them. Luckily, Bubba's own strike was enough to hold the door shut, and I quickly put myself back in position.

Whoever was on the other side slammed against the door with constant, frantic blows. They were powerful, even with the runes reducing their power, but between my vampiric strength and Bubba's hefty body, we were able to keep the door shut through the first wave of attack.

"Damn, I'm really missing my weresteed form right about now," Bubba panted from my side. He was bracing the door with his arms, heels dug into the carpet and sweat already beginning to drip down his face. "Nobody moves a horse that don't want to be moved."

A huge *slam* hit the door as one of the would-be intruders threw their entire body at it. The door held, thankfully, though I had to wonder how much more the frame could take. Sooner or later, they'd knock it off its hinges. All I could do was hope it would be later.

"I'm missing your weresteed form too. I'm no good at this sort of job."

Bubba snorted and shook his head. "Coulda fooled me. Seems like at least once a month you're yanking somebody out of trouble."

"I assure you—" Another huge blow struck the door, followed immediately by a second, and Bubba and

I both focused on keeping our only barrier of safety in place.

"I assure you, it's almost always happenstance and coincidence."

"Whatever you say." Bubba didn't seem like he believed me, but his face was red from effort and sweat poured freely down his collar. Arguing, clearly, was a luxury he could not spare the energy for.

Amy emerged from the opposite side of the cube, a faint halo of swirling, colored lights around her head. "I've got a mixed bag of news. Pretty sure I found a way to open a gate in this thing, but I'm equally sure it's not going to let in anyone but a dragon. Also, I'm going to be dropping in about another minute here, so it's doubtful I'll figure out any other entrance."

"That really seems like all bad news," I told her, gritting my teeth as another shower of attacks fell on the door at my back.

"It probably is, but we do have one shot: that dragon blood in you has kept you safe from suppressing runes and draconic auras. There's a fair chance that you might be able to pass through whatever gate I can open."

"Well then, sure, let's give that a try."

"Hang on, wasn't done," Amy said. "It might let you through, but remember what I said about dragon magic being unpredictable? Trying to pass through the warded gate might also blow you up, or turn you into a bunny, or any other of a million possibilities. One drop of blood does not a dragon make."

"Forget it, we'll just have to tear the damn thing apart the old-fashioned way," Bubba grunted, face still staring at the floor.

He wouldn't hold much longer; neither would the door, for that matter. Amy was going to be passed out and helpless in under a minute, and even if I were in any way good at fighting, there was still no way I could look out for both of them in that sort of situation. If I'd had time to think about it, I certainly would have tried to find a solution that posed less risk, but in that moment, the most hard-wired piece of my mind took over: the accountant.

Two of my friends' lives, plus Gideon's, plus the ones up in the gala, all weighed against my own. The math was simple.

"Open the gate," I told Amy, readjusting my feet to keep the door in place for what I hoped would be long enough.

"On it." Amy scrambled over to the cube, running her fingers along it in patterns I didn't recognize. Having her consciousness on a clock helped her understand the urgency of the situation. Bubba, however, was not so inclined to accept my decision.

"Fred, don't be an idiot. Gettin' yourself destroyed doesn't do a damn thing to help anyone."

"Amy said I could pass through."

"Amy said you *might* be able to pass through. Maybe. As in, there is some chance," Bubba said. "And even if it does work, you have no idea what's through there. For all we know, you could end up trapped just like Gideon."

"I'm aware of the risks."

"Then why are you doing this?" Bubba's words were somewhere between a yell and a groan as he pressed against the warped frame of the door with all his might, driving back the attackers who'd started to gain ground.

"I don't know!" I was yelling too, trying to be heard over the steady thundering of our adversary's attacks. "I don't have a good reason. I'm not stupid; I know it's probably going to backfire or mess me up. I know I'm not the guy who saves the day. But . . . but I guess I'm also not the guy who can do nothing while the people he loves gets hurt."

"Fred!" Amy hollered from her position across the room. "It's go time!" As she spoke, a panel in the cube slid away, revealing a rectangle filled with orange light. Not even my enhanced vision could make out what was on the other side—which didn't surprise me in the slightest.

I started to move forward, then felt the door buckle behind me. I'd nearly forgotten that without me holding the door, they'd easily overpower Bubba. That would leave both him and Amy completely defenseless.

"Go. I got this," Bubba snapped. He took a long, deep breath, and then shuffled over slightly, putting himself dead center on the door.

"Bubba, not even you can—"

"I *got* this. Trust me."

For a moment, I hesitated. Then I saw the look in his eye—more ferocious and determined than I'd glimpsed even a hint of before. He was telling the truth. He would hold this door with everything he had. It was on me to make it back in time.

"Thank you," I said.

Then I was off, dashing through the room before I had a chance to think about any of it. If I let my brain kick into gear, it would find a reason to take me off course. It always did. The only shot I had (that any of us had) was my body moving before my brain really understood was going on.

I tore through the room at top speed, passing Amy as she settled on the floor and the lights around her head started to fade. I didn't slow down—not for her, not even when I got close to the orange doorway in the middle of the cube. There was no slowing down, no stopping. This was all or nothing.

I hit the doorway still going top speed. All the sound from the room died out instantly as I hurdled through what felt like an eternal, empty orange void. Come what may, I was across the threshold.

Everything dissolved, and I fell into nothingness.

7.

"WELL, THIS IS CERTAINLY UNEXPECTED."

The voice was the first thing I'd heard since plunging through that orange doorway. Only when my ears registered it did I notice that I was also touching the ground; I could feel it pushing against my body where I was sprawled out. Carefully, I peeled my eyes open, overwhelmed to see something other than that strange abyss I'd stepped through. It was impossible to say how long it had taken me to cross over. I could only hope it was on the shorter end of the spectrum.

Pulling myself up from the ground, I took in my surroundings. The inside of the cube was lined with more runes, which ran across the floor and ceiling as well. They wove through the interior, stopping only in the floor's center, where they formed a wide circle encompassing a single occupant. Sitting in the middle, legs crossed and wearing a bored expression, was Gideon. At least, I hoped he was the real Gideon. By this point, I was starting to take nothing for granted.

"Are you okay?" I asked, finishing the act of rising and adjusting my now rumpled jacket.

"Just peachy. I love being locked up like this. Might have Sinorah make me one of these to replace my bed."

I relaxed momentarily. If Gideon could be snide, then he probably wasn't hurt, just stuck. My ease quickly ended when I recalled that there was a soon-to-be-overpowered Bubba and a defenseless Amy waiting for assistance. We didn't have time for pleasantries.

"I'm here to break you out."

"And here I assumed you just wanted to come visit."

"Gideon, enough." I raised my voice ever so slightly, all too aware of the fact that I was speaking to a being who could probably destroy me with little more than a thought. "Please, there isn't time for you to be glib. Amy and Bubba are in danger right outside, and who knows what the other dragon is doing to everyone else. I don't know anything about how all this magic stuff works, so I'm going to need your help to get you free."

"The other dragon's name is Sinorah," Gideon said, tone still flat and bored. "And she may not be as old or strong as I am, but she still weaves a fine spell. It will take another dragon or an archmage to break me out of here. I appreciate the sentiment of what you're trying to do; it's just not enough."

"But . . . there are people out there who need you." My eyes searched around frantically, trying to find something, anything, my brain might find familiar. As they scanned, I realized I didn't even see an orange doorway like the one I'd entered through. The entire interior was smooth and unbroken.

"Some of whom will certainly die," Gideon agreed. "I dislike it, but there is nothing to be done. Sinorah managed to trick me, and now, I've been removed from the game board. It is embarrassing, and perhaps a bit humbling, but it has happened. There is no undoing what has been done."

"How can you be so calm about this? What about everyone up there? What about Sally? Richard told me you're engaged or something, doesn't at least she matter to you?" I was grasping at straws by this point, my mind already filling with horrid images of what was happening to Bubba and Amy just outside the metal walls.

Gideon's eyes flashed (and I mean that literally) as his expression warped from bored to fierce. I practically saw the fire in his mouth as he spoke (and again, I'm speaking quite literally here). "Sally Alderson is more valuable than you could possibly fathom, blood-eater. Not just to me, but to all of my dwindling kind. Sinorah would not dare try to harm her. She will have taken up my duties as guardian, just as she assumed my identity."

"Are you sure about that?" I was prodding a dragon at this point, but it wasn't like I had much in the way of options. "Sally wasn't at the gala, even though 'you' were. Krystal told me she'd taken ill over the last few days, right around the time you probably vanished. That sure doesn't seem like Sinorah keeping her close and safe."

By this point, I had seen a limited array of emotions from Gideon, King of the West. Disdain, annoyance, dismissal, anger, boredom, and even kindness when he was talking to Sally. That day, however, I saw something I had never witnessed cross Gideon's face, something I wouldn't have suspected was even possible.

That day, I saw fear in Gideon's eyes.

He rose from his sitting position, the momentary hint of terror gone as a building rage took it's place. "That whelp. She dares to let the Tiamat fall into illness, or, worse, she is trying to drain that magic herself."

"The what?" I liked where this was going, but it had suddenly become hard to follow.

He paid me no mind, eyes flashing as he looked around the room, seemingly seeing it for the first time. Finally, those eyes settled on me, and Gideon let out a long, slow breath.

"Blood-eater, how badly do you wish to save your friends?"

"Bad enough to probably agree to whatever crazy thing you're going to ask of me."

Gideon smiled, a dangerous baring of teeth that sent a wave of terror through my stomach. "You understand well how these things work. My earlier words were true: this cage cannot be broken by anything save for another dragon or an extremely skilled user of magic. Of the two of us, I happen to fit both criteria, but cannot leave my circle. You can walk in and out freely, yet you lack the necessary power and skill to affect anything outside of it."

"Yes, yes, I know, I'm useless. Now, tell me how we can break you free."

"Not useless, just weak." Gideon's hands shimmered as long claws extended from his fingernails. "Your type has a unique trait, though. You can take strength from more powerful creatures. With a little magic of my own, and a healthy dose of blood, you can be turned into a suitable vessel for me to work through."

"How . . . how much blood are we talking?" A single drop had left me so strong that it took me days before I got the hang of it. I couldn't imagine what a full dose of Gideon's blood would do to me.

"Enough." He lifted his right arm and gently ran a claw down his left forearm. The flesh parted, revealing a small red river drifting lazily down his arm. "Bear in mind, this is not a boon or a blessing. The power needed to break apart this cage will likely consume all that I can give you, and perhaps a bit more. This is powerful magic, and as you should know by now, magic always comes with a price."

I stepped forward, walking across the room and stepping over the circle, into the heart of Gideon's cage. "Just promise me you'll save my friends. That's *my* price."

"You are a strange one, blood-eater. Most would ask more from a king." Gideon's claws shrank away, and he dipped a fingertip in the blood. Reaching upward, he began to draw something on my forehead with it.

"I don't need more. My friends are the only valuable thing I have. If you save them, that's enough. And my name is Fred, not blood-eater."

"Very well then, Fred." Gideon finished his drawing and lifted the still-bleeding arm up to my face. "I will honor your bargain. No matter what may become of you, know that I will personally protect your friends. And, if I am too late to fulfill that duty, I will avenge them with great prejudice."

I didn't want to think about that part; in fact, I was trying hard not to dwell on any of what was happening. Instead, I focused on the one thing I knew I had to do to save my friends. For once, I was thankful for the vampire instincts that came bundled with my body. They were screaming at me to drink the dragon blood whose scent was filling my nostrils. That primitive voice was drowning out the rest of me, the parts that were too scared of what might happen if I did, or worried about whether or not I'd survive. Those were all concerns of the human side of me, the part that valued survival over everything else. All the vampire inside me knew was blood. Sweet, powerful, dripping blood. I'd spent so much of my time trying to ignore that aspect of who I was, but in that moment, it was my closest ally.

I'll skip the specifics, because I've yet to find a way to talk about drinking blood that doesn't come across as . . . unsavory. The point is, I drank, and as I did, I could feel Gideon's power flowing through me. A single drop had made me nearly lose my mind; the first mouthful plunged me beyond a state of thought. Still, my body continued working on autopilot, drinking all it could from the still flowing wound. I have no idea how long we stood like that, there was no time when I was in that state. All I know is that when Gideon drew away, I felt as though I had swallowed a dozen suns. The power radiating through me was beyond reason. To know that this existed in the same world I occupied, to truly understand it, would have driven me to the ground in a fit of sheer existential panic. Thankfully, I was not the one in the primary pilot's seat at that moment.

Gideon was in my mind, just as his blood was in my body. I could feel the tingle of the rune on my forehead as my legs turned and walked out of the circle. I was aware of it; I was aware of so much that it threatened to drown me in madness. I could feel the very spin of the earth beneath my feet, hear the sound of raindrops from states away. If this was how Gideon lived every day of his life, I had no idea how he bore it.

"All right, blood-eat . . . Fred. It's time to go to work."

My body complied, reaching for the nearest rune as words I'd never heard before began tumbling out of my mouth.

I can't tell you what Gideon did with my body. Not out of any desire to keep the arcane ceremony a secret or some such nonsense, but because the headrush of his blood, paired with the complete foreignness of what I was doing, means that the memories I do have of that time are hazy and nonsensical. The only part I remember with any clarity is the very end, when my pale hands were laid down on the outer runes of the circle around him.

"Try to hang on," Gideon warned me. "This part might be a little rough."

Then, with no more warning, my world lit up in a flurry of static, pain, and the sensation of being drained. It was thankfully brief, but the intensity was such that it seemed to stretch on for days. I have no idea when, or how, it ended. One moment I was engulfed in the madness, feeling all that power inside me crash itself against an opposing force . . .

And then, there was only darkness.

8.

THE RINGING IN MY EARS ROUSED ME—
incessant bells clanging through my head and pulling
me out of what had previously been a peaceful slum-
ber. As I opened my eyes, I realized that I was no longer
in the cube. Or, rather, that the cube no longer existed
in any recognizable shape. Shattered metal surrounded
me, huge chunks torn away and scattered about. Some
of the shards had even been wedged into nearby walls.
Only minutes before, I would have found such a spectacular display of strength to be mind-boggling. After

holding a fraction of Gideon's power, I was more impressed by his restraint than anything else.

Getting to my feet, I was struck by how much my body ached. Since becoming a vampire, I'd been hurt more than once, but the general pains of wear on a body were a thing of the past. My natural resiliency and rapid healing negated daily damage faster than it could pile up. It seemed that was not the case with channeling dragon magic, however. I was going to need a healthy dose of blood—human, this time—before I was back at a hundred percent.

It was only after standing that I noticed the corpses around me. There were five of them, and I couldn't recognize any from what remained of their faces, so I it seemed like good odds that none were Bubba and Amy. As I began trudging out of the room, it occurred to me that I should have been overwhelmed by the scent of their blood. Instead, it was something I'd had to mentally hunt for, sorting through the smells of the room to pick it out.

Once I made it outside the office, I heard a racket from several floors below. People were yelling, furniture was being smashed, and . . . and actually, that was all I could make out. The ringing in my ears had largely faded, but my hearing still wasn't able to discern what was going on in any fine detail.

I was halfway to the elevator when I finally snapped to what was going on. (In my defense, being piloted by an ancient dragon is a mentally draining experience. But I got there eventually.) The runes in the building suppressed the power of anyone who wasn't as powerful as the caster, or carting around the blood of someone stronger. Whatever Gideon had done must have used up all of the draconic power inside me. I was just a vampire again, and that meant I was as susceptible to the suppression magic as everyone else.

Truthfully, that fact should have terrified me, but, more than anything, I felt relieved. Carrying around even a small piece of Gideon's magic had been a strange experience, more than I really wanted to deal with. Just being a vampire was plenty for me; I didn't need to go augmenting myself like Quinn, my awful sire. It was good to be back to normal. Well, my version of "normal," anyway.

I punched the down button on the elevator just as a giant roar shook the building. I nearly fell over, barely catching myself against the wall in time. Right, no vampire dexterity to compensate for my natural clumsiness. This would take some getting used to.

After the roar, I decided that stairs were probably a safer bet and made my way down the hallway to the nearest stairwell. At this point, I had no idea where I was heading, only that I wanted to make sure everyone was okay. I made it down three flights before I missed my footing. I grabbed for the railing, but my hands were too slow, and I ended up falling forward. I bounced three times before landing on my head.

Vampires can't sleep during the night. It's just one of those things I'd gotten used to over the years. But apparently, dragon magic isn't to be underestimated, because I still managed to pass out at the bottom of the stairwell.

When I came to, the first thing I noticed was the scent of the person who was holding me up. It hit me before I even registered that I was standing, or that I was outside the building, or any other of the inane details that followed. No, the scent came first, overwhelming every other piece of information and telling me exactly who I was near. It wasn't a particularly rational way for my brain to process what was happening, but, then again, isn't love supposed to be irrational by design?

"Easy there, big fella," Krystal said, walking us another few steps forward. "You should start feeling better any minute now."

She was right. Already I could tell that the small pains in my body were fading away, though the pronounced headache I'd suddenly acquired seemed to be taking its sweet time. I probably could have supported myself and stopped leaning on her, but I didn't try. At that moment, I needed the proximity for a support that had nothing to do with the state of my physical being.

Krystal slid me onto a bench, and I pulled her with me. She didn't resist, and the two of us were soon seated, staring at Richard's building. A large chunk of the wall had been blasted out, and the pouring smoke told the story of a fire smoldering somewhere inside. In the distance, I could hear sirens as the various response teams raced to the scene, but none of the gala guests milling about looked particularly worried.

"Is everyone okay?"

"Not *everyone* everyone, but all of the gang made it through fine," Krystal assured me. "Gideon punched into the room with Bubba and Amy in hand—well . . . claw, really—and dropped them with me before attacking the imposter. Arch and I started evacuating everyone, but when dragons fight there's bound to be a few caught in the crossfire. Still, we cleared as many people out as we could. Arch even went and got Sally out of her room personally."

"That was good of him."

"I know Arch comes off rough, but he's one of the good guys. Besides, it was the only way to keep Richard from charging up there himself," Krystal said. "Anyway, we were nearly out when Bubba finally told me that you'd been left behind when Gideon popped out of his cage. I went hunting for you, only to find my boyfriend passed out in the stairs like a freshman after a kegger."

"If only. Merlot hangovers have nothing on what Gideon left me with." My head was slowly clearing as my vampiric healing kicked back into gear, but it was sure taking longer than I would have preferred. Were I a car, my gas light would no doubt have been on.

"Yeah, we're going to have to have a long chat about that, once you're feeling better," Krystal said. "I've grabbed bits and pieces, but this seems like the kind of story I'm going to have to file a report about."

"I'll do my best, but I'm warning you right now that the details will be fuzzy," I told her. My mind wandered back into the cube and the conversation with Gideon. Already, I was trying to sort through it and get everything catalogued into a nice, prepared package for when Krystal asked her questions. As I sifted through, though, something stuck out to me.

"Krystal, do you know what a 'tiamat' is?"

"If memory serves, it's a creature from dragon lore, named after the mythological mother of dragon kind. They're supposed to be a sort of half-breed or something. They were revered because they could birth full-blooded dragons, but with a much higher rate, hence the mother-dragon reference. It's very difficult for dragons to conceive, which is pretty much the only reason they don't rule the planet. Why do you ask?"

Had there been any pulsing blood in my face, it no doubt would have drained away as the implications of her words set in. I might not know the details, but there was no doubt in my mind that I'd just stumbled across something far more important than a man of my level was meant to know. It was the sort of realization that would likely haunt my thoughts for some while, so I chose to veer away from it rather than dwell.

"Just curious. This whole thing has got me interested in dragons. By the way, what was this" —I gestured to the shattered part of Richard's building— "whole thing, anyway?"

"Near as we could figure, a second attempt at a coo. Seems that new leader the other tribe elected had a lot more in common with the first than we realized. He was smarter, at least. Hired another dragon to neutralize Gideon when they made their move."

"I was afraid it would be something like that." I sighed. "Let me guess: this will put something of a damper on their diplomatic negotiations."

"No, Fred. There aren't going to be any more negotiations." Krystal reached over and put her arm around my shoulders, pulling me in closer. "That tribe locked up the King of the West. Even if Gideon were inclined to feel merciful, there are political ramifications to that which he can't let slide."

"You're saying the other tribe will have to find shelter elsewhere."

"I'm saying that, by the time the sun rises, there isn't going to be a second tribe." Krystal kept her eyes trained forward, watching the wind move bits of glass that littered the sidewalk.

I should have been shocked, or outraged, or grief-stricken for all those Gideon was no doubt already hunting down, but all of that would come later. In that moment, I was just too tired to muster up more than a cursory sense of sadness. It didn't seem right to purge an entire tribe of therians based on the actions of a few; however, I could understand why Gideon felt it necessary. It was that fact, more than anything he was doing, that disturbed me.

"When you're feeling better, we can go find the others," Krystal told me. "They're probably with Arch. He was rounding people up when I went back to get you."

"That sounds nice," I said. "After all this, I just want to see that everyone's safe and go back to the apartment."

"Same here." Krystal rose from the bench, keeping her hand intertwined with mine as she pulled me up. She leaned over and kissed me on the cheek, leaving a slight smear of red lipstick when she pulled away.

"Let's get our family and go home."

9.

"YOU'RE SURE ABOUT THIS?" ARCH ASKED. His eyes were narrowed; he was clearly still wary of the offer.

"It was never my decision to make, but she says it's fine, so it's fine," I told him.

"Just be sure you wipe your feet," Charlotte added. "I don't need anyone muddying up my clean floors."

It was three days after the fiasco at Richard's, and I'd more or less gotten myself back to full strength. Admittedly, I still felt a touch off (not bad mind you, just off), but for all intents and purposes I was back in my regular condition. Once the dust had settled, and I'd heard the accounts from everyone about how much Arch had helped, I realized that we were indebted to him. There wasn't much I could offer an agent, of course, but I had hit upon one thing that might benefit both him and someone in need of company.

"I know how to keep clean," Arch said. He and Charlotte had been introduced the evening prior, and I'd left them to chat for a trial night to see if the arrangement suited all those involved. She hadn't tried to kill him, nor he her, and both seemed amiable enough toward the other. I suspected that was as good as I was going to get.

"It's true," Krystal said. "You should see his desk. So organized it makes our records vault look like shambles in comparison."

"Our records vault is shambles," Arch said.

"Cynthia has her system, and I'm sure as shit not going to be the one to try and talk her into changing it," Krystal replied.

Arch said nothing, which I was slowly learning to recognize was his way of yielding a point. Seizing the momentary lull in banter, I made a slight coughing sound in my throat so that we could get the discussion back on track.

"Regarding the matter at hand, I have some paperwork for you both to sign." I reached into the briefcase set before me and pulled out the final sets of documents, sliding them over to Charlotte.

The four of us were in the Charlotte Manor dining room (a place where I'd all too recently been held hostage), hammering out the final details of Arch's new living arrangement. Moonlight shone through the window, but, in spite of the late hour, Charlotte had agreed to make us a celebratory meal, and I could scarcely wait to be done with the meeting and on to enjoying her culinary artistry.

"Feel free to peruse the fine print, but you'll find I worked in the finalized conditions," I said. "Arch will pay a set amount of rent each month to retain one of Charlotte's rooms, whether he is actually in town or not. That money will be used, at Charlotte's discretion, for updating features and incorporating new technology."

"Pretty curious to see what all this internet hub-bub is about," Charlotte muttered.

"In return for the rent, Charlotte will provide Arch with three meals per day, weekly turndown and laundry service, as well as reasonable security," I continued. "Everyone good with that?"

"Still a little insulted that my security is defined as 'reasonable'," Charlotte said.

"Don't take it personally; you should see what he says about The White House," Krystal said. "From Arch, 'reasonable' is about as high of praise as you're going to get."

"Guess I'll have to take it." Charlotte produced a pen from somewhere unseen and scratched her name into the paper before her. When she was done, she moved the pages across the table to Arch, who produced a gleaming metal writing implement and proceeded to do the same.

"Excellent. Now, I'll just need to sign on as caretaker for the funds," I said.

Arch slid the pages across to me, his pen still on top of it, which stopped inches away from where I sat. Like everything else he did, it was eerily accurate and precise. I still had no idea exactly what Arch was, and the more I dwelled on that fact, the happier I was with my ignorance. If my realization about Sally Alderson had taught me nothing else, it was that there was peace to be found in the darkness.

I plucked the pen up from the pages and quickly scrawled my signature across the final line. Looking it over, I noticed Charlotte had forgotten to put the date next to her name. It was a minor matter that I could easily have remedied, but it was better to get her accustomed to how contracts worked. There would doubtlessly be more in her future, as we brought her into the modern age.

"Charlotte, you need to put the date next to your signature." I slid the pages back over to her.

"Sorry." She reached forward, intent on picking up Arch's pen, but when her fingers made contact, she let out a soft yelp and jerked them away. Small wisps of smoke rose from her fingers, and she stared angrily at the table's residents. "What the hell! Why did you give me a silver pen?"

"My mistake," Arch said. "I keep that one in case I need an quick, covert weapon. This one should be fine." He pulled out a golden pen and held it out to Charlotte.

"Yeah, no thanks. I'll use my own." She re-summoned the same pen she'd used the first time, then pointed to the silver one still resting on the documents. "Someone get that thing away from me."

Arch reached forward, but Krystal put a hand on his arm before he made it to the pen.

"Fred . . . why didn't you notice it was silver?" Her voice was soft and low; though, based on the look in her eyes, I could sense that violence was only a few wrong words away. I could hardly blame her. I'd just been wondering the same thing myself. Silver grounded magic, and it was essentially poison to creatures composed of it—like me, or Charlotte. Touching that pen should have smarted like heck, but I hadn't even realized it was made of the stuff.

"I honestly have no idea." I reached over and picked up the pen, bracing myself for a shock, a burn, or even a low-level tingle. Instead, there was nothing. It was like I was holding any other piece of metal.

I heard the click of the gun before I saw that she'd drawn it. Krystal had the sight trained on my head, and at this range, I highly doubted she'd miss.

"Nothing personal if that's really you, Fred, but after that fake Gideon, I'm not taking any chances."

"Did I miss something?" Charlotte asked. She seemed remarkably calm, given that someone had just drawn a gun at her dinner table.

"Fred seems to be unaffected by silver, which should be impossible for a vampire," Arch explained. "Agent Jenkins thus suspects that her boyfriend has been replaced by an imposter, most likely a fey, who doesn't share that allergy."

"Well, she's wrong. This is the same Fred I met a few weeks back, and he's definitely not a fey," Charlotte said. "If anyone has made the veiling magic to beat my detection abilities, I've yet to see it."

"Really? You didn't mention that when you were listing your security features," Arch said. His voice was slightly higher, and it was quite possibly the first time he'd shown genuine interest in something since I'd met him.

"Just one of those things. The mages who built me added a ton of features to make sure I could discern friend from foe. Now, since I only met Fred recently, I can't say that this is the original one you two met, but he's definitely the only one I've ever known."

"Okay," Krystal said, slowly lowering her gun. "But that doesn't explain the silver."

"Perhaps it's only ineffective when applied externally," Arch suggested. Before I could offer an opinion of my own, he had thrown a small dagger across the table and struck me in my shoulder.

"*Gaah*!" My yelp came as soon as the blade pierced my flesh, more reaction than an actual expression of pain. After a few seconds, I realized that the dagger didn't really hurt at all. Reaching up carefully, I wiggled it a bit and found that, while it was certainly not comfortable, it wasn't exceptionally painful either. "Actually, I would like to retract my scream. This isn't really all that bad."

"Pure silver," Arch said. "And it doesn't bother you in the slightest?"

"Sorry . . . but no. The fact that you just ruined my shirt, however, does have me a bit miffed." I pulled the dagger out and set it on the table.

"It has to be a side effect from whatever Gideon did," Krystal said. "I have no idea how that could have happened though."

"Amy warned me several times that dragon magic is unpredictable."

"We'll have to call in a specialist," Arch told Krystal.

"I very much dislike the sound of that," I said.

"Don't worry about it." Krystal reached over and took my hand. If she felt any compunction about such a tender action less than a minute after pulling a firearm on me, it certainly didn't show. "We'll figure this out. You've always been a bit different than most vampires; this is just another thing that makes you one of a kind."

"Though, really, the accounting job is far more bizarre," Arch added.

"I get the feeling that this is sort of a big deal," Charlotte said. "So, if you all want to skip dinner—"

"No," I sighed, shaking my head. "Charlotte, you will learn this sooner or later, but with us, there is seldom a time when there isn't some worry or emergency to deal with. Curious though my silver immunity might be, I see no reason to skip an excellent meal over it. Besides, you and Arch have reason to celebrate. As of today, you have a full-time tenant, and he has a place to live."

"Okay then, let's eat," Charlotte said.

The kitchen doors sprang open and the wait staff filled the dining room, trays of food already giving off aromas that made my mouth water. As they paraded around us, Krystal leaned over and whispered in my ear.

"I'm proud of you, Fred. A year ago, something like this would have had you in fits."

"Sadly, I think I'm slowly beginning to build up a tolerance to the panic-inspiring events that seem to plague us," I whispered back.

"Just don't get too tolerant. I like you just the way you are, panic and all."

"And I love you as you are, death-courting job and all."

That wasn't how I'd ever intended to say it for the first time. In truth, I don't know that I had ever really intended to say it. That was the sort of thing that took more bravery than men like me were born with, but it seemed folly could intervene where courage dared not tread. But there it was—in Charlotte Manor, the sentient house, and surrounded by non-existent waiters and an agent I didn't wholly trust, while still processing the fact that I might not be as back to normal as I hoped— I'd told Krystal Jenkins that I loved her for the first time.

She stared at me for a long moment, then gave me a tomcat grin and slid back to her chair. It wouldn't be until later that night, when we were alone and the environment was more intimate, that she would echo my sentiment with her own voice. That was fine, I didn't need to hear it right away. I'd known it for a long while, just as she had no doubt been aware of my feelings for her. Neither Krystal nor I were the most expressive of people, emotionally speaking, but it didn't mean we were incapable of getting better.

Undead or alive, human or parahuman, everyone is capable of taking steps forward. Ours might have been moving at a lurching, unwieldy pace, but we were taking them all the same. It was irrelevant if we might have been a bit slower than more socially adjusted people.

We were taking our steps together, and that was all that really mattered.

ABOUT DREW

Drew Hayes is an aspiring author from Texas who has written several books and found the gumption to publish a few (so far). He graduated from Texas Tech with a B.A. in English, because evidently he's not familiar with what the term "employable" means. Drew has been called one of the most profound, prolific, and talented authors of his generation, but a table full of drunks will say almost anything when offered a round of free shots. Drew feels kind of like a D-bag writing about himself in the third person like this. He does appreciate that you're still reading, though.

Drew would like to sit down and have a beer with you. Or a cocktail. He's not here to judge your preferences. Drew is terrible at being serious, and has no real idea what a snippet biography is meant to convey anyway. Drew thinks you are awesome just the way you are. That part, he meant. Drew is off to go high-five random people, because who doesn't love a good high-five? No one, that's who.

CPSIA information can be obtained
at www.ICGtesting.com
Printed in the USA
BVHW081942270620
582382BV00003B/378